# EDEN RISING

KEVIN J SIMINGTON

# CONTENTS

EDEN RISING
By
KEVIN J SIMINGTON



EDITORS: Tony Baker, Sandra Simington

✿ Created with Vellum

1

—————

## ALTARIA, 5529

The flitter landed on the grassy headland, its engines switched to silent mode and its lights off. A door slid open and a slender figure emerged. He stood still momentarily, seeming to orient himself in the near-perfect darkness of the moonless, cloud-covered night. Then he began striding purposefully down the grassy slope toward the only house on the small island. Muted lights shone from the curtain-clad windows of the quaint-looking cottage, indicating that someone was home.

*Good. Our intel was accurate.*

He reached the unfenced side garden and walked past orderly rows of vegetables and healthy-looking fruit trees, some of which were laden with ripe fruit. He paused and bent down to examine a particularly healthy ruffel vine, whose elongated black fruit hung pendulously from the green stems.

*How does he get them to fruit so early in the season? My vines have barely flowered.*

He picked one and bit into it, savouring its sweet tang as an errant trail of juice ran down his chin.

He took another bite, then threw the fruit aside and wiped

his chin. He walked around to the front of the neat little cottage and strode up the pebbled front path. The front door was in a small recessed portico. Light shone dimly through a glass panel to the right of the door, illuminating various ornaments attached to the walls of the portico. Figurines of birds and butterflies, obviously hand-made and meticulously decorated. A hand painted sign on the door said, "Welcome to our home".

*He's gonna get such a surprise.*

He smiled in anticipation and pressed the doorbell. A pleasant-sounding chime could be heard from somewhere inside and, moments later, padded footsteps could be heard approaching the door. The door opened and Councillor Drummond stood peering out into the darkness, trying to identify his visitor.

"Yes? Can I help you?" he asked, and then his brow furrowed and shock registered on his face.

"You!" he exclaimed, taking an involuntary step backwards.

"Yes. Me."

"What are you doing here?"

"I've come to give you a message from the reversionists."

"What message?"

"This."

He pulled a laser pistol from his jacket pocket and shot Drummond between the eyes. The laser drilled a neat tunnel through his skull and emerged from the back of his head, drilling a hole through the wall behind him as well.

"Damn!" said the man, as Drummond crumpled lifelessly to the floor, "I set the power level too high."

He stood looking down at his handiwork.

"Nice slippers, Drummond. You always were a homely character."

"Who is it, Gerval?" came a female voice from somewhere inside the house.

He cocked his head to the side and listened.

*Damn! She's not supposed to be here. They told me she was visiting her daughter for the weekend.*

He adjusted the power setting on his laser, stepped over Drummonds body and walked calmly into the house.

*I hate loose ends.*

2

News of a number of overnight assassinations dominated the media services the following morning. Twelve of the sixteen members of the Altarian Federation Council had been murdered overnight, at almost precisely the same time. Nine had been shot in their own homes, along with anyone else present at the time. Two were murdered in public, the assassins blending in with crowds and escaping identification. One councillor had been murdered in her office where she had been working late. Her secretary and a security guard were also found dead at their posts, nearby. The four surviving councillors were all known sympathisers of the reversionists - a movement dedicated to winding back technology and eradicating artificial intelligence.

It was almost exactly twelve months since the destruction of the malevolent artificial intelligence that had tyrannised mankind for centuries. After its destruction, a wave of jubilation had swept across Altaria. Private and civic celebrations took place on every island.

Mankind was set free to live their lives in peace once more.

But the peace was short-lived. Almost immediately, the

reversionists recommended their campaign demanding a reversion to simpler technology that would never again allow a malevolent artificial intelligence to arise. At first it was just demonstrations and rallies, and their cause gained significant support from the general populace. But as the inertia of government policy increasingly frustrated the activists, their campaign became more violent. Destruction of civic property and physical attacks against key opponents increased alarmingly. Several suspicious deaths had also occurred, strongly believed to be reversionist assassinations.

Now, it appeared that the reversionists had taken their campaign to a whole new level by violently removing those from the Council who refused to listen to their demands.

At midday on A1, Altaria's largest island, a live news broadcast was transmitted onto the comm net from the council chambers on the top floor of Federation Tower, in the island's capital. A smiling, olive-skinned face appeared on screens all over the planet.

"Good afternoon citizens of Altaria. My name is Jurd Transid, one of the four surviving members of the Federation Council. No doubt by now, you have heard of the terrible events that occurred overnight; the tragic murders of twelve councillors and various members of their families. I firstly want to assure you that everything possible is being done to identify and bring to justice those who are responsible for these heinous crimes. It was a cowardly act of hate, and those responsible will be punished to the full extent of the law."

"Having said that, we must not let these tragic events interfere with the proper governance of our world. Accordingly, as the senior surviving member of Council, I have enacted the emergency provisions of our Federal Constitution and appointed twelve replacement council members, drawn from a wide selection of our world's islands. The new council has been in video-conference all morning and we have unanimously agreed to the following measures."

"We will begin an immediate, world-wide roll-back of technology in order to protect us from the possibility of hostile artificial intelligence ever developing again. For too long the concerns of a significant proportion of our population regarding the dangers of sentient technology have been ignored. As sad as the deaths of some of our councillors has been, this has opened the way for the appointment to the council of those who have the courage to do what is necessary to ensure our ongoing protection."

Jurd Transid paused, smiling into the camera in what he thought was a conciliatory manner.

"As of this minute, the use of all sentient technology will be deemed to be illegal. This applies to home and hand-held devices, as well as inbuilt technology in larger industrial and transport infrastructure. The global coding that links your cerebral implants to communication and educational technology is being deleted as we speak, meaning that you will now need to interface with technology physically rather than mentally. In other words, you will have to press lift buttons and manually open doors rather command them mentally."

"Obviously, this will cause some initial inconvenience, particularly on dedicated techsav islands where you may have become completely dependent upon implant-based interface with technology. For instance, you may have to climb the stairs if the lifts in your building have no physical interface. You may need to walk if your vehicle has no facility for physical control. We ask that you be patient as we undergo this rollback and systematically replace our dangerous techsav devices with technology that is aligned with reversionist guidelines."

Jurd Transid paused once more and gave the camera hovering in front of him what he hoped was a calm, reassuring look.

"Thank you for your understanding. Let us all move forward together into a safer, more sustainable world."

He smiled again at the camera and remained in that pose until the broadcast light extinguished. Then he turned to the three other surviving councillors, who had been off-screen during the broadcast.

"How was that?"

"Excellent, sir," said one. The other two nodded to the reversionist leader in agreement.

"Good. I think I carried it off with the right balance of empathy and firmness."

He breathed out a sigh of relief and ran his hand through his hair.

"Now, I suppose we'd better actually appoint some more people to the council, seeing I've said we've already done it. We'll choose the eight leaders from the various reversionist factions who have been with our movement from the beginning, but we'll need another four people. Carmen, I want the names of four prospective councillors on my desk within the hour. All reversionists, of course. And try to get most of them from techsav islands so that it has the appearance of fairness. I know there are plenty of reversionist sympathisers living in techsav communities."

"I'll get straight on it."

Turning to the other two he asked, "How are we going with the military? Have we managed to contact General Kellar yet?"

"He's still not answering our comms, sir," replied one of them. "As you know, he is currently at Gateway Station, at the L1 Lagrange point. He may be assessing developments here before aligning himself with our cause."

"What about Commander Bree, the commander of Gateway? Has she responded to our comms?"

"No sir. Gateway Station has remained silent. It appears she is also assessing the situation."

"Let's hope they don't take too long to see the sense of our position. I don't want to be at war with the military."

Jurd Transid walked around to the desk he had inherited this morning from the now deceased Council Chairperson, Gerval Drummond. He reached under the desk and pulled out a bag containing his discarded clothing from last night. He opened the desk drawer and withdrew his laser pistol, which still had a lingering smell of ozone from its recent use. Tossing it in with the clothes, he handed the bag to one of the councillors.

"Get rid of this. Incinerate the whole bag. No traces left. I don't think I'll be needing it again. We've spilled enough blood in the last 24 hours. Let's hope there will be no more."

Unfortunately, it was a forlorn hope.

3

———

**EARTH**

"Keo, you're snoring."

Keo opened his eyes and blinked in the bright sunlight, looking around him as he sat leaning against the tree.

"No, I'm not, bro. I'm just deep in thought."

"Then what was that horrible sound coming out of your mouth?"

"That's an ancient ancestral meditation mantra from my Hawaiian heritage."

"Really? It sounded like some kind of wild animal, dying in agony."

"That's the trouble with you white boys. You have no appreciation for ancient spiritual practices."

Zac smiled at his friend.

"Seems to me that lately you've been doing a whole lot of that 'ancient meditation' as you call it. Especially after a couple of meads."

Keo reached for the travel cup that was sitting in the grass beside him and drained the last dregs, smacking his lips as he finished.

"I'll have you know that Plato once said, 'Mead is the very

essence of life, brewed by the gods and more valuable than gold."

"Really? More valuable than the fish that's been tugging on your line for the last minute while you've been snoring your head off?" asked Zac.

Keo dropped his cup and staggered to his feet, fumbling for his rod which he had left wedged between some rocks. The rod tip was bent at a sharp angle and was jerking violently. He lifted the rod and started reeling the line in as he walked to the river's edge, standing on the pebbled shore and leaning back against the pull of the fish.

"It's a monster, bro! This could be the chinook we've been after!"

"Nice and steady, Keo, not too fast," said Zac, coming to stand beside him.

Keo was grunting as he worked against the strain of the line, and fine beads of sweat had already broken out across his now-bald scalp. Finally, he pulled the salmon flapping onto the pebbled shore and he picked it up, his face beaming with delight.

"It must weigh at least fifteen kilos, man! I told you this was the spot, bro! I told you!"

"Nice work, Keo," said Zac, slapping him on the back. "The girls are gonna be pleased. This'll feed the whole clan."

The afternoon sun was lowering in the sky and a cool breeze had sprung up, so they quickly cleaned their fish, packed their gear, mounted their quad bikes and started the journey back home. Keo's 'secret fishing spot' was six kilometres south-west of their camp. Even though they followed the path of what Keo said had once been a major road, no sign of the old road remained.

In fact, no sign of any former human habitation remained on the Earth. Roads, buildings, entire cities; they had all been completely swept away in the GAE – the Global Annihilation

Event. A catastrophic shockwave had swept across the surface of the planet when the tether lift cable and its orbiting anchor asteroid had impacted the Earth in the aftermath of the nuclear holocaust. The shockwave - an incandescent fireball thousands of degrees in temperature, 150 kilometres high and travelling at over 30,000 kilometres per hour - had raced around the globe, levelling everything in its path. In the nearly 3,200 years that had passed since that fatal day, any rubble remaining from that shockwave had been completely swallowed by the slow, relentless resurgence of the natural world.

When they had arrived twelve months ago, they had discovered a virgin world, reborn and renewed, with no visible sign of previous occupation. They established a settlement in Ahipara Bay, on the north-western tip of New Zealand's north island. It was a place of stunning beauty and tranquillity.

After fifteen minutes of navigating the bumpy terrain, Zac and Keo finally crested a small rise and stopped their quads alongside each other, turning their engines off. They looked down on their tiny campsite in the southern corner of the bay, consisting of a survival drop-pod, a shed, an outdoor barbecue and a gazebo where they ate most of their meals.

Eight of them lived there; Zac and Kit, Keo and Tash, Mel and Phil, Zac's daughter, Dayna and Tash's son, Noah. The rest were now living in the quickly expanding colony in Wellington.

"Looks like we've got visitors, bro."

"Yeh. They don't give up, do they?"

A sleek black flitter had landed on the beach below their settlement, and they could see the visitors sitting in the gazebo, talking with Kit and the others. Dayna and Tash were emerging from the drop-pod with cups of steaming tea in their hands.

Keo looked at Zac and said, "I think they've got a point, my friend. We always knew our time here would be temporary."

"You too, Keo? I thought you, of all people, would be determined to stay."

"I thought so too. But we can't compete with what they have to offer in Wellington. It's a full-blown town now, and we live very basic, isolated lives up here. Besides, I think the girls are hankering for a taste of civilisation. A year of camping has worn a bit thin with them."

Zac grunted.

"I wonder what gifts they've brought with them this time."

"You've got to admit, bro, these quad bikes have certainly come in handy."

Zac merely grunted again and sat looking down on their settlement with a frown on his face. After a few more moments he fired up his quad and said, "Let's go and see what they're offering us now."

He gunned the engine and took off down the slope, with Keo in his wake.

4

Their peaceful isolation on Earth had ended seven months ago. A series of colony ships from Nova and Perdita had begun arriving, packed full of prefabricated building materials and machinery. Wellington, at the southern end of New Zealand's North Island, had been chosen as the site for the new colony because of its deep harbour and fertile soil. Almost overnight, buildings and infrastructure had sprung up. Now, seven months later, there were over 5,000 people living in the town and more were arriving every month.

Three months ago, two colony ships had also arrived from Altaria. The much taller, genetically enhanced Altarians had established an alternate settlement in Hobart, Tasmania, off the southern tip of mainland Australia. It was currently a smaller colony, about half the size of Wellington, but was growing rapidly.

Zac and the others had been hailed as heroes, and both of the fledgling colonies had made several overtures to them, inviting them to relocate. The Wellington colony had been particularly insistent, visiting their little campsite several times over the last few months, bringing gifts and enticements on each visit. Today's visit seemed to have a larger than usual contingent, and Zac wondered what their spiel would be this time.

As he parked his quad bike in the timber shed that he and Keo had recently constructed, Zac had a sense that he was fighting a losing battle. He knew that if he decided to stay, the others would stay with him; such was their love and respect for him. But he had begun to sense that they were pining for civilisation and would leave their idyllic campsite in a heartbeat if he relented. Perhaps it wasn't fair for him to keep them here simply because of his own selfish desire for peace and solitude.

He and Keo walked over to the gazebo and were greeted with hugs and kisses from their wives.

"Hello my love," said Tash, giving Keo a kiss. "What have you got in the sack? Don't tell me you've actually caught something this time."

"Hey, that hurts! How can you possibly doubt my fishing prowess! They don't call me the fish whisperer for nothing!"

Keo opened the sack to reveal the monster chinook, along with two other decent-sized salmon that Zac had landed. There were whistles and exclamations all around as everyone admired the impressive catch.

"Now that, ladies and gentlemen, is a fish!" exclaimed Keo, proudly holding up his prize catch and grunting slightly with the effort.

"You'd better put it back down, darling," said Tash, "You don't want to give yourself a hernia."

"No chance of that, my love! I've got abs of steel."

"Your steel abs seem to have expanded considerably in recent months," replied Tash, poking her finger into his considerable girth.

Keo put on a mock hurt expression.

"Any more of your cheek, and you won't be eating any of the spoils!"

The Wellington mayor stepped forward and reached out to shake Zac's hand.

"Good to see you again, Zac."

"Nice to see you, too, Amanda. You don't give up easily, do you?"

"Not when I know I'm right. The City Council are keen for you to join us."

"Hmm," he grunted, noncommittally, glancing at the four other officials sitting in the Gazebo. "You're calling yourselves a 'City' Council now, are you? It's really still only a town, isn't it?"

"We like to be optimistic and look toward the future; a future that we think you can play a part in."

"I suggest we leave serious negotiations until after we've eaten," ventured Kit, breaking into the discussion. "Why don't we get these fish on the barbecue? Will you all stay for dinner?"

"Of course! That would be lovely," responded Amanda. "We don't have anything to rush back for."

...

Two hours later, the picked-over skeleton of the chinook salmon sat in the middle of the gazebo table and everyone was contentedly sipping mead as the sun began to sink over the western hills.

"I notice you haven't changed your fashion choices, Zac," commented Amanda, referring to his retro-Hawaiian shirt and denim jeans which, by now, were starting to look a little threadbare.

"Why would I? There's nothing cooler than Hawaiian shirts and jeans."

"He's dragged those ridiculous shirts half-way around the galaxy," added Kit. "They're his most precious possession. I have to beg permission to even wash them."

"These are now the only Hawaiian shirts in the whole galaxy," boasted Zac, proudly. "No one else has any."

"Yeh, there's a reason for that, Dad," said Dayna. "It's called good taste!"

"Oh, that hurts! That hurts!" said Zac, holding his hand over his heart.

Everyone chuckled and Keo poured another round of mead for the guests.

"This mead sure packs a wallop," said councillor Sean Gilmour, the burgeoning city's town planner. "What's your secret?"

"Well," began Keo, holding up his cup and preparing to wax eloquent, "it's a highly technical process involving a secret recipe that I'm not prepared to reveal."

"He hasn't got a clue!" interrupted Tash. "Every batch comes out completely different. The last batch tasted like dirty socks!"

"Honey-flavoured dirty socks," corrected Zac. "I've got your back, Keo," he mock-whispered.

"Thanks, bro."

"I'm sure you'll be able to relocate your beehives to Wellington to continue your home brewing enterprise," contributed Amanda artfully.

"Nice segway," said Kit.

"OK," said Zac, "let's talk about that. After all, that's why you're here."

"Yes, it is," answered Amanda. "Zac, you can't hide out here forever. Whether you like it or not, you people are heroes. In fact, considering the EI's galaxy-wide oppression that you managed to bring to an end, you are arguably the greatest heroes in mankind's history. People want to see you. They want to honour you. And, more importantly, I want you, Zac, to have a seat on our council."

"But I can do that and still live up here. I could travel down for meetings."

Amanda shook her head.

"You and I both know that wouldn't work. To play any significant role in our leadership team, you need to live among us. You need to be able to see the issues that need addressing on a daily basis. Plus, because of the high regard in which you are held by the Altarians due to your time living among them, you are the best-equipped person to liaise with the Hobart colony. In short, we need you Zac."

She paused and looked around the table at the others.

"Plus, I get the distinct impression that the majority of your group would be very happy to move to more civilised living arrangements if you were amenable."

Zac looked at the others. They all looked back at him, expectantly. Once again, he was deeply moved by their trust in him and their willingness to follow his lead. He didn't feel worthy of such respect and knew that he couldn't continue to hold out.

"OK."

"OK, what?" asked Kit.

"OK, we'll move."

Kit and the others nodded, a look of relief on some of their faces.

"But on one condition," added Zac.

"What?" asked Amanda.

"That we keep the drop-pod here as our weekend cabin. I want to be able to get up here occasionally to get away from it all."

"Of course," said Amanda. "That won't be a problem."

Sean Gilmour, the town planner, was nodding his head, clearly pleased and somewhat surprised that they had won such an easy victory.

"We've already got your apartments ready, on the top floor of one of the new apartment blocks, right on the harbour's edge, a stone's throw from the council chambers. We can move you in any time you like."

"Maybe give us a couple of days to get things in order here," said Zac, looking at the others and receiving affirming nods.

"No problem," affirmed Amanda. "We'll send a flitter up for you on the weekend. And Zac, thank you. You're doing what's best for the colony."

Later that night, Kit also thanked him. Twice.

Afterward, he lay contentedly on the bed and boasted, "Not bad for an old bloke. I've still got it."

"Yes dear," she replied condescendingly, running her fingers through his thinning hair. "But you are losing it in other places. You might want to consider wearing a cap so you don't get sunburnt up there."

"Humph," he said with mock disapproval, but the smile in his eyes betrayed the warmth of his love for his wife.

**5**

---

"I say we arrest the bastard and shoot him! In fact, shooting would be too good for him. He and his gang are murderers. Every single one of them on that phoney council needs to be locked away in prison!"

General Kellar, head of the Altarian Security Forces, had worked up a full head of steam and wasn't going to be easily placated.

Vorn Ansell, the police commissioner, shook his head.

"It's not that simple, Greville. At this point in time, there is no evidence linking Jurd Transid to yesterday's assassinations."

"Damn it, Vorn! How much evidence do you need!" said the big man, his gravelly voice filling the small meeting room. "That man has been the publicly acknowledged leader of the reversionist faction for years! He has consistently ranted against the inaction of the council, and his organisation has mounted numerous terror campaigns resulting in countless deaths over the years. The man is an outright terrorist!"

"I believe that too, Grev, but unsubstantiated belief doesn't cut it in a court of law. Everything you've just mentioned is circumstantial evidence at best. What we need is solid evidence linking him to at least one murder. Without that, we could arrest him now and he would walk free within the hour."

"In that case, let's not arrest him. Let's just take him out! I have expert sharp-shooters who could nail the bastard without leaving a trace of evidence behind. Problem solved."

"You don't mean that."

"You're damn right I do! I'm prepared to do whatever it takes! You bureaucrats might be prepared to tip-toe around the nuances of the law, but I'll be damned if I'll sit idly by and let an unhinged megalomaniac seize control of our world!"

Starla cleared her throat, and the other two looked at her.

"You got something to say, Commander Bree?" asked Kellar, aggressively.

The three of them were locked away in a secure meeting room on Terminus 8, the geosynchronous satellite station orbiting directly above the Altarian capital. As a commander, Starla was lower in rank to Kellar, but her position as Commander of Gateway Station gave her an equal voice in these situations.

"If we assassinate people because we think they are monsters, we become monsters ourselves. The law exists for a reason, and we can't step outside of it."

"Sometimes the law isn't enough. That's why you need people like me," argued Kellar.

"I disagree, General. You aren't above the law. None of us are."

"Commander Bree is right," said Vorn. "We can't act outside the law. What we need is hard evidence in order to proceed. I have my best people working on the case as we speak. If there is any evidence out there, we'll find it, and then we'll bring them to justice. In the meantime, we need to work out how to respond to this new, so-called council. Have either of you had any contact with them yet?"

"Commander Bree and I have so far refused to answer their comms, but we can't continue that indefinitely."

Police Commissioner Ansell nodded.

"I've spoken to the Attorney General," he informed them. "His advice is that the current council is not constitutionally legitimate. Any appointment of new councillors must be ratified by an election, preceded by a two-week nomination period. The current new so-called councillors are merely nominations and can't take part in decisions. That means that, legally, the current council only comprises four members. Furthermore, the constitution states that council decisions are only legally binding when a minimum of seven councillors have voted."

"Didn't Jurd Transid say something about enacting the emergency provisions of the constitution in appointing the new councillors?" asked Kellar.

"No part of the constitution, including its emergency provisions, gives him the power to do that."

"So that means that this whole technology roll-back thing is not legal?" asked Starla.

"Correct."

"So what do we do about it?" she asked.

Vorn touched the console on the glass table in front of him and an official-looking document was projected onto the wall.

"Two hours ago, the Attorney General issued a cease and desist order, advising the council that they currently have no constitutional power to make decisions, and outlining the procedures necessary for an immediate election to be held."

Commissioner Ansell looked at the other two apologetically.

"I hope you don't mind, but I took the liberty of adding each of our names to the Attorney General's document. I felt it would add more weight to it, presenting a unified front of opposition to their current unconstitutional activities."

"You're damn right!" muttered Kellar.

"No problem from me either," said Starla. "Has there been any kind of response?"

"Nothing so far …," began Commissioner Ansell, but that was as far as he got. An explosion rocked them, emanating from somewhere beyond their meeting room. Bits of the ceiling fell down around them and small arms fire could be heard in the distance.

All three leapt to their feet and Kellar yelled, "I think we just got their response!"

6

---

General Kellar and Commander Bree ran to the closed door of their meeting room, taking up station on either side and unholstering their sidearm lasers. Commissioner Ansell also had a sidearm, smaller but just as deadly, and he took up position alongside Starla. Ansell's heart was pounding furiously. It had been a long time since he had been on the front lines of any sort of action. Starla and Kellar, however, were trained soldiers. Their razor-tuned instincts kicked in instantly and they wordlessly exchanged quick hand signals. The cold glint in Kellar's eyes was matched by an equally focused determination in Starla's. Kellar nodded and swiped his hand across the door activator. As the door slid open the two of them dived out, one to each side, with Ansell following closely behind.

The scene was chaotic. People were running and screaming down the corridor past their meeting room, surging toward the grand concourse and its various transfer booths. The sounds of small arms fire could be heard from somewhere further up the corridor, the distinctive sounding buzz and zap, together with the accompanying smell of ozone drifting down the corridor, indicating that it was laser fire.

The last of the panicked crowd of civilians disappeared down the corridor as the laser fire continued. Without hesitating, all three of them ran up the corridor toward the battle.

The corridor curved gently to the left and opened into a large circular concourse with five other corridors opening into it at equidistant points around the circumference. The other corridors all led to shuttle terminals. Their current corridor was the sole link between the shuttle terminals and the grand concourse behind them, with its booths for instantly transferring to the surface of the planet.

With their backs against the corridor wall, Starla and Kellar sized up the situation. A military meeting room, designated MR1, built into the curved concourse wall between two of the corridors opposite them was now a smouldering wreck, its door blown off and thick smoke billowing out of it into the concourse.

"They got the wrong meeting room," said Starla.

"Lucky us," said Commissioner Ansell.

"Morons!" muttered Kellar, as he continued to evaluate the best course of action.

There appeared to be at least two terrorists holed up inside the destroyed meeting room, firing through the doorway at security personnel who were taking cover in the entrances to several corridors. The security personnel were returning fire sporadically and ineffectually. The circular concourse was filled with smoke, so it was difficult to see anything clearly, but it appeared to the three newcomers that the situation was now a stalemate. Ansell saw an opportunity.

"If we can capture one of these terrorists alive, we might be able to establish a link to Jurd Transid. This could be the evidence we need to convict him."

"I was thinking the same thing," agreed Starla.

"First, we've got to get them out of there," commented Kellar.

He took a step closer to the corridor entrance and bellowed out a command.

"This is General Kellar! Cease fire immediately! I repeat. Cease fire!"

Silence ensued apart from a couple of stray shots emanating from the meeting room. Filling his lungs again, Kellar addressed the terrorists.

"You people in the meeting room. This is General Kellar, head of the Altarian Security Forces. There is no way out for you. We have armed security personnel at every exit. They are trained soldiers and they will shoot to kill if you persist in fighting. Lay down your weapons and walk out backwards with your arms raised. I assure you that you will not be harmed and will be given leniency if you surrender peacefully. This is your only chance to live. If you continue to fight, you will die. That is a promise!"

Kellar's tone left no doubt that he was deadly serious.

There was no response; just an eerie silence.

"Last chance!" he yelled again. "Come out now with your arms raised or die. Your choice."

The silence persisted for a further thirty seconds. Suddenly the chamber erupted with laser fire again as the occupants of the meeting room signalled their rejection of Kellar's offer. He shook his head.

"Like I said, morons!"

Kellar's lapel comm crackled to life.

"General Kellar? This is Corporal Williams, at the entrance to the corridor immediately to your left."

"Go ahead, soldier."

"Sir, there were three of them. They must have transferred up from the surface via a transfer booth. There was a meeting taking place in MR1 – just a briefing for tonight's security detail.

The terrorists opened the door and rolled in an explosive. No one in the room could possibly have survived."

His voice seemed to break as he uttered those last words.

"Steady on, soldier. Just give me the facts."

"Yes, sir. My team and I were about to be relieved. There were two of us on duty here in the concourse. We immediately opened fire. We got one of them. The other two took shelter in MRi. Our reinforcements arrived within minutes. There are about twelve of us now, spread around the various corridor entrances."

"Do you have any flash-bangs?"

"Just a moment sir."

There was a pause.

"Yes sir. Between us we've got six."

"OK soldier. Here's what we're gonna do. We're gonna open fire and when we do, I want two of those suckers lobbed through their doorway. Do you think you can manage that from where you are?"

"Yes sir."

"Good. Then as soon as they go off, we're going to rush the bastards while they're still stunned. Are we clear?"

"Yes sir."

"Good. Inform the others of the plan."

A moment later, Kellar's lapel comm crackled to life again.

"We're ready here, sir."

"Good. On my mark. Now!"

All hell suddenly broke loose. The entire smoke-filled chamber lit up with purple laser fire as a dozen lasers fired simultaneously into the open doorway. Kellar couldn't see the flash-bangs being thrown but their effect was blindingly obvious. A deafening blast issued from inside the damaged room, accompanied by a brilliantly intense white light. Instantly, Kellar charged through the smoky central concourse with impressive speed for a man of his bulk. Starla was right on his heels and, as supremely fit as she was, was only barely able to keep up with him. Without pausing, Kellar charged through the open doorway and crash-tackled one of the terrorists to the ground. The black-clad figure was still holding a laser in his right hand, so Kellar simply grabbed the arm and brought it down it over his knee, snapping both bones cleanly. As the terrorist lay on the ground screaming in agony, Starla dealt with his accomplice who was kneeling to the side of the doorway rubbing his eyes. Starla delivered a swift knee to the temple, knocking him unconscious. She squatted, minimising her profile, and quickly scanned the smoke-filled room looking for further threats as security personnel ran past her into the room screaming, "Down on the floor! Down on the floor! Drop your weapons now!"

But there was no one left alive to hear them. There were over a dozen bodies strewn around the room, with blood and gore splattered everywhere.

Kellar stood and issued instructions, ignoring the groans of the terrorist who was holding his badly deformed arm.

"Williams!"

"Yes, sir."

"Leave two men here with me and take the rest and secure the area. Contact your station security chief. Tell him to lock down the entire station. No one gets in or out until we've checked every single person for weapons. There may be more of these bastards wandering around."

"Yes, sir."

Commissioner Ansell was speaking into his lapel comm, advising police in the capital and locking down the ground transfer booths.

Turning to Starla, Kellar gestured toward the unconscious terrorist at her feet.

"How long until he'll be mobile?"

"Immediately," she replied, bending down and effortlessly hoisting the prone man over her shoulder.

The general nodded approvingly. He reached down and dragged his own prisoner to his feet by the shirt collar. The dark-clad terrorist continued to moan and wail in agony, so Kellar jammed his laser pistol under the man's chin, saying, "You shut the hell up right now, sunshine, or I swear I will drill a hole through your throat and out the top of your skull."

The man shut up.

"Ok, let's move! We need to get these two pieces of pond scum to a secure area where we can have a nice little chat."

They exited the room, with Starla carrying her unconscious prisoner over her shoulder and Kellar prodding his own prisoner forward with a laser jammed against the middle of his spine. They were half-way across the concourse when the situation suddenly became a whole lot worse.

**7**

---

Another explosion shook them violently, knocking one of the security personnel to his knees. It had come from the corridor they had been heading toward; the one that led past their own meeting room and on to the grand concourse. A moment later there was a rending, groaning sound, like metal twisting and distorting.

One of the soldiers who had been left with them addressed Kellar.

"Sir, that's the central connecting corridor, linking the two halves of the station. If that blows ..."

Kellar nodded.

"I hear you, son. Change of plan, everyone. Let's head down here to Shuttle Bay 4. On the double!"

They began running toward the nearest corridor, as the screeching and groaning behind them was suddenly joined by a high pitch whistling that was rapidly rising to a crescendo.

"Hull breach!" shouted Starla above the din. "Must be a small hole, but it's getting bigger. That corridor's gonna blow any second!"

They reached the corridor leading to the docking bay and

were half-way along it when there was a further explosion. This time they were flung violently against the side of the corridor and remained pinned there as the whole universe seemed to start spinning out of control. A violent wind raced past them until the decompression ended with a reverberating clang and they were suddenly in total darkness.

"The main corridor has blown!" yelled Starla. "The safety airlocks must have engaged, shutting off our corridor, otherwise we'd all be dead by now."

"Why are we spinning?" asked Commissioner Ansell, who was finding it difficult to breathe.

"I think we've been completely severed from the other half of the station," Starla answered. "The sudden decompression acted like a rocket engine, imparting thrust and spinning us on our horizontal axis."

She heard Vorn's breathlessness and felt her own.

"We've lost pressure. We're all going to have to breathe as deeply as we can and get to the shuttle as soon as possible – provided it's still there. We can't stay too long in low pressure air like this, or we'll die."

The lights had gone out when they were severed from the other half of the station, so the two soldiers who were with them donned headlamps and switched them on. No one else had made it into their corridor before it had sealed itself off.

The constant spin had turned the side of the corridor into the floor, and it was creating a delta-V of almost two Gs. They stood up and staggered along the side wall, feeling twice their own weight. Starla now needed assistance from one of the soldiers to carry her prisoner who had begun to regain consciousness. As they staggered down the corridor, emergency lights flickered into action, glowing a dull orange – obviously powered by some kind of generator or battery system. They reached the end of the corridor which opened into a small circular docking bay approximately fifteen metres in diameter. On the far side was an airlock and through its small glass windows they could see the interior of the shuttle.

"The good news is, the shuttle is still here," said General Kellar.

"What's the bad news?" asked Commissioner Ansell.

Starla explained.

"Our spin means that the docking bay floor that we would normally walk across is now a vertical wall. Our corridor ends half-way up that new wall, and the airlock to the shuttle is directly opposite, halfway up the wall on the other side."

"I'm completely confused," confessed Ansell.

"You're also deficient in oxygen, Vorn, which doesn't help," said Kellar.

"We'll have to move fast," said Starla. "We can't stay too much longer in this low air pressure."

"So how do we get across?" asked the Commissioner.

"We don't," answered Starla who, as Commander of Gateway Station, was used to taking command in matters relating to off-world habitats. She continued her explanation.

"We'll have to go down what used to be the circular wall, but which is now the curved floor, and we'll go up the other side. Like a giant half pipe. It's almost vertical at the 'top' of both sides but there are hand holds all the way along the old wall, which have now become a ladder."

"I'm not sure I can make it. I'm ... having ... trouble breathing, and I feel twice as heavy as normal."

"Vorn, you don't have a choice," said Kellar, gruffly. "If you stay here, you'll die."

They began the difficult climb. Kellar led the way, moving well for such a big man, but panting excessively in the thin air. He made it to the top on the other side and opened the inner door to the airlock chamber, using the emergency manual override mechanism. The door swung out over their ladder and was the final obstacle in their climb, needing to be climbed around and over in order to enter the airlock.

It took thirty minutes before they were all safely inside the airlock. Starla felt exhausted and she suspected that the two soldiers felt the same, after manhandling the Commissioner up the final climb and virtually having to carry the two prisoners, neither of whom were able to climb in their current state.

By the time they stumbled through the final airlock door into the shuttle, Commissioner Ansell was in a bad way. The low air pressure had taken its toll on him and he was lapsing in and out of consciousness. Once full cabin pressure was reached, they laid him down as comfortably as they could and placed an oxygen mask over his face. Meanwhile, the prisoner with the badly broken arm was clearly in agony and was making a lot of noise with his groaning. Starla broke open the med kit and jabbed him with a heavy sedative. She noticed that the other prisoner was now fully alert and he looked as though he was watching for a chance to make a move against them. Without thinking too much about it, she grabbed another dose of sedative and jabbed him as well.

"Hey! What was that for?" he yelled, rubbing his upper arm.

"That's just because I don't like the look of you. Sweet dreams."

A few moments later he slumped into unconsciousness and peace descended on the shuttle. They strapped down those who were sleeping and then everyone else climbed into seats and fastened lap belts. Starla climbed awkwardly into the pilot's chair which was an accomplishment in itself. It was like climbing into a chair that is mounted sideways half-way up a wall when you weigh twice as much as normal. Eventually she managed to get into the chair, panting with exertion. The co-pilot's chair was even higher up the wall and was effectively out of reach, so Starla was going to have to pilot the shuttle single-handedly. She fired up the engines and the onboard nav system, going through start up procedures that she hadn't been through for several years.

"Pardon me for asking, ma'am," said one of the soldiers, "but you do know how to fly one of these things, do you?"

"Yes, corporal. I was a pilot before I was a Commander. Don't worry. I'll have you home, safe and sound and tucked into your little bed by dinner time tonight."

The other soldier laughed and punched his mate in the arm. Starla turned back to her instruments and as she went through her final start-up procedures, she called back over her shoulder.

"You boys might want to hang on tight. This little tub doesn't have artificial gravity. Things might get a bit funky for a few moments after we undock as I try to cancel out our residual spin."

"Yes, ma'am," the two soldiers both said in unison, tightening their lap belts even further.

"Anything I can do to help, Commander?" asked Kellar.

"Nothing at the moment, General. I've got this."

Starla activated her comms and made a call.

"Terminus 8 Control, this is Commander Starla Bree, on board the shuttle in Bay 4. Do you copy?"

"Copy Commander. It's good to hear your voice. What's your status?"

"On board with me are two prisoners, both unconscious, two security personnel, Police Commissioner Ansell and General Kellar. The commissioner is unconscious and extremely unwell after decompression and low air pressure. We need to get him to a hospital ASAP."

"Roger that. You are cleared to depart as soon as you can."

"Do you need us to assist with any rescues?"

"Negative Commander. There are multiple shuttles already involved in rescue attempts. Your priority needs to be getting the commissioner to medical help."

"Roger."

"Good luck, Commander."

In the end, Starla surprised herself. She wasn't as rusty as she feared, and ninety minutes later they landed safely at the spaceport in the capital.

But by then, Commissioner Ansell was barely alive.

**8**

———

The view from the top floor of the apartment block was spectacular. They were situated right on the water's edge and looked across Wellington Harbour toward the hills in the east. There were four apartments on the sixth floor, each with a balcony overlooking the harbour, and these had been reserved for the four couples. They arrived around midday along with their meagre belongings and after only an hour they were completely unpacked. They had shared a communal lunch with their family members and members of their original expedition who were housed on the floor below: Dayna and Noah, Kia and Harv, Raj and Delta, Jaz and Karl. Each of those couples had been living in the colony for many months, hoping that Zac and the others would eventually join them.

Keo and Tash were now sitting with Zac and Kit on their balcony, admiring the view together.

"I sure hope I don't go stir-crazy cooped up in an apartment," said Zac. "I'm not sure how I'm going to cope with this."

"Me too, bro. Although there is an excellent gym two floors down. Plus we've got our fishing gear, and the water's right at our doorstep."

"I suppose so," said Zac, unenthusiastically.

"And don't forget the quad bikes that the council have provided us with in the basement garage," added Tash. "Any time you boys start to climb the walls you can jump on those and go exploring the hills and forests to the west."

"She's right, bro. The flitter pilot told me there are streams and rivers all through those forests. Enough for a lifetime of fishing and exploring."

"Yeah, I guess so."

Somehow, Zac didn't seem convinced.

Kit jumped to her feet and clapped her hands.

"It's time, people! We need to get changed. We don't want to be late for our own reception."

"Oh, great," complained Zac.

"Cheer up, grumpy bum!" said Kit. "Anyone would think they were gonna roast you on a spit! This dinner is simply the council's way of welcoming you. I'm sure you'll enjoy yourself once you get there."

"Well, I hope it's just a small affair. I don't feel like facing too many people."

"Don't worry, my love," she said, ruffling his hair. "Amanda promised it will just be the council members and their partners."

Half an hour later, as the sun set in the west, the eight couples met in the ground floor lobby. The four recently-arrived couples had been provided with more formal clothes that fit them surprisingly well, apart from Keo's jacket which wouldn't do up at the front. When Zac pointed this out, Keo merely responded with, "They underestimated my abs of steel, bro."

The dinner was to be held in the town hall, just one hundred metres from their apartment, and as they walked up the gentle hill toward it, they noted the complete absence of people in the streets. They entered the small foyer of the Town

Hall and were met by what appeared to be a waiter in formal attire.

"Welcome, honoured guests. Allow me to show you to your seats."

He ushered them across the small foyer and opened a set of large double doors that led into the main hall. As the doors opened, a crowd of at least two thousand people rose to their feet and burst into thunderous applause. The four newly arrived couples stopped in their tracks, stunned, mouths literally hanging open. The other four couples had known what was going to happen and had not said anything.

The applause went on and on, as the citizens of Wellington honoured those whose heroic deeds had liberated the galaxy. Zac shook his head in wonder and glanced at Kit, who had tears in her eyes. She reached out and grabbed his hand then leant close and said to him, "Come on, Zac. You can do this."

The usher led them down the central aisle, taking his time, allowing the crowd on each side time to look upon their heroes, and all the while the thunderous applause continued. Zac noted a number of tall Altarians in the crowd and realised that this was a combined, trans-Tasman reception. It was completely overwhelming and by the time the usher had led the entire group up the steps to their seats on the stage, there was not a dry eye among their group.

Finally the Mayor, Amanda Robinson, walked to the lectern and the applause died away as the crowd sat down. She gave a brief speech of welcome and then invited a series of individuals to come forward to speak. Each one, Novan, Perditan and Altarian, spoke briefly of the heartache and grief of living under EI domination and then of their jubilation when the EI's demise became apparent. To make it even more personal, each of the speakers mentioned the names of loved ones who were still living but who would not be alive today without the actions of the heroes on stage.

Finally, Amanda Robinson took the lectern again, her button microphone amplifying her voice around the large hall.

"These sixteen people on stage behind me are heroes beyond description. In the words of a great orator of the past, 'never before have so few, done so much for so many'. With great risk to their own lives, they destroyed the Enhanced Intelligence that was based on Mars and which had, via its Hive Relay Units, controlled the technology on all of our worlds and caused the premature deaths of countless people." Turning to face them directly, she continued.

"I know you did not ask for this, and I respect your desire for privacy. But you have done mankind a great service. You risked your lives and undertook an almost impossible journey. And against all odds, you defeated an enemy whose cruel domination has caused immeasurable misery for generations. Tonight we honour you for your bravery and present each of you with these symbolic keys to the city."

Amanda then read out each of their names and as each one stepped forward, she placed a gold medallion carved with the outline of a key around each of their necks. Throughout this process, the crowd were once again on their feet, applauding and cheering.

Once the ceremony was over, the group was invited to share dinner with the council members and their partners in an adjoining room. Getting there, however, proved problematic. An hour later, Zac and the others were still in the main hall, surrounded by crowds of people wanting to shake their hands and even hug and kiss them. Finally, the mayor stepped in to rescue them. She shepherded them through a side door into a corridor and, after allowing them to freshen up in the public bathrooms, led them to a large meeting room where thirty guests were seated around eight circular tables, awaiting their arrival. Once again there was a standing ovation which Zac quickly quelled by raising his hands and saying,

"Please! Please stop! I don't think I can take any more of this. There is just one thing I need."

He paused, and all eyes were on him.

"I'm starving! Can we please eat?"

The crowd laughed, and shortly afterward the food arrived. The heroes were spread around the tables, and the rest of the night was a blur of faces and names as the newcomers were swamped with conversation. At one point, Zac drew Amanda aside and said,

"You lied to me."

"How so?"

"You told me that tonight was just going to be dinner with the council members and their partners."

"It is!" she said smiling and opening her arms wide to encompass the small dining room.

"No. I'm pretty sure you said 'just' a dinner. You didn't mention the public ceremony."

"Didn't I?" she replied with a twinkle in her eye. "It must have slipped my mind. I've been so busy lately."

"If I'd known this whole thing was going to happen, I wouldn't have come."

"I know, dear. That's why I didn't tell you."

She leant forward and gave him a peck on the cheek.

"Now, be a good boy and keep circulating. Everyone wants the chance to talk with their hero."

"Hummmph!" grumped Zac, but the smile on his face betrayed his good humour.

Later that night, as he and Kit lay snuggling in bed, he tried to maintain an air of grumpiness over the ambush that had taken place, but Kit was having none of it.

"You can't fool me, Dr. Perryman – introspective historian that you pretend to be. I think you actually enjoyed yourself tonight. And you can't deny these people the chance to officially celebrate the cause of their new freedom. Tonight was important for them."

"I guess so."

"And Amanda told me that the whole ceremony was recorded, compressed and streamed via a short-burst transmission through an open wormhole connection to Altaria. By now it has probably also been transmitted to Nova, Perdita, Polaris and Altaria. All four of the human worlds have shared in witnessing the ceremony and adding their own local celebrations to it. Tonight was important for everyone, Zac."

She rolled on top of him and ran her hands down his body, kissing his neck as she did so.

"And you were such a good boy tonight, being nice to all those strangers, I think you deserve a reward."

"Do I? Oh, goody!"

**9**

---

Police Commissioner Vorn Ansell was rushed into an emergency theatre at the hospital in the Altarian capital. He was diagnosed with a life-threatening cerebral oedema and an emergency operation was performed to relieve the pressure on his brain. His blood was also pumped full of nanobots which began their cellular repair work of his body and brain. The doctors in charge of his treatment stated that if he had arrived an hour later, he would almost certainly have died, but they were confident that he would now make a swift and complete recovery.

In the meantime, the two sedated prisoners were taken to a secure military base attached to the spaceport. Commander Bree and General Kellar accompanied them and oversaw their placement in separate adjoining holding cells.

"What's your next step, General?" asked Starla as they stood together in the central monitor room, watching the video feeds from the cells.

"Now we wake them up and get them to sing like canaries."

"What about medical treatment? That looks like a seriously broken arm."

"There'll be no medical treatment until we've got the information we need."

Starla just nodded. General Kellar was Head of Security and this was now his show. She wasn't entirely comfortable with the denial of medical treatment but chose not to say anything.

Turning to his aid, Kellar ordered that the prisoners be given a fast-acting antidote for the sedative. Ten minutes later, both prisoners were wide awake, the injured one moaning loudly again.

"Send in the interrogators," ordered Kellar.

For the rest of the evening they watched trained interrogators tag team each other, questioning the prisoners in shifts, at times threatening and at other times flattering them, but to no avail. The prisoners remained completely unmoved and silently defiant. At the same time, news filtered down to Starla and Kellar from Terminus 8. A space tractor had captured and stabilised the spinning section of the satellite station and all survivors had been safely removed via shuttles. Sadly, six security personnel had died when the corridor ruptured, sucked into space through the gaping hole. At least a dozen civilians had met a similar fate on the other side of the space station before the emergency airlock had sealed their end of the corridor.

In the hours since the attack, the duty chief on Terminus 8 had pieced together a rough outline of what had taken place. As well as the three terrorists dealt with in the shuttle terminal concourse, a further three had arrived shortly after via the transfer booths. They had rolled an explosive into MR2, the meeting room that Starla and the others had barely vacated. All three newly-arrived terrorists had perished when the explosive charge blew the corridor apart. Clearly, they had bungled the timing. If they had attacked simultaneously with the first three terrorists, Starla, Kellar and Ansell would be dead now. General

Kellar's contempt for the terrorists stemmed not only from their violent actions, but also from their apparent ineptitude.

"The morons couldn't even get a simple coordinated attack right!" he grumbled, shaking his head in disbelief.

By dawn the next morning, no progress had been made with the prisoners, who refused to say a word. Kellar finally called a halt to proceedings and dismissed the interrogators.

"Now what do we do?" asked Starla, who had stayed alongside the general watching the interrogations all night. "Without a confession linking them to Jurd Transid, he remains completely untouchable."

"Now we stop playing nice."

"What does that mean?"

"You don't need to know what it means, Commander. Go to the barracks and get some shut-eye. I'll take it from here."

"General, if you're planning what I think you're planning ..."

"Commander, I've deliberately NOT told you what I'm planning. That way you have plausible deniability. Let's keep it that way. You're dismissed."

Starla glanced at the comm officer who was the only other person in the control room and saw that he was studiously staring at the video screens, pretending that he hadn't heard the exchange. She recognised the pointlessness of protesting any further. She nodded her head and left the room without saying another word.

On her way to the barracks she called the hospital and was told that Commissioner Ansell was doing better than expected and was making a speedy recovery. When she reached her temporary quarters at the barracks, she stripped off down to her underwear, lay down on the army-issue bunk, and was fast asleep within seconds.

# 10

Starla woke feeling disoriented. It was dark and when she called up the time on the comm panel built into her side table, she saw that it was 03:15 am. She had slept all day and most of the night! Needing to blow some cobwebs off, she left her uniform where it was, donned some generic fatigues that were supplied with her room, and walked down the corridor. The night duty sergeant in the foyer directed her to the gym, located in an adjoining building. At this time of night she had the place to herself and she spent ninety minutes working out, pushing herself hard. Returning to her room, she showered and changed into her uniform and went in search of the officer's mess. She was starving but had to wait until 05:30 until breakfast was available. She hadn't eaten for over 24 hours and she wolfed down two servings of a full fry-up, washed down with two mugs of steaming hot black juvo.

There were several other officers up at this time of the morning but they gave her a wide berth. News of yesterday's events on Terminus 8 had spread around the base and, as Commander of Gateway Station, Starla was a well-recognised figure among the military. She was also an intimidatingly beautiful woman, with a figure seemingly cast from a perfect mould, although on the short side of average for an Altarian – barely two metres tall.

After breakfast she checked out of the barracks, signed out a base transport vehicle and drove to the hospital. She entered the ICU but was told that Commissioner Ansell had just discharged himself. The doctor in charge appeared nonplussed.

"He refused to stay any longer. We couldn't keep him here."

"Is he safe to leave?" she asked, concern written on her features.

"Yes. He's fine. The nanobots have basically completed their repair work. But we would have preferred to keep him here for a further twelve hours just to complete our tests."

"Where is he now?"

"He only just went down in the lift. You might still catch him at the reception desk."

Starla did catch him, just as he was walking out through the main entrance.

"Can I give you a lift somewhere, Commissioner?"

"Starla! Perfect timing. I was going to call up some transport."

"Are you sure you're well enough to be leaving?"

"Never felt better. Those boffins wanted to poke and prod me for another day. Never gonna happen."

"I'm heading to the interrogation rooms to speak with General Kellar," she stated. "Where can I take you?"

"That's my destination as well. Let's get going."

On the way she filled him in with the details of last night's unsuccessful attempts at interrogation, and then hinted at Kellar's planned changed tactics. The commissioner shook his head.

"Let's hope the pig-headed fool hasn't done something we'll all regret."

A few minutes later they found out that he had.

**11**

---

"I got a confession from both of them," Kellar announced without preamble.

The three of them were in a private conference room attached to the interrogation centre.

"What did they say?" asked Starla.

"They were acting under direct orders from Jurd Transid. They met with him almost immediately after he received the 'cease and desist' notice from the Attorney General. Transid ordered the hit on the three of us. He'd received intel regarding the location of our meeting."

"That, in itself, is a concern," said Starla.

"Yes, it is," agreed Kellar, "and I've already launched an investigation to try to find the leak. But the good news is that we've got the bastard by the short and curlies now."

"I presume you have videos of their confessions," said Ansell.

"Damn right I do!"

"Let's have a look."

Kellar fiddled with the glass topped touch screen built into the conference table and then a video began playing. The scene showed the injured prisoner and Kellar himself walking into the cell. Kellar walked straight up to the seated man and punched him in the face, knocking him onto the floor. Kellar dragged him back into the chair. His nose was clearly broken and blood was pouring down his face. Kellar then spoke, with a menacing tone in his voice.

"I'm gonna give you one chance, and one chance only, to tell me who planned this attack. If you don't, you're gonna find yourself in a world of pain. I promise you, son, you WILL tell me. It's just a matter of when and how much damage you're gonna suffer before you do. So tell me. Who was behind this?"

The prisoner spat blood at the general's face.

"Go stuff yourself!"

Kellar merely nodded, as if he had expected that kind of response.

"Your choice, pal."

What followed was brutal, even savage. Starla, a hardened soldier herself, had to look away. Commissioner Ansell had stopped looking as well, staring down into his lap and shaking his head in disbelief while listening to the screams of the prisoner.

"Stop! I've seen enough."

As Kellar stopped the video, Ansell got to his feet and walked around the room with his hands on his head.

"Did your other 'interview' take a similar course?" he asked.

"You're damn right it did!"

"General Kellar, we can't use these videos. They're no good to us."

"But we got their confessions, damn it! They both identified Transid as the instigator."

"Yes, but confessions that are coerced or obtained under duress are not admissible in a court of law. These videos would be thrown out the moment we show them."

"What about if we just show the end bits, where they confess?"

"What state are the prisoners in by then?"

"They're not exactly looking in the prime of health."

"No, I imagine they aren't. Look, Greville, defence attorneys would have a field day with these videos. Not only would all charges against Jurd Transid be dismissed, but you would be up for a court martial."

"What about if we just use the audio? Pretend we didn't video the interviews."

"Is there audible evidence of the prisoners suffering, perhaps in some kind of pain as they give their confessions?"

Kellar sighed.

"Probably."

Ansell shook his head.

"Sorry, General. Unless you want to end up behind bars yourself, we can't use any of this."

"Damn it!"

Kellar smashed his already bruised fist down onto the table and got to his feet. He began pacing the room.

"But we've got him! We've got him, Ansell! We know for certain that it was him now."

"Yes. We do," agreed the commissioner. "But we have no legally acceptable evidence to prove it. And until we do, we can't do a thing about it."

A stony silence prevailed in the room as they each desperately tried to think of a way of resolving the situation.

The silence was broken by knock at the door.

"Enter!" said Kellar, gruffly.

An aide entered and said, "General, there's some breaking news regarding the newly appointed council. You might want to tune in to the news."

Kellar switched to the live news channel and they watched and listened to what was unfolding. The self-appointed Federation Council had instigated a wave of arrests on a number of techsav islands. Innocent citizens were being taken into custody simply for accessing supposedly outlawed technology. The screen switched to a video of Jurd Transid standing alongside the Deputy Police Commissioner, with Transid announcing that due to Police Commissioner Ansell's current incapacitation, he was promoting Deputy Commissioner Warland to the top job and that with his cooperation they would stamp out any continuing unlawful behaviour.

Now it was Ansell's turn to thump the conference table in frustration.

"He can't do that! I'm not even close to being incapacitated! He's gone way beyond the scope of his jurisdiction! The role of Commissioner is an elected position, not an appointment from the Council!"

A comm line buzzed and Kellar took the call, placing it on speaker a few moments later. It was the Attorney General who confirmed what Ansell had just said. Transid had stepped outside the bounds of his constitutional power. Not only was he constitutionally unable to appoint a new Commissioner, but he was acting outside the law in arresting citizens. The prohibition against the use of certain technology was illegal and so were the arrests. The AG signed off after promising to immediately dispatch a formal legal briefing to them, spelling out his definitive decision on the matter.

"That's it!" exclaimed Kellar. "We've got the bastard now! We can arrest him and his cronies!"

"Yes," agreed Ansell. "But we'll have to be careful how we go about it. The law is firmly on our side, but we want to avoid precipitating some kind of civil war. The last thing we want is to set in motion a wave of reprisals. I want to make sure that when we take Transid and his council out of circulation, we don't start some kind of war."

"I've got an idea about how we might proceed," said Starla.

They both looked at her expectantly.

"It involves Earth."

**12**

———

Zac and Keo were both in a mellow, philosophical mood. This tended to happen when they had consumed several meads each. Today, they were onto their fourth cup and they were now engaged in a deep philosophical duel as they sat on Zac and Kit's balcony, gazing across the harbour.

Zac looked at Keo.

"Does expecting the unexpected make the unexpected the expected?"

Keo nodded, and a moment later responded.

"If two mind readers read each other's mind, whose mind are they reading?"

Zac acknowledged the comment with a nod and responded.

"If your shirt isn't tucked into your pants, are your pants tucked into your shirt?"

Keo nodded.

"Is there a synonym for synonym?"

Zac raised his glass and took a sip in honour of the comment.

"Why is it called quick-sand if you sink slowly?"

Keo toasted him in return.

"If I try to fail and succeed, which one did I do?"

Zac nodded in appreciation.

"If Cinderella's shoe fit perfectly, why did it fall off?"

Keo toasted him and took another sip.

"What was the best thing before sliced bread?"

Tash and Kit were in the lounge room enjoying a late-afternoon drink as well. Tash shook her head and said,

"I swear, those two are as mad as each other. Do you understand the rules of this stupid game, Kit?"

"I think so. You can't say anything apart from philosophical conundrums, and you only have fifteen seconds after the other person has finished speaking to think of something yourself. The first person who doesn't think of something profound to say in that time, loses."

Tash shook her head in amusement, and they listened for a bit longer.

"What if oxygen is just a deadly gas that kills us really slowly?"

"What if we all used to be zombies and there was a human apocalypse?"

"If the fountain of youth makes you live forever, what happens if you drown in it?"

"If a King farts, is it a noble gas?"

"If a cockroach can survive a nuclear blast, what the hell is in cockroach spray?"

"If moonlight is just reflected sunlight, why doesn't it kill vampires?"

Despite themselves the girls couldn't help chuckling with each new comment, and the boys, knowing that they had an audience, kept up their performance for another twenty minutes.

"If I hit you with a dictionary, is that physical or verbal assault?"

"If revenge is a dish best served cold and revenge is sweet, does that mean that revenge is ice cream?"

"If you're waiting for the waiter, doesn't that make you the waiter?"

"If a genie grants you three wishes but says you can't wish for more wishes, can you wish for more genies?"

Finally, Zac faltered, just failing to get his next comment out in time. Several minutes of friendly arguing then ensued regarding when the fifteen seconds should officially start. Eventually they sat together in easy companionship, enjoying the warm afternoon breeze and chatting about whatever came to mind.

"Those two boys are inseparable. They're like brothers," said Tash.

"Even closer than most brothers, I would say," replied Kit. "I don't know how Zac would have coped with the last few years, without Keo."

"Keo would be absolutely lost without Zac, too," said Tash.

The boys had been silent on the balcony for some time when Zac spoke again.

"It's bizarre being back on Earth isn't it?"

"Sure is, bro."

"I mean, we were here 3,177 years ago! There are only nine human beings left alive in the whole galaxy who have previously set foot on Earth – and that's only because of the weird time distortion we went through with that black hole."

"Twice!" added Keo helpfully.

They both sat shaking their heads in wonder.

Keo looked across at Zac.

"How do you think Mel is coping, being back at Wellington? After all, this is where you rescued her."

"Yeh. I wonder that too. Her mother, Elizabeth Canning, president of the whole damn western world, showed up at the last moment as our shuttle was about to take off. I remember trying to tell her that there was no more room on board, but she was determined to save her daughter. She literally threw Melody through the hatch as I was closing the door."

"Yeh, bro, I remember. I was on that shuttle too. That's how I met you. And I remember little Mel, crying hysterically for her mum. We only just managed to gain enough altitude to escape the shockwave."

"Having a heavy bloke like you on board didn't help, Keo."

"Easy, bro! Easy! My soul is light."

Zac smiled at his friend.

"It certainly is, Keo. No doubt about that."

They both took another sip of their drinks.

"Mel was just twelve, wasn't she?" said Keo.

"Yep. Just twelve years of age. That's a tough age to become an orphan. Her mum must have perished along with everyone else on the Earth."

"So, do you think she has any memories of that day? Has being here brought back those bad memories?"

"I don't know. Kit and I were talking about that last night. Kit is thinking of having a chat with her about it."

"Good idea, bro. If she wants, maybe we could take her to where the airport used to be. She might want to revisit the last place where she saw her mother."

Little did both men realise that taking Mel to revisit her past would result in a discovery of such stunning magnitude that it would turn the whole world inside out.

**13**

———

The flitter landed on the flat, grassy plain that stretched between Wellington Harbour and the Tasman Sea on the other side of the peninsular. As far as Zac and Kit could remember, this was where the airport had been. There were eight of them on board today: Zac and Kit, Keo and Tash, Mel and her husband Phil, Jaz and Karl. Jaz had wanted to see the place where Zac had found the lost little girl whom they had taken under their wings.

They all disembarked and stood on the grass in the bright morning sunlight, looking around as if trying to identify some familiar landmark. Of course, nothing of the old airport remained. It was just an unremarkable, if picturesque, grassy plain, dotted with trees and shrubs that had grown up in the intervening years. Perhaps the only hint that it might once have been an airport was the fact that it was perfectly flat – unnaturally so, in fact.

"This has to be it," said Zac.

"It definitely is," confirmed Kit. "I remember coming tearing in across the harbour, way too hot but with no spare time to burn off the excess speed. I banked hard left to line up with the runway and came down hard and fast, pretty much right where we are standing now."

She paused and looked around in something approaching awe.

"Zac, do you realise that you and I probably stood on this very spot over 3,000 years ago?"

Zac shook his head in amazement.

"I know. It's a head spin isn't it?"

He pointed to his right.

"The terminal building was just over there. We loaded evacuees into the shuttle as fast as we could. And then as you were firing up the engines and I was starting to close the door, that big old yellow bus came crashing through the chain-link gates over there."

He turned to Mel.

"It was your mother and her political advisors, with you in tow. Do you remember?"

She nodded. Tears welled up in her eyes as she stared where Zac had pointed, as if seeing into the past.

"I didn't want to leave my mother. I couldn't understand why she wanted me to go. When she threw me onto the shuttle, it broke my heart."

Tears were streaming down her face now, and Phil held her close, his arm around her shoulders. Jaz walked to her side and held her hand.

"She saved your life, Mel. She wanted you to live."

Mel nodded.

"And she'd be very proud of the person you've become," added Zac.

A tiny sob broke from her lips, and more tears flowed down her face.

They stood silently together for a while, respecting Mel's memories and letting her reflect and grieve in her own way.

After a respectful period of time, Phil asked Mel tentatively,

"Do you think this is where she died? Would you like to lay some flowers down here as a memorial?"

Mel dried her eyes and shook her head.

"No. I'm pretty sure this isn't where she died."

"How do you know?" asked Zac.

"I'm fairly certain she was going to try and make it back to the Strategic Command Bunker."

"The command centre you'd just come from?"

"Yes."

Zac frowned.

"You've never told us that."

"I guess we never really talked about it."

"What makes you think she went back there?"

"My last memory of my mother is of one of her advisors grabbing her arm and saying, 'Ma'am, we have to leave, right now!' And my last glimpse before the shuttle door fully closed was of her turning and running back toward the bus."

Everyone was silent for a moment as they digested this new information. Finally Phil spoke up.

"So, could she have survived the shockwave inside the bunker?"

"I'm certain of it," said Mel. "My memory of the bunker is that there were at least six levels underground, and the first level down was at least fifty meters below the surface. If they made it there in time, they definitely would have survived the initial blast."

"Wow!" said Tash, speaking up for the first time. "That sure puts a different spin on things."

Turning to Zac, she asked, "You're the historian and I know you've written about the previous war in your book. How long could they have survived in a bunker like that?"

"It depends on a lot of things – how well it was stocked, what sort of power they had, air filtration, water, what provision there was for food production. Theoretically, they could have survived for years. Plus, New Zealand wasn't directly targeted with nuclear bombardment, so they might even have been able to access the surface after a period of time. But I guess the first question is, did they even have time to make it back to the bunker at all?"

Kit asked, "Do you remember roughly how far away it was, Mel?"

"It was on top of a hill, north-west of here. I remember it took us about ten minutes to get here in the vintage Dodge bus."

"Ten minutes," repeated Kit, digging back through her memory. "It would have been very tight. It was about ten minutes after we took off that we encountered the outer edge of the shockwave. I guess it's possible that they might have just made it."

"I'd like to try and find the bunker," said Mel. "Do you think it could still be there?"

"The underground part of the bunker would almost certainly still be there," answered Zac. "But whether there is anything visible on the surface after more than 3,000 years is highly unlikely."

"Still, it won't hurt to go and have a look," said Kit, frowning at Zac. "We might at least be able to pinpoint the right hill."

"Sure," said Zac, quickly catching the hint. "The council have given us the flitter for the whole day, so we may as well use it. It will be the colony's first archaeological expedition!"

Melody nodded and smiled.

"Thanks. I'd like that."

"If we're going to do this properly, I suggest we go home and get some food and drink for lunch," said Tash.

"Yeh, and some bottles of mead," suggested Keo.

Tash slapped him on the back of head.

"No mead for you today! The last thing we need is for you

and Zac to have another one of those ridiculous philosophical battles!"

Zac smiled and said, "Why do we call things that are sent by car, shipments, and things that are sent by ship, cargo?"

Tash shook her head and muttered, "Heaven help us!"

**14**

"So what's your plan, Commander?" asked General Kellar.

The three of them were still sitting around a conference table in the capital's military base.

It was Starla's turn to stand up and start pacing the room.

"The way I see it, we have enough to immediately remove Jurd Transid and his cronies from office. We may even have enough to give them jail time, although that is by no means certain. At the moment, all we can effectively pin on them are constitutional breaches. Not murder. Not terrorism. Just procedural breaches of the Federal Constitution. They will no doubt hire a team of expensive lawyers who will mount a strong case against a custodial sentence. At best I can only see them getting six months in a comfortable low security island facility. Realistically, they will probably walk free with a commuted sentence and a hundred hours of community service."

Commissioner Ansell nodded in agreement.

"Unfortunately, I think you're right. Which will leave them free to agitate and continue their campaign of terror."

"Precisely."

"So, what do you suggest?" asked Kellar.

"I suggest that we remove them permanently."

Kellar sat up with a fiery glint in his eyes.

"Assassination?"

"No, General, as tempting as that might be, I don't propose that we stoop to their level."

"That's a shame."

"You're suggesting that we transport them to Earth?" said Ansell.

"Yes. I am. It would be the ideal place for them, as it is currently the kind of low-tech world that they are agitating for. Our colony in Hobart, Tasmania, is deliberately low tech and is committed to staying that way. That is why the vast majority of the colonists are what we might call passive reversionists. In my role as Commander of Gateway Station, I have access to the complete manifests of any vessels travelling through the subspace portal, and I can tell you that over 95 percent of all colonists who have migrated to our Hobart colony are from reversionist islands. Plus, I happen to know that the Hobart City Council is strongly committed to reversionist principles. The mayor is a staunch reversionist supporter. Jurd Transid and his buddies will feel right at home. In fact they'll have nothing to agitate against anymore."

"Plus, they'll be out of our hair for good," added Ansell.

"Precisely."

Kellar wasn't looking particularly impressed.

"So, these guys murder a whole bunch of innocent people, and we simply give them a free holiday on Earth? Is that it?"

"I don't think we've got a whole lot of choice, General," answered Starla. "It's either that or they walk free and stay here to continue wreaking havoc."

They were silent for a moment, and then Ansell spoke up.

"So how do you propose we go about this. Do we abduct them or arrest them?"

"I think we've got to do this by the book. If we abduct them it would simply make them martyrs and add further fuel to the reversionist flame. No, I think we have to arrest them and charge them, and then give them a choice."

Ansell frowned and shook his head.

"But if they know they are likely to only get a minimal sentence if they stay here, and quite possibly just a rap over the knuckles, surely they won't agree to transportation?"

"They will if we bluff them."

"How do we do that?" asked Kellar.

"We present them with a seemingly water-tight case for a murder and terrorism conviction. We get our current two prisoners to sign a written confession, pointing the finger at Transid and his gang. I'm sure that in their current weakened state, they'll sign anything you put in front of them, General."

"You're damn right they will!"

Starla continued.

"We arrest Transid and the rest of the Council, present them with the written confessions and charge them with terrorism and murder. The written confessions will be enough to warrant immediate incarceration. Obviously, their legal team will demand to see the video confessions. We assure them that we have the video evidence, but we aren't legally obliged to give them access to any of our evidence until one month before the trial date, which could be in another twelve or eighteen months. We can ask the AG to use his influence to push for a long delay on the trial. We'll let them stew in their juices for a few weeks, staring down the barrel at the possibility of being locked up for the rest of their lives. We then offer them a deal; agree to transportation and we drop the charges. They will be able to live out their lives as free citizens on Earth."

"Won't they smell a rat?" asked Ansell. "After all, it seems too good to be true. Surely their lawyers will suspect that we possibly don't possess the evidence that we claim to have."

"Not if we play our cards right. We justify our offer on purely pragmatic grounds. We use the argument that we would much rather ship them off-world permanently than pay for their food and lodging for the rest of their miserable lives. We could also argue that we want to negate any possibility of them exerting a continued influence over the reversionist movement from prison. Both arguments are entirely reasonable and believable."

There was silence for a moment as the other two digested all this, and then Kellar spoke up.

"I dislike the idea of these scumbags living a life of ease in an island paradise. They should be locked up. They don't deserve freedom."

"I agree, General. They don't deserve it. But we've got a bigger picture to consider. This is the best possible outcome for our world. Removing Transid and the key reversionist leaders will effectively defuse their whole movement. With one stroke we will effectively end the conflict that has plagued us for decades."

Kellar nodded, stroking his chin as he contemplated the full ramifications of Starla's plan.

"I think you're right. It's a good strategy, Commander."

"Thank you, General."

"I agree," said Ansell. "Do you mind me asking you, Commander, how do you know so much about the legal system?"

She smiled.

"That's simple. I trained as a lawyer, prior to joining the military."

**15**

—————

The flitter flew in a slow, steady search pattern, criss-crossing the low hills about seven kilometres north-west of the old airport and three kilometres due-west of the current colony. According to their calculations, this was the most likely location of the now-ancient bunker. They had stocked up on provisions for the day and Phil Lambert, through his scientific contacts, had managed to borrow a sophisticated ground pene-trating scanner. The scanner operated at ground level, so they needed to land the flitter in order to use it. So far, they had investigated three promising hills with no success.

Melody pointed through the window on the right side of the flitter.

"There's a small reservoir down there. I remember driving past a small lake of some kind soon after we left the bunker. The bunker can't have been more than two hundred metres west of the lake."

Kit banked back around, to do a lower fly-by.

"It's hard to say how much the shockwave would have reshaped the Earth's surface," she said as they bled altitude. "Who knows if that's the same lake you saw three thousand years ago, but if it is, then that hill immediately to the west looks promising. It's pretty clear of trees, too, so we'll land and take a look."

The flitter touched down on the grassy knoll, and they all clambered out.

"Does it look familiar, Mel?" asked Zac.

"Not really. But then nothing really looks familiar anywhere. I was only twelve and I guess I wasn't particularly taking notice of my surroundings."

Zac nodded.

"That's understandable. Let's wander around and see if we can see anything that might indicate previous human presence."

As the group spread out and began searching the hilltop, Phil set up the ground-penetrating scanner and booted up its operating system. It was the fourth time he had used it that morning, so he was now very familiar with its operation. After a few moments, a green light lit up accompanied by a pleasant-sounding ping, indicating that it was fully powered up and ready for operation. He grabbed its two handles and pointed its canon-like projector toward the ground with the scanner's screen facing toward him. He thumbed the activation button and waited while the scanner sent a series of varied-frequency electromagnetic pulses deep into the ground below. A moment later his eyes opened wide in disbelief.

"Holy crap!"

Everyone came running.

"What? What have you found?" asked Mel.

"H-O-L-Y crap!" repeated Phil, beginning to move around while staring at the screen.

"Yeh, OK, we got the message about divine defecation," said Tash. "You wanna try to enlarge your vocab a bit for us?"

"Take a look," he said, holding out the scanner so that everyone could see the screen.

They all leaned in, staring intently at the screen.

"I can't see anything," said Zac. "It looks like a whole lot of nothing to me."

"Precisely!" enthused Phil. "There's nothing there!"

"What are you saying, my love?" asked Mel, touching his arm and looking at his face expectantly.

"What I'm saying is that this whole damn hill is hollow!"

"Hollow?" she said, excitement lighting up her face. "So this is it? We found it?"

"Sure looks like it!"

"How far down does it go?" asked Zac.

"I don't know," admitted Phil. "This is a hand-held, portable scanner with limited range. It can only scan down to about a kilometre. But these readings are showing multiple hollow levels all the way down to the limits of its range."

"Underground levels down to a kilometre?" said Mel, perplexed. "That ... that ... can't be right. The bunker we were in only had about six levels that went down about one hundred metres."

"Well, I'm looking at this screen, and it's definitely telling me a kilometre or more."

"So what does that mean?" asked Mel, looking around at the others.

"There are only two possibilities," said Zac, immediately engaging his logical faculties. "The first is that we've stumbled upon a much bigger, more extensive bunker that existed at the same time and in the same area. That's highly unlikely, though, because if that was the case, the president would have utilised this much deeper and safer bunker as her command post."

He looked at the others to make sure they were following his logic.

"That leaves us with the only other logical conclusion. This is the same bunker that you were in, Mel, and it was gradually enlarged over time."

"So that means ...?" she began, suddenly afraid to say the rest out loud, lest the truth somehow evaporate when it was given voice.

"I'd say it means that your mother and her team survived the blast," Zac finished for her. "In fact, they may have lived and thrived here for many years."

"She made it," Mel whispered, her eyes glistening.

She looked around, trying to imagine her mother racing into the bunker just in time and sealing herself in as the world above her was destroyed.

"How do we get in?" asked Tash, ever the pragmatic one of the group.

"We won't get in from where we are standing here, that's for sure," said Phil. "There's over a hundred metres of solid earth between us and the first level."

He began walking across the hilltop, scanning as he went.

"There's got to be an access shaft of some kind. If there's one here, this thing will find it."

For the next thirty minutes, Phil walked in ever-increasing circles, bombarding the earth below with invisible microwaves. At first the others all followed, like sheep behind a shepherd. After a while, however, they split up and began scouring the hilltop for any signs of previous human habitation.

The hill was elongated in shape, about eight hundred metres long and five hundred metres wide, with numerous undulations and small rises, dotted with trees and rocky outcrops. They roamed across the hilltop, searching the ground, kicking aside rocks and peering into bushes and undergrowth. Kit was just about to suggest that they stop for lunch when Keo cried out from a grassy knoll fifty metres down the eastern side of the hill.

"I've found something! Come and have a look!"

They arrived to find Keo holding up a piece of crumbling concrete about the size of a baseball. Dotted around his feet were smaller pieces of the same ancient concrete. He had a huge grin on his face and was clearly very pleased with himself.

"Nice work, Keo!" said Zac.

"I can't take all the credit, bro. It was my ancestral connection with the land that did it; a deep mystical and spiritual oneness with the universe that has been passed down to me from my distant ancestors."

"If you say so, my love," said Tash, giving him a kiss on the cheek.

Phil pointed his scanner at the ground.

"Bingo! This is it! There's a shaft directly under us that goes all the way down to the first level."

"How far beneath the surface is the top of the shaft?" asked Zac.

"We'll have to dig through about two metres of soil to reach it."

Zac pondered the implications for a moment.

"Seeing we didn't bring anything to dig with, I suggest we come back tomorrow with some earth moving gear and do a proper job."

"I agree," said Kit. "Besides, I'm starving. Let's find a nice spot in the sun and have lunch."

They walked back to the flitter, spread out a couple of picnic blankets and ate a lunch of cold meat, freshly baked bread and crisp apples. As they ate, they talked excitedly about tomorrow's excavation and what they might find in the bunker below. It was an idyllic lunch in a beautiful location.

Little did they realise that it would be the last meal they would all have together.

**16**

---

The arrests were planned for 0200 hours, when Transid and his fellow-reversionists would be least expecting it. The Attorney General had issued indictments for all sixteen council members as well as seven other reversionists who had been identified via the confessions of the current prisoners as having been involved in the recent assassinations. As evening fell across the capital, the whereabouts of each person listed in the indictments was being closely monitored by a team of highly trained, covert operatives who were part of an elite military unit. At the instigation of the AG, the Supreme Court had declared a state of martial law until a constitutionally legitimate council could be elected. This was not made public knowledge, however, as they did not wish Jurd Transid and his followers to have any inkling that something was wrong. Martial law gave full policing powers to the military, bypassing the now compromised police department. In fact, the Deputy Police Commissioner was the subject of a last-minute indictment, issued secretly late that afternoon, as his ongoing unauthorised actions made it clear that he was part of the subversive reversionist movement.

By 0150, all the arrest teams were in place. General Kellar was coordinating the operation and had placed himself on the team that would arrest Jurd Transid. Although he was not part of the military, Police Commissioner Vorn Ansell had been invited to head up the team that would arrest Deputy Commissioner Warland, and he was quite looking forward to bringing his subordinate to justice for the swathe of unlawful arrests that he had authorised. Commander Starla Bree had been given command of the team arresting Carmen Orlando, Transid's long-time lover and his most-trusted lieutenant. She was a particularly nasty piece of work and had been one of those involved in the assassinations. Carmen had left Transid's apartment shortly after midnight and was now in her small downtown apartment, apparently fast asleep.

At 0155, Kellar asked for a status update from all twenty-four team leaders over their secure comm channel. They all indicated a go for engagement. The remaining minutes ticked by and at 0200 precisely, Kellar whispered,

"All teams, go, go, go!"

All but one of the arrests went smoothly. Twenty-three people were sound asleep when black-clad elite service men and women stormed into their bedrooms, yelling aggressively and pointing deadly weapons at them. Commissioner Ansell thoroughly enjoyed the look of sheer terror on his deputy's face and suspected that the wet patch around his groin when he was handcuffed and marched outside was a very recent leakage. General Kellar derived an equal amount of enjoyment from his arrest of Transid, although in his report the next day, he had to apologise for a moment of uncharacteristic clumsiness when he apparently tripped in the dark and accidentally head-butted Jurd Transid, breaking Transid's nose. His accident was later excused by the Security Forces Review Board as 'an acceptable minor instance of unintentional collateral damage'.

The arrest of Carmen Orlando, however, did not go so well. Starla and her squad of six soldiers silently approached the front door of Orlando's ground floor apartment. They were all dressed in full battle gear, including body armour and helmets. With a nod from Starla, the master sergeant placed an electro-magnetic code breaker against the door sensor panel and activated the decoder.

And then all hell broke loose.

The panel above the door exploded, leaving the door intact but shooting jagged metal shrapnel down on the soldiers. The explosion blew most of the team backward, leaving them dazed on the ground. Starla and the master sergeant, having been hard up against the door, were least affected, receiving only minor cuts to their faces, but the two soldiers who had been directly behind them took the full force of the blast and were clearly out of action. The three in the rear were also injured but appeared to be still operational.

"Master sergeant! Break that door down! Take two soldiers in with you!"

As they moved quickly toward the front door again, she turned to the remaining soldier.

"You! Come with me!"

They ran down the side of the building and paused at the rear corner as they heard the sound of the front door being blown inward. Starla took a small mirror with an extendable handle from her battle belt and poked it around the corner. It disintegrated in a blinding laser blast. A second blast dissolved a chunk of the building near her head.

"Damn! She's already out!"

She heard the distinctive sound of a streaker engine firing up.

"Oh no! That's not good!"

Starla turned and sprinted back the way she had come,

knowing from her previous reconnaissance of the property that the only exit for the hover cycle was via the driveway on the other side of the building.

*Damn it! I should have stationed one of the team to guard the driveway!*

She reached behind her as she ran and extracted her micro-tag pistol. She only just made it to the front in time. As she rounded the front corner of the building the streaker raced out of the driveway on the other side of the building, its antigrav unit throwing a blue light under its wheel-less chassis and a purple tongue of flame issuing from its rear super-charged thruster.

Starla dropped to one knee, took aim with a straight-armed double grip, and fired. She saw a red dot briefly appear on a rear panel of the fuselage and then the streaker turned left and roared up the street.

Starla ran to the street and turned in the opposite direction, sprinting toward the flitter they had parked one hundred metres up the road. While she was still fifty metres away, she remotely opened the door and activated the engine, tossing aside her micro-tag pistol as she did so. She heard the footsteps of the soldier behind her, trying to keep pace but falling further back.

Reaching the flitter she threw herself into the driver's seat, engaged the drive and used maximum acceleration. The flitter rocketed forward as she closed the door, gaining altitude as it did so, leaving the slower soldier panting in the middle of the road behind her. She flicked on the tracker and got an instant reading on the tag. Two clicks and heading south-west. She had a feeling she knew where Orlando was going. It's where she would go if their places were switched.

Starla changed course and made a direct line for Central Terminal, leapfrogging the patchwork of streets below her. She saw the terminal dead ahead, lit up with spotlights even at this time of night, and she began a power descent, coming in way too hot for comfort. As she drew near, she saw Carmen Orlando's streaker pull up in the empty street at the terminal entrance. Orlando spotted the flitter as it raced down toward her and fired off two rapid laser blasts before abandoning her streaker and running into the terminal. Both blasts went clean through the flitter, the closest shot burning a neat hole in the floor next to Starla's right foot and exiting through the roof centimetres from her head.

She dropped the flitter down onto the empty street, hard and fast, the whole craft shuddering with the impact. She already had the door open before she landed and was out of the craft and running instantly. As she sprinted through the entrance, she spotted Orlando running across the large circular concourse toward the transfer booths in the centre. Starla paused and peeled off a shot, the beam narrowly missing its mark and, instead, damaging a booth slightly to the left of the fugitive. She started running again and saw Orlando enter a booth. The door slid closed and the green light above the door turned red. A few moments later, the light turned green again and the door slid open, revealing an empty booth.

Starla ran into the same booth. As the door closed behind her, she placed her wrist against the ID pad and said,

"Repeat last transfer. Security Override Clearance Code 499512."

A calm voice replied, "Welcome Commander Starla Bree. Request accepted. Processing. Transfer complete. Welcome to D327."

The booth door slid open in the small island's terminal building, and Carmen Orlando fired her laser into the booth from point blank range, firing from side to side from just beyond the door's threshold. Finally she took her finger off the trigger and stood staring at the smoking wreckage of the empty booth, a look of puzzlement on her face. Starla dropped down from her spread-eagled position across the ceiling, pivoting from the top of the door frame and swinging her legs through the open doorway to connect squarely with Orlando's midriff.

Orlando staggered backward, involuntarily bending over in pain, but she was a professional and didn't drop her laser. Ignoring the pain in her stomach, she began to straighten up, raising her arm to aim her pistol at Starla. Starla's own laser was tucked into her belt behind her back, but there was no time to reach around grab it, arm it, aim and then fire. She would be dead before then. Her well-trained military brain processed the situation in a fraction of a second and she did the only thing she could do. She executed a flying roundhouse kick with her right leg, connecting perfectly with Orlando's right wrist and hearing the satisfying crack of breaking bones as the laser pistol was sent flying.

But Starla wasn't finished. She allowed her momentum to complete the movement, her right foot now coming down to land on the ground as her body continued to twist to the left. As she landed on her right foot, she pivoted sharply, with her back now to Orlando, bringing her left leg up and behind her in a beautifully executed spinning-crescent back kick. Her left foot connected perfectly with the side of Orlando's chin and dropped her like a sack of potatoes.

Orlando lay flat on her back, out cold. Starla knelt down and checked her pulse and breathing, then rolled her over and cuffed her. She stood up and retrieved Orlando's pistol, switching it to safety and stuffing it in her belt beside her own. Then she looked around the small terminal, wondering where the cameras were.

*I'd like to take a look at that footage. Two kicks in one move. Not bad. But I think the spinning crescent kick was a bit sloppy. Might need to work on that one a bit more.*

Orland was conscious again, so Starla rolled her over onto her back. Orlando lay there looking up at her in amazement.

"Who are you?"

"I'm Commander Starla Bree and you're under arrest."

"Holy crap, you're good!"

"Yeh. I know."

**17**

———

One of Starla's arrest squad died at the scene, her jugular vein ripped open by a jagged piece of shrapnel. A second soldier lost an eye and also came close to losing his life from blood loss from a severed artery in his arm. The rest of the squad had cuts and abrasions of varying severity, but nothing life-threatening. Starla required stitches to a gash on her cheek that she hadn't noticed until she arrived back at the capital with her prisoner in tow. All twenty-four prisoners were now locked in separate cells at the military base attached to the spaceport, although Orlando's broken wrist and Transid's broken nose had been given appropriate medical treatment first.

By 0500 each of the arrest team leaders had submitted their electronic reports to General Kellar who signed off on the operation, deeming it to be an overwhelming success. At 0600 General Kellar, Police Commissioner Ansell and Starla met in a secure conference room on the military base to map out the way forward from here.

"Don't beat yourself up, Commander," said Kellar, after Starla had lamented the casualties her team had suffered. "The casualties were not your fault. The door was obviously rigged to automatically respond to any attempt at forced entry. You weren't to know."

She shook her head.

"It doesn't make me feel any better about it, though."

Kellar leaned back in his chair and absently touched the slight bruise on his forehead.

"Given the fact that we've effectively rounded up the entire reversionist leadership and their hit squad, I'd say the level of casualties is entirely acceptable."

He glanced at a data screen built into the desk in front of him.

"The collateral damage to public property, however, is another matter. Damage to the front and rear of the apartment building. A transfer pod at Central Terminal shot up by laser fire from your own pistol. A transfer pod on D327 completely destroyed. A flitter shot to hell and its undercarriage bent out of shape by your less-than-subtle landing. Have you got any comment to make about all of that, Commander?"

She stared at Kellar for a few moments before responding.

"I also had some trouble tuning to the classical music channel during my flight. You might want to get the entertainment system looked at, General."

The two soldiers looked at each other with steely expressions until Kellar finally cracked a smile and chuckled.

"I like your style, Commander. I'm just blowing smoke up your arse. That was exceptional work. I don't know of many people who could have accomplished what you did last night. I've got no problem with any part of your operation."

"Thank you, General."

"In fact, I'm promoting you to Colonel, effective immediately."

"Thank you, sir."

"You might be interested in the video of your arrest. It's quite spectacular."

He touched his interface and a video started playing on the wall beside them. The camera was obviously located somewhere up high in the small island's terminal, looking down on the transfer booth. As they watched, the light above one of the booths began to blink red. A moment later, it turned green and the door slid open. Carmen Orlando emerged, breathing heavily and looking harried. She immediately spun on her heels and pointed her gun back at the booth. The door closed again and a red light came on. Nothing happened for about thirty seconds, then the red light started flashing. The light turned green and the door slid open and Orlando went to work with her laser, the brilliant bursts of light momentarily dazzling the camera. She stopped firing and stood still, with her firing arm still extended. Starla's entrance onto the scene was spectacular, swinging through the doorway with the grace of a gymnast and knocking Orlando backward. Her double kick manoeuvre was equally impressive, a single fluid movement executed with the grace of a ballerina and the ferocity of a martial arts expert.

"Pretty impressive, wouldn't you say, Colonel?"

Starla cocked her head to the side.

"The spinning crescent kick was a bit off. I need to work on the extension. I'm a bit rusty. Too much desk work."

Kellar chuckled again.

"Well, if I even attempted what you did, I'd be in a back brace for a month. But enough of that. We've got some decisions to make. Vorn, are you happy with how things have gone so far?"

"Yes, General. Couldn't be happier. The arrests were all by the book. I assume that the prisoners are all demanding to see lawyers."

"Yep. They're all whining like babies. But with martial law now in place, I'm not in any rush. Plus, according to the Terrorist Act, I can keep them locked up indefinitely without any access to legal aid. I'm planning to let them stew in their own juices for a while yet."

Kellar turned toward Starla.

"From this point forward we'll be following your plan, Colonel. We'll present the prisoners with the signed confessions. We'll paint a grim picture, set a distant trial date, leave them stewing for a couple of weeks, then offer them the deal; permanent banishment to the new colony on Earth."

"Do you think they'll take the deal?" asked Ansell.

"I'm certain they will. Particularly if I add some further incentives. I'll make sure the food they are served is barely edible and their cells are cold and uncomfortable. They won't get showers or access to anywhere outside their cells. I guarantee that after two weeks of that, plus staring down the barrel of decades more of the same treatment, they'll be begging to sign up for the colony. It's a no-brainer really."

Starla looked at Ansell.

"How are things shaping up in your department, Commissioner?"

"All the civilians that were wrongly-arrested have now been released and I've stood down a number of officers pending criminal investigations into their recent conduct. I suspect we'll be adding several more names to the list of people being transported to Earth."

"Speaking of which," said Starla, "I think we need to consider the fact that there are almost certainly still some reversionist agitators who remain at large. It would be naïve to think that we got all the trouble-makers last night. I suspect that we arrested the main leaders, but there will be others on the fringes who could step into the vacuum once the current leaders are gone."

"So what do you suggest, Colonel?" asked Kellar.

"Enticement. I think we need to mount an advertising campaign, painting the virtues of the new colony, aimed specifically at reversionists. After all, the colony is everything the reversionists have been demanding for decades; a pristine world without AI technology. We can simply offer free passage to anyone who wants to go."

Kellar grunted and nodded.

"In other words," he interpreted, "we're saying, 'If you don't like it here, piss off!'"

"Well, I wouldn't put it quite so bluntly, General. But, yes, that is effectively what we would be saying. The existence of an AI-free world now means that there is no reason for people who feel strongly about the issue to try to change *our* world. They can simply leave."

Ansell spoke up.

"Colonel, as the head of Gateway Station, you are in regular contact with Earth. We know that our colony in Hobart is committed to a society free from artificial intelligence, but what about the other colony in Wellington. What if they have AI technology? By sending a whole group of reversionists to Earth won't we just be exporting our problems to them?"

Starla shook her head.

"I am in weekly contact with Amanda Robinson, the Mayor of Wellington, and she assures me that the Novans and Perditans, who founded the Wellington colony, are equally determined that Earth remains free from any technology that might allow for the future development of artificial intelligence. Quite honestly, Earth is going to be a reversionist heaven. Transid and his gang will have no reason to start making trouble there, and we can transport them with a completely clear conscience. I can't foresee any problems at all."

Starla was a clear-thinking leader who rarely made mistakes, but in this instance, she was completely and utterly wrong.

**18**

———

The first flitter touched down on Wrights Hill shortly after 0900, followed soon after by two more. Overnight, Zac had searched through the historical records that had been on board Genesis when it left Earth and which were now part of the colony's data base. He had identified the name of the hill and had discovered that there had been an underground bunker built there during World War Two, in the mid twentieth century; a system of shallow underground tunnels servicing a large gun, strategically placed at the top of the hill. Zac surmised that the government of his own era, the Democratic Alliance of Nations, had chosen the same site to construct the much deeper and more extensive bunker in which Mel and her mother had sheltered. And now, yesterday's scans had revealed that the bunker had apparently been transformed even further in subsequent years, enlarged into a labyrinth of tunnels and multiple levels extending much deeper beneath the surface. It was an astonishing discovery. People had survived here after the GAE! Today was going to be an exciting day. He only hoped that there would not be any gruesome discoveries to upset Mel.

Given that two metres of earth needed to be excavated to

reach the head of the access shaft, the colony had supplied them with an earth-nibbler, a small remote-controlled machine that removed soil and redeposited it several metres away via an extended chute, grinding any rocks in the process. The City Council was extremely excited to learn of the bunker's discovery and had stocked the flitters full of equipment, along with some additional personnel. An engineer, a scientist, an archaeologist and two soldiers had joined Zac and the others for today's exploration of the bunker.

As the people unloaded and sorted their gear, Phil and the other scientist began mapping the extent of the bunker, roaming across the hilltop, each armed with ground-penetrating scanners. Meanwhile the engineer fired up the earth-nibbler and began eating away at the soil and rocks that were covering the ancient access shaft. It took twenty minutes before he made contact with the top of the shaft, and a further thirty minutes of excavation until he had uncovered the entire concrete slab. The concrete square, four metres on each side, now sat at the bottom of a deep hole, two meters deep on the high side and about one metre deep on the low side of the slope. The nibbler took a further ten minutes to remove additional soil on the lower side, so that people could access the slab without needing ladders.

By now the entire group were gathered around the site. Everyone from yesterday was present, along with Dayna and Noah.

Zac and the archaeologist, Wilford Albright, were the first to walk onto the slab, and they spent some time searching its surface for any historical markings.

"It's just a blank slab," said Zac. "No markings, no writing. Nothing."

"Yes," agreed Wilf, rubbing his hand across his completely bald dome. "It's just the top of the shaft. I'd say the shaft was originally exposed on the side of this slope, with a door on the lower side."

A decision was made to keep digging in the hope of finding an access door. The nibbler was fired up again and after another hour, the side of the shaft on the lower side of the slope was exposed to a depth of an additional two meters. A large metal door was built into the side of the shaft, obviously made of some kind on non-corrosive metal. Once again, Zac and Wilford were the first to examine the structure and this time they found something of note, although they didn't need a close inspection to find it. The centre of the door was dominated by two large embossed letters that stood out in stark relief; 'NE'.

"Any idea what 'NE' stands for?" asked Zac.

"North-east?" suggested Wilf.

"No entry?" ventured Zac.

"No eating?" added Keo helpfully.

"That'd be right," said Tash, shaking her head. "Always thinking of your stomach."

"In his case, there's a lot there to be thinking about," quipped Zac.

"Very funny," said Keo in a tone of mock indignation. "I'll have you know it's been nearly two hours since I've eaten. You light-weights might be able to get by on minimal rations, but my heavy-duty chassis requires regular fuel intake to maintain its supercharged performance."

"Yes dear, whatever you say," said Tash.

Zac turned to Mel who was directly behind him.

"Mel, does this look familiar to you at all?"

"The shaft looks identical; exactly the same size. And the position on the side of the hill looks about right, too. But that door is new. The old door was a rusted iron door with a central locking wheel."

"I guess that's to be expected," answered Zac. "An iron door would have completely rusted away by now."

Phil stepped forward with a small electronic device and scanned what appeared to be a touchpad on the shaft wall near the right side of the door. After a few moments he shook his head.

"This keypad is completely dead. I guess it would be too much to expect it to be still powered after thousands of years."

There was a simple handle on the side of the door. Zac pulled on it but, of course, the door didn't budge.

"Any ideas?" he asked, turning to the engineer in the group.

Erik Karlsson scanned the edge of the door near the handle with a hand-held device.

"There is a locking tongue in place. I'll have to cut it, as long as it's OK with you historical egg heads."

Zac nodded.

"It's the only way we're going to get in. Go for it."

Erik quickly retrieved a laser cutter from his nearby kit bag, donned a protective face mask and gloves, and began cutting while everyone else stayed at a safe distance. It took less than a minute to cut through the door's edge including the solid metal locking tongue. Stepping back, Erik asked,

"Who wants the honour?"

Zac turned around.

"Mel? I think it's only fair that you open the door. That's if you want to."

"Sure," she said, stepping forward.

She grasped the simple handle and pulled. Nothing happened. She pulled again, this time putting all her strength into it. Again, nothing. Erik ran his scanner around the entire edge of the door and shook his head, clearly puzzled.

"I'm not sure what the problem is. Maybe the hinge is seized up after all these years. I suggest I just cut a big hole through the middle of the door, big enough for us to fit through."

Several moments were spent brainstorming any other possibilities but, in the end, Erik's suggestion was agreed upon. He stepped forward again, fired up the laser cutter and began outlining a large oval-shaped hole in the middle of the door. As he finished the cut at the top a few minutes later, the whole piece fell inward and smashed onto the floor with a reverberating clang. A cloud of dust issued from the dark hole and everyone's ears were ringing.

"Well, that certainly would have woken the natives up," said Kit, facetiously. No one really expected there to be anyone left alive down there after three millennia.

Zac stepped forward and peered into the structure. It appeared to be a standard access shaft, with concrete steps leading down from the entrance landing. Mel was beside him and confirmed that it looked identical to the shaft of the command bunker that she had once sheltered in.

"OK, folks," said Zac, turning to the group behind him. "Headlamps on. Gloves on as well. And keep your oxygen masks handy in case our air samplers identify a problem."

Zac, Phil and Erik were the first to step across the threshold. Phil checked a small hand-held device and announced that the air was safe to breathe. Meanwhile, Erik had turned and examined the inside of the door to determine why it hadn't opened.

"Zac, you'd better take a look at this."

"What?" asked Zac, adding his own head lamp to the investigation.

"There's a solid weld all around the inside of the door."

Zac's brain started spinning its wheels.

"So, that means...?"

"It was welded shut from the inside," finished Erik for him. "People were still alive when they shut themselves in."

**19**

---

The group walked down the stairs in single file, their footsteps leaving imprints in the chalky white dust and their headlamps shining through clouds of tiny suspended particles that sparkled like fireflies in the darkness. The stairs continually bent back on themselves, their descent punctuated by a series of square concrete landings.

"It's just like a set of fire stairs in an old-fashioned building from the 21$^{st}$ century," said Kit, her voice echoing up and down the shaft.

They counted twenty sets of stairs before they finally reached the bottom which opened out into a larger landing facing a concrete wall with another metal door.

Mel looked around, scanning the area with her headlamp.

"Yep, this is the same as I remember, except the door is different."

The two embossed letters, NE, once again dominated the door's centre.

"New entrance?" suggested Kit.

"Nasty eels?" ventured Tash.

"Nearly exhausted?" said Keo, panting after his descent.

"Sounds like your high-performance chassis could do with a tune up, dude," said Zac.

"I'm just savouring the air, bro."

The laser cutter was utilised again – at the door's edge initially, with the same negative result. Once again, they waited while Erik cut out another large hole in the middle of the door. As the cut was completed, the centre-piece fell out, this time falling back toward them, into the access shaft, crashing to the floor with an ear shattering clang that echoed up and down the shaft like an ancient church bell calling devotees to worship.

"Wow!" said Kit, rubbing her ears and blinking in surprise. "That was loud enough to raise the dead!" Then she realised what she had just said and turned around to Mel.

"Sorry Mel. I didn't mean ... um ... I wasn't thinking."

"That's OK," said Mel. "My mother is thousands of years dead. I've come to terms with that. There's no need to tiptoe around my feelings."

Zac was the first to step through into the darkened interior beyond, but as he did so, rows of ceiling lights flickered to life, suddenly illuminating a large vestibule. Immediately to their left were two lifts whose operational lights came to life at the same time. To their right was a glass walled room with a long conference table surrounded by black padded chairs. Straight ahead, the vestibule ended in a similar glass wall that looked down onto what was clearly an operational control room, with long rows of workstations, each with old fashioned computer screens. The far wall of the recessed command centre was dominated by a huge screen that was now lit up with the words, Democratic Alliance of Nations Command Bunker.

"Oh my gosh!" said Mel. "This is it! This is really it! This is the conference room where mum had her meetings. And that's the control room, down below!"

The conference room's side wall was also made of glass so

that its occupants could look directly down on the activities of the sunken control room.

"But this railing definitely wasn't here," Mel added.

A curved, glass-panelled, waist-height metal railing extended around the vestibule, rising up from the floor and holding them back about one metre from the entrance to the conference room and from the glass wall overlooking the sunken control room. The floor on the other side of the railing was painted bright red, with the words "No Entry" repeated at intervals around the perimeter.

"So, NE means 'No Entry'?" asked Jaz, who until now had had very little to say.

"I don't think so," said Zac. "I think it's just coincidental."

"This is weird!" said Tash. "It's like a ... like a ..."

"Museum," finished Kit.

"Yes! Exactly right! It's like a museum!"

"Check this out, guys," said Keo.

A plaque was mounted on the railing directly opposite the entrance to the conference room. Keo read the words out to the rest of the group.

"This is the conference room where President Elizabeth Canning and her war cabinet met immediately prior to The Scorching. The room has been restored to its original condition, including coffee mugs and 23$^{rd}$ century data pads. President Canning sat at the head of the table, closest to the door."

"There's a similar explanatory sign over here," said Phil, standing at the railing overlooking the sunken control room.

"It's not just like a museum. It *is* a museum," whispered Zac, in awe.

"The Scorching. That's what these people called it," said Kit.

"Yes, but who were they? How long ago did they set this museum up?" asked Zac.

No one had an answer.

"Has anyone noticed anything odd about the floor?" asked Karl, Jaz's partner.

They all immediately looked down at the polished floor.

"What do you mean?" asked Jaz, coming to stand beside him.

"No dust," said Karl, succinctly. "It's perfectly clean. In fact, everything is in pristine condition. It's completely different to the stairwell. It's as if it was all cleaned yesterday."

Keo was munching on a muffin that he had stolen from the lunch provisions, and he spoke with his mouth half full.

"Maybe it's just not dusty down here?"

As he spoke, some crumbs fell from the corner of his mouth.

Immediately, a flap at the bottom of the wall behind them opened, and a small disc-shaped object emerged. It glided across the floor, dodging people's feet, and sucked up the crumbs that Keo had dropped, then rapidly disappeared back into its cavity.

"There's your answer," said Zac. "There aren't any ancients left alive, wandering around with mop buckets."

"Where do I get one of those things?" asked Tash. "It would have a full-time job just following Keo around!"

"How are they powered?" asked Dayna. "In fact, how is this whole place still running after thousands of years?"

"The whole place must be nuclear powered," offered Karl, drawing on his technical knowledge as a shuttle pilot. "It will probably keep on running for thousands more years."

One of the two soldiers that the council had supplied had pressed the button on the nearest lift and it opened with a pleasant-sounding chime.

"Let's keep heading down," suggested Zac.

It was a large lift and they all managed to fit in easily. The display panel indicated that they were on Level 6. They pressed the button for the next level down and moments later they walked out into an almost identical vestibule, this time looking through a glass wall into the operational command centre that they had seen from above. The vestibule was similarly ringed with a glass panelled, waist-height wall with a plaque describing the function and operation of the command centre.

"I'm surprised they didn't have recorded holograms to describe the various rooms," said Kit.

Zac shrugged.

"Maybe they were trying to keep the experience authentic; sticking to old-fashioned text."

The next level down, Level 4, proved to be accommodation and a small gym. Rather than a single vestibule, the group were able to wander through corridors and look into bedrooms, living quarters, communal lounge areas and kitchens, with glass panels blocking each of the doorways. Elizabeth Canning's quarters were given special attention, with a detailed plaque at the doorway. It was here that they gained the first real clue as to how long she had survived down here. The last sentence of the plaque stated,

"This remained President Canning's quarters for the first twelve years after The Scorching."

Mel was transfixed at the doorway, trying to imagine her mother existing down here for that long.

"Twelve years!" exclaimed Tash. "I don't know how she did it. I would have gone stir-crazy!"

"But what happened after twelve years?" asked Dayna. "Did they leave the bunker and venture back out onto the surface? There's no evidence of human habitation anywhere on the planet – at least not that our scans have been able to detect."

"I don't think twelve years would have been long enough to make the surface habitable," Zac answered. "I'm guessing they went down, not up."

"Let's keep doing the same," said Kit, who was curious to see more.

The next level down was entirely devoted to food production. There was an extensive aquaponics area, that still appeared to be operational, with healthy-looking plants being fed from drip lines. Small robots were scurrying around, tending the plants and harvesting the crops.

"It's still operational!" said Dayna, incredulously.

Plaques throughout the facility drew attention to the various processes being undertaken.

"What happens to the crops when they are harvested?" wondered Keo, eyeing some particularly juicy-looking pears.

"I'm guessing it all gets recycled and used as fertiliser," suggested Phil. "This whole facility has probably been running on an endless automated cycle for centuries."

Another section on the same level was devoted to protein production from yeast.

"Was all this down here when you were here, Mel?" asked Jaz.

"Yes. Mum told me about it, but I never came down here."

The next level down, Level 2, was dedicated to power generation, recycling and waste disposal. As Phil had previously suggested, the facility was powered by a nuclear power plant, although a very ancient one. They wandered through the level, reading the plaques and trying to imagine what it would be like to live out your life in a limited subterranean world such as this.

As they walked back into the lift and pressed the button to descend to Level 1, Dayna asked, "Have you noticed that they numbered the levels from the bottom up? I would have thought it would make more sense to number them from the top down. After all, that's where you enter the facility. I wonder why they did it that way?"

Her question was never answered. The doors opened and

they gasped in astonishment. Mel's hands flew to her mouth and her eyes immediately glistened with tears.

There, standing directly in front of them, was her mother, Elizabeth Canning.

**20**

———————

The likeness was uncanny and the statue was amazingly lifelike. They stepped out into a large room, twenty metres by twenty metres, with various displays around the walls. The centre of the room was dominated by two statues of Elizabeth Canning, the closest one facing the lifts and the other one, about six metres further into the room, facing the large double doors on the far side of the room. An illuminated sign above the doors stated, 'Exit'. Both statues of Elizabeth Canning were life-sized and captured her in different poses. They approached the first statue and read the inscription underneath it:

"President Elizabeth Catherine Canning, First President of New Eden."

The group stood in front of the statue, absolutely stunned.

Dayna was the first person to speak.

"New Eden. So that's what 'NE' stands for."

Tash was confused.

"But she was the eleventh president of the Democratic Alliance of Nations, wasn't she? I'm pretty sure she was the eleventh."

"She was," confirmed Zac.

"So ... what the hell?"

Zac pondered for a moment.

"It seems as though they regarded 'The Scorching', as they called it, as the starting point of a new chapter in Earth's history. Elizabeth effectively became the last president of DAN and the first president of the new community of survivors."

"New Eden," said Keo, mentally chewing over the name as if savouring some new flavour. "I like it. It's biblical. I think it's very appropriate."

Mel was standing transfixed in front of the statue. She had almost forgotten what her mother looked like.

Jaz moved to stand beside Mel and placed her arm around her shoulders.

"How are you feeling?"

"Strange. It's been over thirty years since I saw her. And now I look older than her. She's so young."

"And she looks pretty determined," said Kit.

"Oh yeh," said Mel, smiling. "She certainly was! She was strong and courageous, clear thinking and incredibly intelligent. She was a good mother, too."

The group broke up and wandered around the large room which was effectively a shrine to Elizabeth. The walls were lined with recreations of some of her clothes, her hand-written notes, her laptop and notepad. There were also images of her in the conference room as well as others of her in various places around the facility. Mel's favourite was an image of her mother in the hydroponics farm, dressed in dirty clothes and harvesting beans, smiling at the camera as if she had just shared a joke.

The group finally came to the double doors at the far side of the room. Both doors under the exit sign swung smoothly inward as they pushed gently on them. The walked through into a moderately-sized rectangular vestibule, with the longer sides to their left and right. Straight ahead was another set of double doors, with an illuminated sign above them saying, THANK YOU FOR YOUR VISIT. The right-hand wall was a feature wall declaring the name of the museum, featuring huge, embossed metal words: 'THE ELIZABETH CANNING MEMORIAL MUSEUM'. Underneath, in smaller embossed letters, was the declaration, 'Sponsored and Maintained by New Eden City Council'.

Along the left wall of the vestibule was a reception counter with a small door behind it leading to some other internal room. There were various electronic images shifting and changing on the wall behind the counter and a stack of what looked like data pads on the counter.

"What's that smell?" asked one of the soldiers.

"Smells like coffee," said his counterpart.

Karl walked over to the counter and lifted a cup that was sitting there. It was half full and still warm.

"Um ... guys ... I think we might have a problem ..."

At that moment the doors on the far side of the room opened a crack and a small metallic ball rolled in, coming to rest in the middle of the floor. A light started blinking rapidly on it and one of the soldiers shouted,

"It's a bomb! Everyone down on the floor, now!"

The explosion that took place seconds later had a devastating impact, not only in that enclosed space, but also around the globe and throughout the galaxy.

## 21

The bomb exploded with terrifying ferocity, but most of them were saved by the fact that it was designed to momentarily incapacitate rather than wreak absolute destruction. Those who survived later surmised that the bomb throwers wanted to minimise the damage to their beloved museum. As it was, however, it did more than enough damage to the colonists. The concussion momentarily overwhelmed their senses and deafened them. The majority had heeded the soldier's warning and flung themselves on the ground, thus saving themselves from significant injury from the flying shrapnel, but most still ended up bleeding from lacerations.

At the same time as the detonation, the vestibule lights went out and they were plunged into darkness. The double doors opened and human-like figures entered, armed with laser rifles, their headlamps shining through the smoke-filled darkness. It was difficult to tell whether they were battle-suited humans or robots, because they were clad from head to foot in a shiny bronze-coloured exterior, including either a face-hugging helmet or a full-blown robotic head-piece. The colonists didn't have time to ask questions, however, as the bronze-clad attackers immediately opened fire on them.

The two soldiers were quick to respond, opening fire with their own laser rifles, and yelling at the others to stay down. The others continued to lie flat on the ground, while the two soldiers returned fire. Fortuitously, the soldiers had been on different sides of the room when the bomb went off, so they were able to set up an effective field of crossfire, bringing down two of the attackers and keeping the rest pinned down on the other side of the doors. The soldier nearest to Zac managed to undo his pistol holster and throw his pistol to Zac while still getting off shots with his rifle.

"Here! Help us out!" he yelled.

The soldier on the other side of the room managed to give his sidearm to Karl, so they quickly had a crossfire of four weapons. But they knew they couldn't keep the attackers at bay for long. As laser fire lit up the dark, smoke-filled room, two more attackers managed to gain entry and take up position behind a small statue of Elizabeth just inside the doors.

One of the soldiers yelled at the rest of the colonists,

"Get out of here! Everyone! Up off the floor and back through the museum!"

No one needed a second invitation. As the four men with weapons lay down a field of intense covering fire, lighting up the billowing clouds of smoke with purple laser beams, the rest of them crawled, ran or stumbled through the double doors. As the last of them made it through, the four remaining men began making their retreat, firing as they went. For a moment it looked as though all four would make it, but as they reached the doors one of the soldiers was hit by two shots simultaneously, one through his upper left shoulder and the second through the middle of his chest. He dropped to the ground dead. As the three remaining men backed through the doors, firing as they went, Zac bent down and picked up the dead soldier's rifle. They made it through and as they closed the doors Zac slid the rifle through the looped handles on the two doors, effectively stopping the doors from opening from the other side.

"That won't hold them for long, but it will give us a bit more time," he said. "Let's get out of here! Is everyone OK?"

"Phil! Phil!" yelled Melody. "Where's Phil? He's not here."

"He didn't make it," said Karl. "I saw him go down."

"Nooo!" screamed Mel, trying to run back to the doors.

Zac didn't have time for pleasantries.

"He's not coming, Mel. He's dead. He was shot in the head. I saw it too. Now we've got to go!"

He forcibly propelled her back up the room. Kit grabbed her and kept her moving as she continued to sob hysterically.

The lights were out in the larger statue room as well, so they switched their headlamps on as they ran and stumbled their way toward the lifts. They were only half-way through the room when they heard the attackers begin battering the doors and firing their lasers into them. The doors started to splinter as they reached the still-open lift and began piling in. Tash was at the control panel, already pushing the button for the sixth floor as the last of them entered. The attackers finally broke open the double doors with a splintering crash. Immediately they began firing toward the lifts as Tash repeatedly pressed the symbol for closing the door while Zac, Karl and the remaining soldier returned fire. Finally, agonisingly slowly, the doors started closing. But as they did so, two things happened at once. A laser blast from the attackers scored a direct hit on one of the colonists. At the same time Zac slipped back out through the closing doors, into the darkness of the statue room.

"Nooo!" screamed Kit.

She threw herself toward the lift control panel, trying to stop it and reopen the door, but it was too late. Zac was gone and the lift had started its ascent.

## 22

'Plan' was a very loose term for what Zac was trying to do. In fact he had acted instinctively, almost without thinking. He knew that unless the second lift was taken out of action, or at least slowed, the bronze-clad attackers would use it and would quickly catch up to the struggling colonists, killing or capturing all of them before they made it to the surface.

As soon as he was out of the first lift, he punched the call button for the second while simultaneously firing his laser pistol toward the oncoming attackers. He knew that if the lift was on one of the higher floors, he was probably a dead man. But he had taken a chance that these lifts returned to the first floor when the building was empty, because the last people to leave the museum would surely have to go down to the bottom floor to exit.

He was right. The lift door opened immediately and he threw himself in, pressing the button for the sixth floor as he did so. He heard the sound of the attackers running toward him as the lift doors remained stubbornly open. Flattening himself against the side of the lift he pressed the symbol for closing the door and then dropped flat to the floor. He started firing continually and was sure he saw two of the running attackers go down. Meanwhile the lift was getting hit from every angle with laser fire, including the side wall where he had been standing only seconds ago. As the lift doors finally closed, he peeled off a last shot, drilling an attacker through the middle of the face, only a couple of metres from the closing door.

The lift started rising and Zac sat up. He was trembling all over and he could barely keep hold of his pistol as the nervous reaction set in. He watched the display panel, counting up through the levels until Level 6 lit up and the doors opened. Karl and the surviving soldier had their guns levelled at him, unsure who or what would be emerging. They lowered their weapons with relief but before Zac could say anything, Kit stepped forward and grabbed him by the front of his shirt.

"What were you thinking, Zac!" she screamed, then flung her arms around him. "Don't you ever do that again!"

"I'm not planning to, my love."

"We've got to move!" said the soldier.

"Before we do, we need to take these lifts out of action," said Zac.

"We've already taken care of the first one," said Karl, indicating the burnt-out control panel, still smoking from multiple laser blasts. He moved to the lift that Zac had just vacated and raised his pistol to fire at that control panel as well.

"Wait! Don't fire!" yelled Zac.

"Why not?"

"I'm not sure, but I just don't think it's a good idea to permanently disable the second lift. We might want to use it again at some point. Get out of the way, and I'll show you what I'm thinking."

Karl stepped away from the lift and Zac approached the still-open doors. He dialled his laser pistol down to fifty percent power and widened the aperture, then fired a long burst at the base of one of the doors. The door and its track melted together and fused. He did the same with the other door and then stepped back to admire his handiwork.

"That lift's going nowhere for a while."

Karl noticed a small door, just to the side of the second lift and opened it to see where it led.

"This is a stairwell! I can hear footsteps! They're coming up the stairs!"

Zac turned to the others and yelled,

"Everyone get going! Hurry!"

Karl slammed the door shut and adjusted his pistol as he had just seen Zac do. He began fusing the door to its metal frame. Zac joined him and started from the other side and in a few moments the door was welded shut.

"I don't think they'll be getting through that any time soon," said Karl.

"Zac! We've got a problem here!" called the soldier.

He was standing next to Keo who was slumped on the ground, with his back against the wall near the entrance to the access shaft. Tash was kneeling beside him, and Keo was holding his side. There was a pool of blood on the floor beside him.

Zac came running to up them and Tash looked up at him with fear in her eyes.

"He was shot when we were in the lift. It looks bad."

Zac knelt down and noticed how pale his friend looked.

"Keo, can you walk?"

"No problem, bro. It's just a little scratch."

He tried to stand up but barely moved his backside off the ground before sagging back against the wall.

"On second thoughts, I might just sit here for a few minutes and catch my breath."

As he spoke, they heard pounding and banging commence on the other side of the door that they had just fused.

"I don't think we've got a few minutes, dude. We're gonna have to move you."

Karl and Zac pocketed their pistols and knelt on each side of Keo.

"Just put your arms around both of our shoulders, Keo, and we'll do the rest," said Zac.

"Are you sure you skinny little white boys are gonna be able to carry a heavy-duty chassis like mine?"

"As you once said to me, 'you ain't heavy, you're my brother'."

They lifted Keo and started the long haul back up the stairs, with the soldier bringing up the rear, his rifle at the ready. Ahead they could hear Melody sobbing hysterically as she was propelled up the stairs by the others. There were splashes of blood on the steps too, indicating at least one bleeding wound among the survivors.

Zac and Karl had barely reached the top of the second flight of stairs when they heard the sizzle of lasers burning through the door that they had only just fused in the vestibule.

"We'd better pick up our pace, Karl," said Zac, who was already breathing so heavily he could barely speak.

The soldier stopped at the next landing and told them to keep going.

"I'm going to lay down some suppressing fire. Give you guys some more time."

"OK, but don't do anything dumb, man," said Karl. "You get the hell out of there when you need to."

"Will do."

Zac and Karl kept going as fast as they could, breathing raggedly with sweat pouring off them.

"Hey Keo?"

"Yeh, bro?"

"You know what I said about you not being heavy?"

"Uh huh."

"I take it back, dude. You've gotta ease up on those muffins."

"It's Tash's fault, bro. It's all those muffins."

They had reached the half-way point in their ascent when they heard laser fire from below. The exchange heated up and the echoes of a ferocious gun battle reverberated up the shaft. The battle continued while they ascended two more flights of stairs and then the firing ceased and they heard the sound of numerous sets of boots pounding up the stairs.

"That doesn't sound good," gasped Karl.

"I've heard better sounds," agreed Zac.

The staccato echoes of boots on the stairs below them sounded like machine gun fire and it was gaining rapidly.

"Bro, you're not gonna make it. Put me down."

"Never gonna happen."

"Damn it, Zac, put me down! Don't do this, man!"

"Why don't you do something useful and pray?" said Zac, gasping for breath.

At that moment Erik, the council engineer, emerged from the stairs above.

"I got Melody to the top," he said. "Thought I'd come back and see if you boys need a hand."

He squeezed past them to the step below, put his shoulder under Keo's backside and started pushing. Suddenly, they were running up the stairs. The sound of boots below them were still gaining, but not as quickly anymore.

Sooner than they expected, they reached the top landing and squeezed through the doorway into bright sunshine. They turned and stumbled up the hill toward the flitters, about fifty metres away, expecting at any moment to be caught in laser fire from the pursuers when they emerged from the bunker. But it never happened. They reached the flitters safely. One had already lifted off carrying Noah, Wilford, Dayna and Mel. A second flitter was powered up and waiting for them, with Kit, Tash and Jaz already on board. They eased

Keo in and lay him down on a med bed that had already been unfolded.

"Anyone else?" asked the pilot.

Zac shook his head.

"No. The rest didn't make it."

The flitter took off, quickly gaining altitude and velocity. The access shaft was visible below them, rapidly diminishing as they rose higher, but no sign of the pursuers could be seen. The third flitter, which had carried most of their gear, lifted off just behind them, leaving most of the gear strewn across the hillside.

Keo was in a bad way, drifting in and out of consciousness and mumbling deliriously. He'd lost a lot of blood. Jazz's medical training immediately kicked into gear. She had opened the med locker while she was waiting for them to arrive and had all the necessary gear ready. She quickly inserted a cannula into Keo's arm and started a plasma drip, then gave him a shot of pain relief and an injection of antibiotics. Meanwhile, Kit was applying pressure bandages to his stomach wound and Tash was monitoring his vitals. Zac, on the other hand, felt utterly useless. All he could do was hold his friend's hand and keep talking to him.

"You hang in there, Keo. Do you hear me? You fight this, brother. Don't give in. Stay awake. We're safe now. We'll be at the hospital in a minute and you're gonna be fine. Can you hear me? Stay with us man."

Keo opened his eyes briefly and looked straight at Zac. He squeezed Zac's hand and leaned his head towards him to speak. Zac sensed that Keo was about to say something profound.

"My turnips are itchy," he said, and then he slumped back into unconsciousness.

**23**

———

Keo was rushed into surgery. The laser blast had drilled a hole clean through his left side, destroying his kidney, perforating part of his large intestine and slicing through some major blood vessels. He was in surgery for nearly four hours while they removed his kidney and repaired the rest of the internal damage. For the next 24 hours, Keo's life hung in the balance. He was kept in an induced coma while the nanobots they had injected into his bloodstream did their repair work, engineering new cells in damaged areas. As he lay unconscious the rest of that day and throughout the night, Tash, Kit and Zac didn't leave his side, apart from Zac's attendance at a brief emergency council meeting.

On the second day, Keo turned the corner. He came off life support and regained consciousness, but he had no memory of the flight to the hospital.

"What's the last thing you remember?" asked Zac.

"I remember telling you about Tash's muffins, and after that it's a complete blank."

"My muffins?" asked Tash, incredulously. "You were basically dying and all you could think to talk about were my muffins?"

"Well, they are exceptional muffins, my love."

"He was blaming you for how fat he is," added Zac, helpfully.

"Woah, bro! You've overstepped the mark there!"

Tash poked the side of his butt and said, "Zac's right. I'm putting you on a diet, effectively immediately. No more muffins for you!"

Keo groaned.

"Oh man! I must have died and woken up in hell!"

There were other injuries among the survivors. Kit had needed stitches to a gash in her thigh, probably from shrapnel, and Erik had sustained a cut to his forehead which had bled profusely but was not serious. Zac had been nicked by a laser blast which had gouged a furrow across his shoulder. He had no memory of being hit, and there had been only a little bleeding because the laser had cauterised the wound. The medical staff at the hospital indicated the need for plastic surgery to remove the scar tissue and stitch the wound up, but Zac refused. He was rather proud of the scar it would leave and saw no need to remove it.

Mayor Amanda Robinson was at the hospital as the flitters first arrived and she continued to be a regular visitor, giving comfort to the injured while at the same time trying to piece together what had happened and determine what ongoing threat the colony might face. No one was as regular a visitor as Zac, however, who maintained an almost permanent presence at his friend's bedside for the four days of his hospital stay.

An emergency meeting of the City Council was held on the evening of the attack. Zac was present, along with Karl, and Erik, the engineer. Together, they provided a detailed description of the events that had unfolded. At the conclusion of their account, the mayor stood and began pacing around the large oval table in council's meeting room.

"There's a bunch of questions I'd really like the answers to. Who or what were they? Why did they attack? And what is the ongoing risk to our colony? In regard to the first question, what is your opinion? Are they human or robots?"

"It's hard to tell," answered Karl. "At first I thought they were robots. They were metallic, burnished bronze or gold coloured figures, and I automatically assumed they weren't human. But as they chased us toward the lifts, there was something about their movements, too fluid and perfect, that made me think they had to be human."

"I agree," said Zac. "The last attacker I shot was only two metres away and as I put a hole through his head piece, I'm sure I caught a glimpse of a human face."

"Well if that's true," said Amanda, "How the hell have they survived here for thousands of years without leaving a trace of their existence on the surface?"

Erik spoke up, offering an opinion from his engineering expertise.

"I can tell you that the access tunnel we dug up hasn't been used for centuries at least. It was buried under two metres of compacted earth and rock. That tends to suggest that they have survived totally underground."

"Unless there are other access shafts that are still open to the surface," added Zac.

"Yes, that's yet to be determined," agreed Amanda. She sighed deeply.

"OK, that brings us to the next question: why did they attack?"

"That's just as puzzling," answered Zac. "We weren't acting aggressively. We didn't pose an obvious threat. Most of us were unarmed. I can't see what would have prompted such a hostile act."

"Although we did destroy two doors on the way in," said Karl. "That wouldn't have looked particularly friendly."

"Granted," agreed Zac, "but even so, their reaction was completely over the top."

"I agree," said Amanda. "There is clearly some kind of underlying issue at work there that we are currently unaware of. I guess the most important issue for our immediate concern, however, is whether our colony is now at risk of imminent attack."

There was a pause as they all considered the question. Finally Zac spoke up.

"What puzzles me is why they never emerged from the bunker. They must have been only a couple of flights of steps behind us by the time we got to the top. They could easily have emerged and blasted the crap out of us. But they didn't. We made it all the way to the flitters without further engagement, and there was still no sign of them as we took off."

"So are you saying you think they're afraid of being on the surface?"

"Perhaps. Or maybe it's not fear. Maybe it's a philosophical objection of some kind. Whatever the reason, there's a very strong motivation at play here that caused them to weld up those doors so securely in the first place."

"Unless they just didn't want to use that particular access shaft any longer because it is attached to their sacred museum," said Karl.

"That makes sense as well," said Amanda. "In which case there could be numerous other access shafts still in use that we simply haven't found yet. I think we have to assume that to be the case and prepare accordingly."

Amanda nodded toward a silver-haired military figure with a buzz cut and a clipped moustache.

"Colonel Carlisle, what's the state of our security forces?"

"We have a company of 112 soldiers who I've already

deployed around the perimeter of the colony in squads of six to eight. They will all remain on duty throughout tonight until 0800 tomorrow, at which time we will revert to eight-hour shifts. I've also deployed motion sensors every hundred metres around the perimeter as well as laser canons with flood lights. If any of those bastards come at us, we'll be ready."

"Thank you, Riff. I appreciate your quick action. At first light tomorrow, I'm ordering a fleet of our colony's flitters to begin a grid search of the hills to our west, using their onboard scanners. If there are any operational access shafts out there, we'll find them."

"And what do we do if we find some?" asked Zac.

"That's a good question. We'll jump that bridge when we come to it."

24

There was no attack that night. Nor the next day. Nor even the day after. Three days of continuous searching of the hills by the flitters, using their most advanced multi-frequency scanners, did not uncover any trace of other access shafts or any other kind of human-built structures. The hills were completely bare. On the morning immediately following the attack, two squads of heavily armed soldiers landed at the excavation site to retrieve the equipment that had been abandoned. All the gear appeared to be untouched, but the door into the access shaft had been welded closed again from the inside. It seemed as though the people who had attacked them simply wanted to be left alone.

On the fourth day after the attack, a memorial service was held for the three who had lost their lives. It was a difficult day for the colony. The town hall was packed and the grieving families were surrounded by people offering their comfort and support. Colonel Riff Carlisle gave a eulogy for the two soldiers who had lost their lives protecting the civilians in their care. Zac felt ashamed that he had never even bothered to find out their names. Dayna – Jaz and Zac's daughter – gave a moving eulogy for Phil, whose death had deeply impacted their circle of friends.

Mel, of course, was devastated. She was a mess. Her relationship with Phil had been late to blossom, but it had become the central grounding point of her life. He had been a stabilising influence for her, moderating her more incendiary personality and bringing a certain stability to her life. Mel had become a softer, more considerate person under Phil's calming influence and they had shared a love deeper than she had thought possible. But now he was gone and her grief was overwhelming. Jaz and Dayna stayed with her continually in the days after the attack, taking over the practical necessities such as cooking and cleaning and, more importantly, just being there for her.

At the conclusion of the memorial service, Zac and Karl made a point of introducing themselves to the families of the deceased soldiers, telling them that their loved ones were heroes who had saved their lives and the lives of everyone else who had survived.

Afterward, the circle of friends gathered in Tash and Keo's apartment to share a meal together and to continue to support Mel. The doctors had wanted to keep Keo in the hospital for another 24 hours but he had insisted on attending the memorial. He was now reclining on a deck chair on the balcony, playing up to his role as an invalid.

"Tash, my love!" he called over his shoulder. "I'm starving! Can I have something to eat?"

A moment later she came out with a plate containing a raw turnip and a single piece of lettuce.

"Very funny," he said, grimacing.

"Welcome to your new diet, sweetheart," Tash said with a sweet smile.

"And you'll be pleased to know," added Zac who was sitting beside him, "we've scratched the turnip thoroughly, so it shouldn't be itchy anymore."

They weren't going to let Keo forget the bizarre comment he had made during his delirium. While he was in hospital, his friends had signed a huge 'get well' card that they had made together, featuring a sketch of a turnip cleverly drawn by Tash and featuring the words, "We hope all your turnips stop itching soon." Keo, of course, had no memory of his delirium-inspired comment, but that didn't stop his friends from making regular references to it.

Amanda Robinson, the mayor, arrived as lunch was about to be served, apologising for her lateness. Most of them sat around the large dining table, with the overflow sitting on lounge chairs and balancing their plates on their laps. Keo finished his meagre serving quickly and looked longingly at the food overflowing other people's plates.

"That was a very tasty entrée," he said, licking his lips. "What's next?"

"Dinner, in about five hours," replied Tash.

"You can't possibly expect me to survive on that paltry amount of food, my love!"

"Of course not, sweetie. I'm relying on your blubber to keep you alive. There's enough there to feed an army for a month."

The table erupted into laughter, with a variety of hilarious comments being added to the conversation at Keo's expense. Tash joined in with the jocularity but underneath the humour was a steely resolve to enforce Keo's new diet. The months ahead were going to be very interesting, indeed.

After lunch, Amanda drew Zac and Karl aside to speak about a concern. Karl had proven himself to be resourceful and extremely useful during the laser battle, and his experience as a shuttle pilot on Nova warranted his inclusion in the discussion.

"I would value both your opinions regarding the way forward from this point," she began. "It would seem that we aren't in any danger of attack. Every indication is that the Subterrans, if that is what they are, want to be left alone. If they were going to attack, they would have done it by now."

"It does seem that way," agreed Zac.

"But I'm not sure we should leave them alone," Amanda continued. "It doesn't make any sense for humans to be living in such close proximity and have nothing to do with each other. Particularly as there are so few of us on the planet. We all need to be working together, sharing resources and doing everything we can to build a new civilisation here. My worry is that if we allow this separation to continue, it could boil over into violence again at some point in the future. Clearly, there is some kind of underlying misunderstanding at work here, and it has to be resolved before it results in more deaths."

"So what are you proposing?" asked Karl.

"That's the problem: I'm not sure how to go about it. I just know that we need to somehow make contact with them and try to negotiate peace."

"The only way we can make contact is via the access shaft, which they've welded closed again," said Zac.

"And if we break the doors down again," added Karl, "they'll interpret that as another act of aggression and probably launch another attack."

"You see my problem," said Amanda.

"What about trying to broadcast a message to them?" asked Zac.

"We've been trying that for the last few days, with no success. We suspect that their city, if that's what it is, is too far underground to receive any surface transmissions. The fact that even our most sensitive receivers haven't been able to pick up tell-tale signals from their city seems to confirm that."

"It doesn't seem like we have much choice," lamented Karl.

"If we want to make contact, we have to cut through those doors again."

"Colonel Carlisle agrees," said Amanda. "He's pushing for sending a whole platoon down there."

"That would be a disaster," interrupted Zac. "That will only exacerbate the situation. While I agree that we have no choice but to break through those doors again, I think we need to leave a message in the vestibule and then beat a hasty retreat."

"What kind of message?" asked Amanda. "What if they can't read or understand our language?"

"We could leave a written message in as many languages as possible, including 21$^{st}$ century English," said Zac. "As an historian and someone who was born over three thousand years ago, I can certainly help with that."

"What about a voice recording or video message?" asked Karl.

"We could try," responded Zac. "But any electronic recording or video may be problematic, as their technology may not be compatible with ours. Written messages would be the surest way forward."

"Don't forget food," added Kit who had been eavesdropping.

"You mean some kind of gift?" asked Amanda.

"Definitely. Nothing says, 'hello, nice to meet you', better than presents. We should leave them a selection of fresh produce – fruit and vegetables – and perhaps some venison."

Amanda sat thoughtfully as she mulled over the suggestions. Finally, she nodded.

"I like it. It's a good plan. Zac, can you write a peace message?"

"Sure. I'll draft something and get it to you by tonight."

"Thanks. And Kit, seeing it was your suggestion, can you coordinate the gathering together of a peace offering? You can use council funds to secure whatever provisions you want."

"Absolutely. Tash and I will work on it together."

Amanda left shortly afterward.

"You know, I've got a good feeling about this," said Zac. "I really think this is going to work."

But sometimes, good feelings don't translate into reality.

**25**

The two flitters landed on the hilltop shortly after midday the following day, and two squads of soldiers quickly disembarked and moved into position. One squad set up a covering field of fire in a semi-circle facing the entrance to the access shaft. The second squad of six soldiers swiftly moved toward the door. Five of them took up covering positions on either side of the door, with one of them carrying a box containing the colony's peace offerings and messages of good-will. The remaining soldier approached the door directly, carrying a laser cutter.

Colonel Carlisle was supervising the operation personally, from his position among the encircling squad. The soldier with the cutter examined the door closely and activated his comm.

"It looks safe to proceed, Colonel. They welded a piece of the same metal across the inside of the door. I should be able to cut through it pretty quickly."

"Roger. You have a green light."

The soldier was already wearing protective welding gear, so he quickly set to work cutting another hole, following the recessed outline of the previous hole. The laser bit into the door, its incandescent beam melting the metal and sending out a kaleidoscopic spray of sparks. Within two minutes he completed the section and the inner piece of metal fell inward with a reverberating clang. The soldier who had done the cutting stepped to the side; his job now complete. The closest soldier on each side of the door edged closer and peered in, their headlamps lighting the dust-filled darkness. They nodded and signalled to the other two armed soldiers, then the four of them quickly entered the shaft, scanning to left and right with their torch-lit laser rifles. They signalled the all-clear and the soldier carrying the peace offering entered. Those outside waited, listening to the diminishing sound of their comrades' footsteps as they descended the stairs. The idea was to leave the peace offering at the foot of the stairs, near the door to the museum vestibule.

They didn't have to wait long. A massive explosion sounded from within the shaft, and a cloud of choking dust and debris spewed out of the hole in the door. The Colonel didn't hesitate. He was up and running immediately, yelling,

"Bravo squad, on me!"

As they ran toward the entrance to the shaft, they lifted their breathing masks and battle goggles into place. The squad entered the smoke-filled shaft without hesitation, with Carlisle in the lead. Their headlamps and rifle lights cast eerie beams in the thick smoke and dust, giving the whole scene an apocalyptic appearance. It took them four flights of stairs before they reached the carnage below. The bomb had sent barbed shrapnel slicing through the faces, necks, arms and legs of the alpha squad members. There was blood splattered all over the walls and steps, and two soldiers were clearly dead, their necks having been sliced open.

"Retrieve and exfiltrate!" yelled Carlisle. " Duffy, you're with me!"

He and Duffy took up a covering position a few stairs below

the decimated squad, training their rifles on the stairs below. Meanwhile the other five soldiers bent and lifted a comrade over their shoulders and began carrying them up the stairs. Carlisle and Duffy covered their retreat all the way to the surface, without encountering any sign of further attack. As they exited the shaft, they continued straight to the waiting flitters without stopping. The two pilots already had the engines running, and a medic on board each flitter began processing the casualties.

There were four dead. Two whose throats had been torn open, one who had lost a leg and bled out, and another who, at first glance, appeared to have superficial cuts, but who could not be revived. The lone survivor had lost an arm and had half his face blown off, but he was clinging stubbornly to life.

As the flitters raced back to the colony hospital, Colonel Carlisle felt a rising rage. He had now lost six good men and women, and that body-count might possibly increase to seven before the day was finished. This couldn't go on. The colony needed to step up and take retaliatory action. He vowed that the deaths of these soldiers would be avenged.

He would make it his personal crusade.

**26**

---

The sole surviving soldier did not die, but it was a close thing. He received many litres of blood and was in the operating theatre for several hours before the doctors could confidently predict that he would live. Eventually, he was wheeled into the intensive care unit and the surgeons advised his worried family that several more operations would be required to rebuild his damaged face.

An emergency meeting of the City Council was called to determine what had gone wrong and what they needed to do now. Colonel Carlisle began by describing each step of the operation. After he had finished a bare-bones description, Amanda asked,

"So, what do you think happened down there?"

"The bomb may have been set to go off automatically in response to some kind of sensor – either movement or body heat. The other possibility is that it was detonated remotely, in response to some kind of video feed."

"But why a quarter of the way down the shaft? Why not on the top level?" asked one of the councillors.

"My guess is that they wanted to get as many of us as possible. If the bomb was detonated on the top landing, a lot of the bomb's energy would have been expended out the door, and perhaps only one or two who had already entered would have been injured. Detonating it further down the shaft ensured maximum killing power and maximum reach in terms of the number of victims."

There was silence around the conference table. The Colonel's cold tone hinted at the simmering rage that boiled just below the surface.

"Colonel, I'm very sorry about the loss of your men," said the mayor. "I know you must feel their loss very deeply."

"I'm not interested in talking about my feelings. I'm only interested in action from this point on."

Amanda nodded.

"I can understand that. Which is why we're here now. How likely is retaliation this second time around?"

"From them or us?"

"I'm talking about from them at this point."

"I'd say very likely. We've now demonstrated that we're not going away. In their minds we probably pose an ongoing risk. I wouldn't be surprised if there is some kind of strike against us now."

"So how do we guard against that?" asked another councillor.

"Same as before," responded Carlisle. "Patrol the perimeter of the colony. Motion sensors. Laser canons. Flood lights. The works. We'll be ready for them if they come. Matter of fact, I hope they do come. My troops are itching to get these bastards in their sights."

"That's understandable, Colonel," said Amanda. "But where does that leave us, in terms of our peace overtures?"

"I'd say that chapter is finished," replied Carlisle. "We've gone to them in peace twice now, and we've been mercilessly attacked. Only a fool would keep going back for more of the same. The time for love notes and fruit is over. Our peace offering has been rejected. I say we go to war."

"I disagree, Colonel," ventured Zac. "Our peace offering hasn't even been received by them yet. They know nothing of our peaceful intentions. All they know is that we've broken down their front door twice. In their minds, they are merely defending themselves. They probably see us as the aggressors who are invading their home."

"You're kidding me! We've got six dead soldiers, a dead civilian and several more injured, and you're taking their side?"

"I'm just trying to put their actions in context. They've got dead soldiers too: they've got families who are grieving their own loved ones. I am convinced this whole thing is a terrible misunderstanding – one that has to be corrected before it escalates out of control."

"So what do you suggest, Zac?" asked Amanda.

"I think we should try to send them another peace offering."

"You've got to be joking!" scoffed Carlisle. "And just how do you propose we do that?"

"I'm not sure," admitted Zac.

Carlisle laughed out loud and looked as if he was about to respond aggressively, so Amanda decided to change the direction of the conversation before it got out of hand.

"I suggest we leave the issue of another peace offering in abeyance for the moment. Let's see how the next twenty four hours unfold and then re-examine the idea. In the meantime, there is some new information from our science team that we need to hear. I've invited Dr Simon Kessler to address Council."

She nodded to her secretary who opened the door and invited Dr. Kessler in.

Simon Kessler was not what Zac was expecting. Instead of a bearded, ageing scientist, the man who walked in looked like he was a personal trainer at a gym. He looked to be in his late thirties and was obviously extremely fit. Simon took the seat next to Amanda and began confidently.

"My name is Simon Kessler, head of the science department. You are no doubt aware that over the last few days, aerial scans have been carried out of the hills west of our colony, looking for signs of additional access shafts. None have been found. What you probably don't know is that survey teams have also been placed on the ground with ground-penetrating scanners. We have thoroughly investigated the area surrounding Wrights Hill and have made an important discovery."

He paused, looking around the table.

"The underground habitation at Wrights Hill is not the only one. There are three others of roughly equal size and depth, in a curved distribution to the west of the existing subterranean habitation. We have also been able to identify what looks like tunnels linking all four areas – I'm going to call them suburbs – together."

There were exclamations of surprise all around the table.

"Each suburb is underneath an area on the surface which is about two square kilometres. But the size of these is made much more impressive by the fact that they are also at least two kilometres deep, with, as yet, an unknown number of levels. There could be twenty or more levels in each suburb."

"That's at least 160 square kilometres!" said Zac, quickly working out the math. "That's thirty or forty times the size of our little colony!"

"So they could outnumber us by a factor of forty?" asked someone else.

"Not necessarily," cautioned Amanda. "We don't know if all the suburbs and all the levels are inhabited. For all we know, some or even most of them could have fallen into disuse. We just have no way of knowing at this stage."

"Which is why it would be foolish to blindly rush into a conflict with them," said Zac. "One of the maxims of warcraft is

'Know your enemy'. And in this case, we know absolutely nothing about them."

"I agree," said Amanda. "We need to do nothing preemptive for the time being and find out as much as we can about them while we consider our options very carefully. Let's see if anything develops over the next 24 hours. We'll meet again tomorrow afternoon, same time. Let's hope that peace and common sense prevail."

Unfortunately, it was a naïve hope.

**27**

———

Ludd was late for the quadracil. By now, all four Primes would be there, along with their chosen Seconds. All except him. His father would be disappointed. As the Second for District 1, he should be setting an example. Instead, he would have to walk into the chamber and apologise, knowing that they could not start the meeting without him. He had been in the city archives again, down in the $2^{nd}$ Elevation, and had lost track of time. He raced along the corridor and reached the bank of lifts. The indicators showed that one of the lifts was already on this elevation, waiting empty. He pushed the call button and a set of lift doors opened immediately. He ran in and placed his wrist against a reader built into the wall.

"Quadracil authorisation. Emergency express to the $20^{th}$ Elevation, Level 10."

The doors closed and the lift shot upward at a velocity that was much faster than normal. A pleasant male voice said, "Emergency express commenced. Are you sure your father would approve of your use of the quadracil authorisation in this way, Ludd?"

"I'm sure he would," he lied. "After all, today's quadracil is an emergency meeting, and they can't start without me."

The Sentium's lack of response expressed silent disapproval. No doubt Ludd's commandeering of the lift like this would add further fuel to his father's anger when he found out. But at least this would reduce his lateness by a minute or two. How could he have lost track of time so badly? He was angry with himself and ashamed that he would be causing his father to lose face in front of the other Primes.

He watched the indicator panel, willing the elevator to rise faster through the elevations. It was a journey of nearly two klicks, and today it seemed to last forever. Finally, the elevator approached Level 10 on the 20th Elevation and braked aggressively, bleeding off the excessive velocity so quickly that Ludd was almost weightless for a few seconds. Then the doors opened and he was sprinting down the central corridor toward the quadracil chambers. At least the archives were almost directly underneath the chambers and he didn't have to traverse any great horizontal distance. People were staring at him as he raced past. Primes and Seconds were supposed to conduct themselves with dignity and decorum, and he was doing anything but that at the moment.

He reached the door of the quadracil antechamber and ran in, receiving a scowl from his father's secretary who was sitting at her desk.

"You're late."

He didn't bother answering. He paused at the arched double doors of the chamber and composed himself, trying to get his breath back, then he pushed open one of the doors and walked in.

All eyes turned to him. The four Primes were already seated, spaced evenly around the circular table like the four points of a compass. His father was closest to the double doors, with his back to Ludd; Prime of District 1. Sterv was to his father's left, Prime of District 2. Seated on the far side of the table was Avril, Prime of District 3. And on the right side was Gord, Prime of District 4. Although the Primes were seated, the Seconds were not. The First-Borns were standing in their places, to the right of their respective Primes. And the reason they were standing was because of him. They could not sit until he, the Second of District 1, sat. His face grew red with shame.

"I apologise for my lateness. It is inexcusable, and I deeply regret that I have inconvenienced you and brought shame upon my district."

He took his place to the right of his father. Lystrall and Garran smiled awkwardly at him, sensing his shame and trying to encourage him. But Myla, Avril's Second at the opposite end of the table was almost sneering with scorn. He could almost feel her animosity burning into him from across the table. The Seconds all looked at him, waiting for his signal. He nodded to them respectfully and sat, and the others all followed. He wasn't game to look to his left at his father's face.

The table at which they sat was made of brilliant polished metal and was hollow in the centre, forming a circular ring. They sat around the outside, facing in.

Joram stood, ignoring his son's late entrance, and commenced the quadracil with the formal words of welcome.

"Primes and Seconds of the four districts, you are welcome here. As Prime of District 1 and President of New Eden, I declare the quadracil complete. Let the meeting begin."

He resumed his seat and now that the formalities had been dispensed with, the meeting took on a slightly more relaxed feel.

"I am sorry to have called a quadracil at such short notice, but these are exceptional circumstances that require immediate attention," he began. "You are all aware of the basic facts. There was a breach from the surface yesterday into our beloved museum. The invaders were successfully repelled at the cost of five lives and injuries to several other defenders. The breaches were resealed last night. Then, today, a second attempted invasion occurred, this time foiled by means of a movement-activated bomb that we planted in the stairwell during our repairs last night. The outer door of that access shaft has now been resealed a second time, and further explosive devices have been planted in the stairwell."

He paused and looked around the table.

"As I say, those are the basic facts. Now we are faced with three important questions; who, why and what? Who are they? Why are they invading? And what should we do about it? Let's start with the 'who' question. Any thoughts?"

Gord, to Joram's right, spoke first.

"It's irrelevant who they are. If they're from the surface, or from anywhere else in this solar system, they're infected. We simply can't let them into our city, or they will bring with them the virus that would dement our Sentiums."

There were nods of agreement all around the table. Gord was the bluntest and gruffest of the Primes and often took a hard line, having served in the security forces as a young man. He was short, bald and aggressive, with a prominent scar above his left eye, from a fight in his younger years. He often tended to put people offside with his hard manner, but on this occasion, he seemed to speak for everyone.

"We all seem to be in agreement on that issue," said Joram. "But why are they invading?

Sterv, to Joram's left spoke.

"It's been 2,000 years since we completely removed ourselves from the surface because of the virus. And in that time, there have been no incursions. In fact, until yesterday, we believed ourselves to be completely hidden from the outer world. How did they find us? What gave away our presence?"

"Those questions are irrelevant," responded Gord once more. "What is more pertinent is the issue of why. What is their purpose? I can only envisage one reason for their invasion attempts: they have come to pass on the virus and assume control of our Sentiums. Their minds have become twisted by the virus and they are being driven to spread it here as well."

"Whether they are deliberately trying to spread the virus or not is a moot point," said Avril, on the far side of the table. "The fact that they are living on the surface means that they have the virus. Even if they have noble intentions, perhaps even wishing to join us, the fact remains that they are infected, and cannot be allowed to interact with us or our technology."

Once again, there were nods all around the table. Joram spoke again.

"Well, that just leaves us with the last question: what should we do about it? Have we done enough? Is there some other action we now need to take?"

"Our actions to this point have been effective," offered Sterv. "Perhaps we have done enough to deter them. I say we wait and see what happens."

"I think that's naïve," countered Gord. "Clearly, they are determined. We are fortunate that, up to this point, they have not found any of our main hatchways. But now that they know where we are, they won't give up – not unless we send them a strong deterrent. We need to take the fight to them."

"What do you propose?" asked Avril.

"The first step is to find their location. I say we send up a seeker. If they are within a radius of one hundred klicks it will locate them."

"That means sacrificing the seeker," said Sterv. "It cannot return without infecting us."

"That goes without saying," said Gord. "We will program it to self-destruct once it has relayed its information back to us via tight-beam transmission."

"And if the invaders are nearby?" prompted Avril.

"We will send out some wasps. Two ought to be enough to inflict some heavy damage."

"No ground assault?" asked Avril. "Battle suits with disruptor fields would keep our soldiers safe."

"I am not prepared to risk more lives," declared Joram, authoritatively. "We've lost enough already."

"I agree," said Gord. "Besides, the wasps have inbuilt intelligence. They are more than capable of carrying out an effective attack without us needing to have a physical presence on the surface. Once again, they will self-destruct once they have released their payload."

Sterv shook his head, a look of deep concern on his face.

"If we launch an attack, even a limited one such as you are suggesting, it will inevitably escalate the conflict. We may have already done enough to dissuade them. But by attacking them now, we risk provoking their wrath and precipitating a full-blown war. I say we wait and see."

"Permission to speak?" asked Ludd.

All eyes turned his way, shock registering on his friend Garran's face.

There was a pause as Joram considered his request. Finally he nodded.

"Speak."

"What if there is no longer any virus? It has been two millennia since we left the surface. Anything could have happened since then. Perhaps the virus has been wiped out. These could be innocent people we are about to kill. They could simply be trying to make contact."

"The virus wiped out?" Avril laughed, and Ludd could see her daughter, Myla, smirking with disdain at her side.

"It isn't like influenza!" continued Avril. "You can't kill it with disinfectant! The 'virus', as we call it, is some kind of electronic and biological manipulation engineered by the artificial intelligence that now inhabits this entire solar system. We all know what happened to our people during the Years of Dying. It not only caused the premature deaths of our population, but also demented our Sentiums and other computer systems. It's still out there, and we can't allow it in."

"Avril is right," agreed Gord. "We have to assume that the virus is still there. What I propose is the safest course."

"In that case, let us vote," said Joram. "What say each of you? Gord?"

"Aye."

"Myla?"

"Aye."

"Sterv?"

"Nay."

Joram paused. That meant that he had the casting vote. If he voted 'nay', the quadracil would be tied, in which case his vote, as president, would become two votes. The decision was now effectively his. All eyes were turned his way. He felt the weight of responsibility. The safety and security of the city of New Eden rested upon his shoulders. He must protect his people at all cost.

"Aye."

**28**

A cool wind had sprung up from the south-west and the soldiers on sentry duty had donned warm battle jackets over their fatigues. A full moon had just risen in the East and was hanging newly-born above the harbour, its yellow glow bathing the water below in a soft buttery light. The sky was completely free of clouds, with the result that the temperature had plummeted in the hours since sunset.

Colonel Riff Carlisle was doing a circuit of the perimeter on a quad bike, stopping at each sentry post to speak briefly with his soldiers. He was a good leader, firm but fair, and his soldiers knew that if it came to battle, he would be at the forefront with them, never asking them to do what he was not willing to do himself.

He reached the next sentry post and switched off his quad. Two soldiers were manning the laser canon, directly underneath a spotlight that was sweeping the terrain to the west, the powerful search beam occasionally illuminating the motion detectors that had been placed at intervals, one hundred metres further out. Four more soldiers with high powered laser rifles were peering over the edge of a bunker beside the canon, sweeping the moonlit horizon with heat-sensing binoculars.

"How goes it, squaddies?" asked the colonel as he approached the bunker.

"Very good sir. Nothing to report."

"Cold enough for you?"

"Yes sir, I'm freezing my gonads off."

"If they fall off, just stick them in your pocket; we'll sew them on again later."

"Yes sir," he chuckled.

He was about to turn back to the quad bike when one of the soldiers exclaimed.

"I see something! Due west. It's some kind of launch!"

They could all see it now; something streaking up from the hills to the west, leaving an orange exhaust trail behind it. They watched it as it rose to about one kilometre in altitude, then the trail abruptly vanished. The whole squad had their field glasses trained on the spot where the trail had last been visible, adjusting the apertures and spectral settings on their glasses, trying to pick out the object.

"I've got it!" said a soldier. "I'm locked on! I'm sending the coordinates and settings to your fields glasses now. It looks like some kind of probe, just hovering now."

They all zeroed in on the object. It remained stationary for almost a minute, then moved directly toward them, maintaining the same altitude. It came to a stop again about a kilometre west of their position and remained hovering there.

"Is the canon locked onto the target?" asked Carlisle.

"Yes sir. We've got the sucker zeroed in our crosshairs."

"Are you confident you can make a direct hit at this distance?"

"Yes sir."

"Take it out, soldier."

"Yes sir."

A moment later a brilliant blob of purple light shot across the night sky, momentarily dazzling them with its brilliance. The laser found its mark and the probe exploded, sending a cascade of sparks and glowing pieces of metal floating down to the ground like a fireworks display on New Year's Eve.

Carlisle was immediately on his comm.

"All squads! This is Colonel Carlisle. We've just taken out an enemy probe. I want everyone on high alert. I've got a feeling things are about to get interesting."

The colonel then spoke directly to the squad stationed on top of the town hall. They had been a last-minute addition to his defensive plans for the colony.

"Gamma squad. Keep your eyes peeled. They may have more flyers."

Soldiers all along the perimeter and in the town centre prepared for battle. Field glasses swept the perimeter and scanned the skies above. Weapons were checked and then checked again. But an hour later, their defensive positions were still undisturbed and the colony continued to sleep peacefully as midnight approached.

The Colonel was doing his rounds again, speaking with a soldier who was manning a canon, when a soldier nearby yelled,

"Contact! Two UFOs coming in low and fast from the north-west!"

He had barely finished the words when two disc-shaped objects flew out of the darkness and streaked past them before they had time to even shoulder their weapons. It was later estimated that they were travelling at over 600 kph but the only sound they made was from the wind resistance they encountered.

The colonel was straight on his comms.

"Gamma squad! Incoming! Two UFOs from the north-west. Low and fast! Delta squad, reposition to the town hall.

Repeat: move back to the town hall and assist Gamma squad!"

As he spoke, he leapt onto his quad bike and raced toward the town centre, hoping his soldiers could bring down the threats before they did any damage.

The squad on top of the town hall only had a few seconds to react before the two objects came into view, barely clearing the tree-tops to the west. As they approached the town they suddenly split up. One turned toward the northern end of the town and the soldiers quickly lost sight of it, but the other one came straight toward them. They managed to get a single canon shot off but missed.

The object suddenly dropped below the level of the roof tops and streaked up the main street of the town, coming to an instant stop at about head-height, directly opposite the entrance to the town hall. The soldiers manning the laser canon on the roof of the building couldn't depress the gun far enough to bring it to bear on the target, so they took up their rifles and started firing, but either their shots kept missing or the object had some kind of shield that protected it from small arms fire.

As the disc hovered in mid-air, five tubes suddenly extended from it at equidistant points around its circumference, making it look a bit like a starfish. It then started spinning on its horizontal plane, so fast that its tubular arms became a solid blur. A moment later a myriad of large golden globs of light flew outward in every direction smashing through the walls and windows of the buildings all around it. The object stopped spinning and retracted its tubular arms, and all was quiet for a moment. Suddenly, the town centre seemed to erupt. Dozens of huge explosions rocked the immediate area. Some buildings simply collapsed. Others were reduced to rubble on the inside. Meanwhile the hovering disk shot up to a height of about fifty metres and blew itself up, sending a deadly shower of shrapnel over the town hall roof top and in a wide circle beneath it.

By the time Colonel Carlisle arrived back in town, it was all over. The scene was chaotic, with rescue teams pulling the dead and injured from the rubble and trying to extinguish the fires. The Colonel stood for a moment in the main street, shocked, realising that he had grossly underestimated the enemy.

**29**

———

"How bad is it?" asked Amanda. "Do we have a final figure on casualties from last night?"

"It's bad," confirmed Dr. Tanya Reynolds, the town's Chief Medical Officer. "Currently there are seventeen dead and over forty injured. Some of those may not make it. Most of the casualties were sustained in the attack in the northern residential district. The device unleashed its bombs among several blocks of apartments. The attack in the town centre did a lot of damage but there were only a few casualties as most people were home in their beds at that time."

There was a moment's silence as the councillors digested the devastating news. Several minutes of intense discussion then followed, identifying immediate action steps that needed to be taken in order to rehouse people and begin to put their town back together again. Amanda then turned her attention on Colonel Carlisle and, from her opening salvo, it was clear that she wasn't happy.

"Colonel, I've received a report that you initiated the conflict, firing upon and destroying a probe that had made no move to provoke or attack us. Is that correct?"

"It was moving toward the town. In my estimation it represented a threat."

"It had stopped moving toward the town when you took it out, Colonel! It made no further move, it fired no weapons, it didn't act aggressively in any way. In fact, it gave every indication of being merely a passive surveillance drone."

The Colonel wasn't used to being spoken to in this way. The colour rose in his cheeks and he retorted angrily.

"My job is to make tough decisions on the front line. While you sit back here in comfort and security, my team and I are out there putting our lives on the line to defend our colony. I made the best decision possible, given the circumstances."

"No you didn't, Colonel! It was the worst possible decision you could have made! You were specifically instructed by this council *not* to provoke an attack, and to only fire weapons if you were fired upon first. You have directly disobeyed those instructions, and in so doing, may have just started a major conflict! Your unilateral, gung-ho actions have jeopardised the safety of this entire colony!"

"That's your opinion. As Head of Security for the colony, I would make the same decision again."

They had reached an impasse, with neither willing to back down. Amanda realised that if she kept pushing, she would have no choice but to dismiss the colonel from his position as commander of the colony's armed forces. It might still come to that, but she was not quite ready to travel down that path just yet. She decided to change tack.

"Where did the drone and the attack weapons originate from? We installed video cameras in the trees around the access shaft yesterday and I've viewed the footage from those. Those things didn't come from there."

The colonel was glad for a change of topic.

"There must be another access point for the city. I've got soldiers searching the hillsides as we speak."

"Let's move on," said Amanda. "The most pressing issue now is how to respond to last night's attack."

The colonel was quick to offer his advice.

"We might differ on what should have happened last night, Mayor Robinson, but there can be little doubt what needs to happen now. We need to strike back quickly and decisively."

"Why?" asked Zac

"I would have thought that was obvious. We are now at war. And we can expect more attacks of this nature unless we convince them that we are too strong an enemy to continue to engage."

"What sort of decisive action are you talking about?" asked Amanda.

"A strike from space. We have a dreadnaught-class destroyer from Perdita in orbit around Earth. Over the last few hours since the attack, it has moved down to a geosynchronous orbit, directly above our colony. It has a ground-penetrating plasma canon that, if fired down through their precious museum, would drill a hole to the very bottom level of their city in a matter of seconds. Then there is a choice of MDBs – mass destruction bombs - that could be dropped down there, anti-matter or thermo-nuclear, both of which would completely annihilate them. They may have picked a fight with us, thinking that we are just a tiny colony, but in reality, they've poked the bear, and the bear is much bigger and far more powerful than they ever imagined."

"How nice to know that we can completely destroy them," said Zac, sarcastically.

"I take it that you have a problem with the colonel's proposal, Zac?" Amanda intuited.

"Yes. I don't agree that we are at war. Quite the opposite, in fact. I think this attack was meant to deter us from *starting* a war. I think it is the final warning from the Subterrans to leave them alone. If we do absolutely nothing from this point forward, I suspect that we will never encounter them again."

"So you suggest we let them get away with this?" asked Carlisle, incredulously. "They have killed a total of twenty of our citizens now! They've injured over forty! They've destroyed parts of our town! These are crimes that can't go unpunished!"

"We've killed some of them too," said Zac.

"In self-defence!" yelled Carlisle. "And now we must hit back harder and stronger!"

Zac shook his head in frustration.

"Colonel, there are bigger issues at stake here than punitive reprisals. We are dealing with the first meeting of two very different civilisations – a meeting which, in my opinion, has gone pear-shaped very quickly because it has been plagued by serious misunderstanding. The answer is not to turn around and blow the crap out of them. I don't believe we are at that stage yet. I think there is still a chance to resolve this situation and foster a positive relationship between the two societies."

Amanda spoke again.

"I've got to say, Zac, I think there is currently a lot of support in the colony for the kind of strategy the colonel is proposing. There's a lot of grief and fear out there among the population. They want this threat neutralised."

"So do I!" said Zac, with exasperation in his voice. "But blowing them to kingdom come isn't the next step! I haven't travelled half-way across the galaxy to arrive back on Earth, only to nuke everyone who was already here!"

"So what are you proposing?"

"The first stage of my proposal is very simple, but you probably won't like it. In fact, most of Wellington will disagree with it. But I honestly believe it's the best possible thing we could do at the moment."

"And what is that?"

"Nothing."

"You're proposing that we do nothing at all?" asked Carlisle.

"Yes. I'm proposing that we simply wait."

"And what will that achieve?" asked Amanda.

"As I said before, I believe that this attack was a final warning; a kind of 'back off or else' message. If we do nothing for a while now, it shows that we've got the message. And I strongly suspect that their response will be to do nothing as well. I don't think they want to go to war any more than we do. If they wanted to wage all-out war on us, they would have sent dozens of those things to attack us. The fact that they only sent two, gives me hope. Doing nothing for a while will allow the situation to de-escalate."

"What if you're wrong?" asked Carlisle. "What if we do nothing and they attack again today? Or tonight? Or tomorrow?"

"Then we have to take more drastic action."

"But you're gambling with people's lives! If you're wrong, more people will die!" cried Carlisle.

"I don't think so, Colonel. If this Perditan dreadnaught is as good as you say, it should be able to track any further launches from space and knock them out before they reach us. Now that it is directly overhead, we are effectively protected from further attack. The way I see it, we have nothing to lose by waiting."

"Except for the goodwill of our citizens, who will be crying out for blood," said Amanda.

"Sometimes the right thing to do is the least popular," replied Zac.

Another councillor spoke up.

"You mentioned that doing nothing is the first stage of your proposal. What's the next stage."

"To be honest, I haven't quite figured that part out yet."

**30**

---

Ludd was down in the archives again. He was still smarting from the tongue-lashing he had received from his father after the last quadracil. By not being there at the beginning to welcome the leaders from the other districts, he had embarrassed his father and brought dishonour to his district. His lateness wasn't just a lapse in protocol, it was extremely bad manners, and his father had let him know it. He and his father didn't see eye to eye on many things, but this was the first time since he was a little boy that Ludd had been on the receiving end of his father's anger, and it shamed him. It shamed him because he knew that his father was right. He needed to grow up and stop day-dreaming. He needed to stop spending so much time digging around in the past and take a more active interest in the day-to-day affairs of the district.

But here he was again, in his favourite place in the city. He couldn't explain it to most people, but he was fascinated about history. He wanted to learn all he could about their past – how the city had been founded and the events surrounding that time. For many months now, he had pored over the ancient archives, watching vids of the early years; the gradual excavation of the city by the founders, elevation by elevation. At first, he had been fascinated by the crude technology. During the first decade of the city's construction, the excavated earth had needed to be moved to the surface and transported to the dump site a kilometre to the west using crude vehicles constructed in the engineering bay. But as time went on, conveyer belts were utilised, transporting the excavated rock and soil to the canyon via underground tunnels.

More than the ancient technology, however, it was the surface life of the early colony that fascinated him most. For nearly two centuries after The Scorching, the surface had been unliveable; burnt, barren and desolate. But as the Earth slowly healed itself, his ancestors had been able to utilise it again, growing certain fruits and crops that fared better on the surface than in their vast underground gardens. They worked their surface gardens by day and retired to the comfort of the city by night. As the Earth continued to heal and the seasons reasserted themselves, a growing percentage of the population established a permanent presence on the surface, building homes and even schools and hospitals. Work on the underground city ceased as the need for further expansion disappeared. For several centuries the population was split between the surface dwellers, 'surfies', and the inhabitants of the underground city, 'grounders'. A healthy trade grew up between the surfie town and the grounder city, with certain produce and meat being traded for machinery and technology that, by then, was being produced by the vast underground engineering facility.

Then the virus struck. They were in regular communication with the struggling colonies on Mars and the Moon – those who had survived the brief but brutal conflict initiated by the Caliphate. Then, over a period of months they learnt of the rise of a malevolent artificial intelligence, calling itself an Enhanced Intelligence, that had arisen on Mars and was systematically taking control of mankind's off-world bases, exterminating the human population. The last off-world base to be infected was Floyd Base, on the dark side of the Moon, its population fleeing at the last possible moment in a starship that was never heard from again.

By then, Ludd's ancestors knew how the virus worked. It was a malevolent code that invaded computer systems, inserting itself into the operating system and wreaking havoc, turning mankind's by-now sentient technology against them. They knew it was only a matter of time before the malevolent coding reached Earth. The surface towns were abandoned and destroyed, removing all trace of their presence from the surface. The entire population retired underground, sealing themselves in.

Over the next few years, several unmanned probes landed in the area, transmitting seemingly friendly messages, but they had learnt from the experience of off-world bases not to respond. The briefest response would open a channel that would allow the Enhanced Intelligence to upload its coding and take control of their technology. They ignored the transmissions from the probes and hunkered down in their underground city, resuming its expansion once again.

Ludd scrolled through some later vids and docs, documenting his ancestors' subsequent attempts to repopulate the surface. Over a thousand years ago, after many centuries without any sign of probes, an expedition was mounted to explore the possibility of reclaiming the surface. Over two hundred brave souls, calling themselves 're-surfies' exited the city. For months, they lived on the surface, erecting temporary shelters and beginning to plant crops. Each night they sent a coded report of their progress to the underground city. By mutual consent, the city never responded, maintaining transmission silence to protect themselves from possible infection. It was determined that a period of twelve months would have to go by until it was deemed to be safe to open the city to the surface.

Then, after ten months, tragedy struck. Overnight, everyone on the surface over fifty years of age died. Their Sentiums – sentient artificial intelligence entities– were taken over by the EI, who communicated with the settlers that death at the age of fifty was the optimal, sustainable life expectancy for the community. It had apparently modified its approach to humanity, choosing to control and limit their lives, rather than destroy them. The settlers deliberately stopped having babies, choosing to die out rather than bring children into a world dominated by such a malevolent overseer.

The EI knew nothing of the existence of the underground city. There was deliberately no reference to the city in any of the surface colony's records. Its Sentiums had only been brought online after the establishment of the surface settlement. New Eden had had no further contact with the outside world since then.

Ludd sat back and scratched his head. Who were these new people who had broken into their world? Were they descendants of the surface colony who had somehow survived? Or were they from off-world somewhere? It was puzzling.

His comm pinged and he accepted the call. Garran's face appeared on his tablet.

"Hi Garran."

"Greetings earth-burrower," said his best friend, the Second of District 4. "I assume you are down in the bowels of the archives again, digging around in the past."

"It's fascinating! I don't understand why it doesn't interest you."

"I'd rather live in the present. Speaking of which, I've managed to get hold of a vid that I thought you'd be interested in watching."

"Not more of your ridiculous dance moves!"

"No. Even more interesting than that."

"Well, that wouldn't be difficult."

"Dude, just shut up and listen! I overheard my dad speaking with the captain of security about the vid recordings of the two recent invasion attempts. The vid is a compilation of recordings from the helmet cams of the defenders and some cameras that were hidden in the stairwell above the museum. The captain gave dad the access code for the vid."

"Don't tell me you hacked into the security server?" asked Ludd.

"Of course not. No hacking involved. I just used the access code. That's not hacking is it?"

"I don't know, but it's surely unauthorised access."

"So, do you want to watch the vid or not?"

"Of course!"

"Thought so. I'm sending it to you now. Happy viewing!"

Garran signed off and a moment later the vid file appeared on his screen. He activated it and watched in fascination. It was just as Garran had said. The action was captured from the viewpoint of the soldiers as they had stormed into the museum and repelled the invaders. The last part of the vid was a recording of the blast in the stairwell which had thwarted the second attempted invasion.

He reached the end and started watching from the beginning again. There was something troubling him; something about the invaders. He froze the playback as the first New Eden defenders burst into the smoke-filled museum vestibule. It wasn't a particularly clear picture. The room was dark and smoke from the blast was obscuring a lot of the scene. But one thing was very clear: only two of the invaders were armed at the beginning. They were obviously soldiers in battle dress, but the rest of the intruders were just as obviously ordinary civilians. This was not an invasion force! These people, whoever they were, could hardly be accused of invading with hostile intent if most of them were unarmed civilians!

As he stared at the scene, something even more disturbing became apparent. He stared at the picture, hardly believing his eyes. He zoomed in closer and moved the view around, examining the faces of a number of the intruders. Some of them were old! He could clearly see grey hair on at least four of them. They had to be older than fifty! He sat back in his chair, shock and excitement coursing through him. If these people were as old as they looked, it could only mean one thing: they didn't have the virus!

He pinged Garran and as soon as his friend's face appeared on the screen, he began talking excitedly.

"They're old! Some of them are over fifty!"

"Thought you'd pick that up. I told you it was fascinating."

"Garran, this is more than fascinating! It's ... it's ... monumental! The virus might be defeated! We might be able to return to the surface!"

"Yeh, but it also means we've killed some innocent people. Did you look carefully at the last scene, in the stairwell?"

"I saw the bomb go off, and a whole lot of carnage, if that's what you mean."

"There's more there than that. Have a closer look. Zoom in on the box that the last soldier was carrying."

Ludd did as instructed.

"It looks like a box of fruit," he said.

"The reason it looks like a box of fruit, is because it IS a box of fruit," replied Garran.

"It's a peace offering," whispered Ludd, almost reverently.

"Yes. It's proof that they weren't invading us. They were simply trying to make contact."

"And we killed them," added Ludd, the shock registering in his voice. He shook his head in disbelief.

"There's one more thing you need to see," said Garran. "It's in the very last frame of the vid."

Ludd forwarded to the end of the vid. It was a picture of the slaughtered soldiers lying all over the stairwell.

"OK, I'm there. What am I looking for?"

"Zoom in on the bottom step in the picture. There's a piece of paper beside the soldier's boot."

Ludd zoomed in and clarified the picture with his editing tools. He enlarged further until the sheet of paper filled the entire screen. He rotated it until he could read the words. It was in standard Terran. Most of the writing was illegible, smeared with blood and gore and covered with grit from the explosion. But the first few words at the top of the page could just be made out. He read the words out loud.

"We come in peace. Please accept these gifts ..."

Both of the young men were silent for a moment as Garran allowed his friend to digest the shocking message. Finally, Ludd broke the silence.

"I don't understand. If we knew this, if we already had these video images, then why did we still send the wasps to attack their colony? That's ... that's murder! We've killed innocent people who were only trying to reach out to us! Didn't the security personnel watch the video carefully enough? Maybe they missed seeing what we just saw."

"No, they saw it, alright," said Garran.

"How do you know?"

"Because I heard the Captain talking to my dad about it."

"What did they say?"

Garran was silent for a moment, indecision and conflicting emotions playing across his face. Then he seemed to reach some kind of internal decision and sighed deeply.

"I heard my dad tell the Captain to not tell anyone and to destroy all the evidence – including the vid file and the letter. I only just managed to grab a copy of the vid file before it was deleted."

"What? Why did he do that? I don't understand! How could he?" exclaimed Ludd.

"You know my father. He refuses to be proved wrong. Plus, as you know, he suffers from surphobia. Like a whole lot of our population, he's terrified of the surface. He's convinced we will all die if we so much as open the door a crack. In his mind, he probably thinks he's protecting us."

"By murdering innocent people and keeping the truth from his own people!" exclaimed Ludd.

Garran was silent for a moment, unable to defend his father's actions. Then he looked imploringly at his friend through the screen.

"What are we going to do about it?" he asked Ludd.

Ludd looked back at him with grim determination.

"We're going to make things right!"

**31**

---

"We'll have to start without him," said Amanda. "We can't wait all day."

The council had been waiting for at least twenty minutes for Colonel Carlisle to arrive.

"It's unusual for him to be late," offered a councillor.

"Yes. Very. But I can't do anything about it. I've left two messages. We'll just have to make a start."

She looked down at her notes.

"The first thing we need to do this morning is thank you, Zac."

"What did I do?"

"You told us to do nothing. You urged us not to strike back, when every fibre of my being felt like doing just that. But we listened to you, and I'm glad we did. It's been four days now, and there have been no further hostilities. Looks like you were right. It appears that all they want is for us to leave them alone."

"Yes, it does," agreed Zac. "But that raises an extremely important question. Why? Why are they so determined to be left alone? So determined, in fact, that they are willing to kill anyone who comes near them. It's extraordinary! It just doesn't make sense – or at least it didn't until I put some pieces of the puzzle together."

"What pieces?"

"Four separate pieces, actually. The first was the fact that when they attacked us in the museum, their soldiers were dressed in space suits or something similar. I saw breathing apparatus on the back of their suits. All they needed in a situation like that was battle dress, not fully enclosed space suits."

"Secondly, there is the fact that they didn't exit the bunker and gun us down after we got to the top of the stairs. They were very close behind us and gaining on us all the time, and after we exited, we were struggling with an injured man up the hill toward the flitters. All the attackers had to do was step out of the bunker and shoot us in the backs from almost point-blank range. Every second while we struggled up that hill, I was expecting to be sliced to pieces with their lasers. But it didn't happen. They never even exited the bunker. Even as we lifted off in the flitters, the doorway to the bunker remained empty."

Everyone was listening intently, trying to see where Zac was heading with this.

"Then there was the fact that their attack on our town was done remotely. Once again, no personal presence on the surface."

"Finally, there is the fact that they have not answered our transmissions. I don't accept that they can't hear us. A civilisation as technical as they are, must be able to receive signals from the outside world. But for some reason, they refuse to respond. Not even a 'go away and leave us alone' message."

"So when you put those pieces together, what did you get?" asked a councillor.

"They think we are infected with the EI virus."

He waited for them to process the thought, seeing some of them nod, while others were frowning, trying to connect the dots.

"It's the only thing that makes sense of all the facts!" he continued. "They used the self-contained suits in order to insulate themselves from any physical or electronic infection. When I shot the last one just in front of the lift, I saw an energy shield shimmer. It wasn't strong enough to stop a laser, as demonstrated by the fact that we were able to kill several of them. So what would be the purpose of the shields? It can only be to somehow insulate them from electronic infection."

Amanda picked up the remaining threads. "And that explains why they haven't wanted to come to the surface or respond to our transmissions."

"Precisely!" said Zac. "I realise that none of these clues individually are completely convincing, but when you stack them all together, I think they are compelling."

"My goodness, I think you're right!" said a councillor.

"It puts a whole new perspective on what has taken place," said another.

"Yes it does," agreed Zac. "We've been interpreting the motivation behind their actions as hostility and aggression, but it's not. It's fear! They're afraid that we're going to infect them."

"So how do we solve the problem when we have no way of communicating with them?" asked someone.

"We do have a way of communicating with them," said Zac. "We've had it all along, but we just assumed it wasn't possible."

"Voice transmission?" asked Amanda.

"Yes. Transmission on all the bandwidths and frequencies. We assumed that because we got nothing back when we first tried that they couldn't hear us. I'm convinced they can hear us."

"So what do you suggest we say?"

"I've drafted a simple message," said Zac, pinging a copy to each of their data pads as he spoke. "It basically covers three main points. One, that we come in peace and wish to be friends. Two, that the EI has been destroyed and there is no longer any virus. And three, that we apologise for the misunderstanding that has caused the recent hostilities. Have a read through and see what you think."

The councillors read the message carefully. Amanda nodded as she finished.

"This is really good, Zac."

The rest of the council agreed.

"You'll see that I have included translations in several of the ancient languages as well as a copy in digital text."

"Excellent," said Amanda.

"When should we start broadcasting?" asked one of them.

"Immediately," said Zac, emphatically. "We've wasted too much time already on unnecessary violence. Let's get the peace train rolling!"

The council formally approved the message. Amanda then sent the message to the comm centre and spoke directly to the senior comm officer, instructing her to begin immediate transmission on all frequencies.

When that had been accomplished, Zac added a final thought.

"You realise, of course, that they won't believe the message when they get it."

There was silence for a moment, as they considered that.

"I suppose they won't," agreed a councillor.

"I know I probably wouldn't if I were in their shoes," enlarged Zac. "They will probably think that the message is some kind of trick."

"I suppose you have a suggestion?" enquired Amanda.

"Yes. A simple one really. As well as our message, they will also need proof. And the only kind of proof that will carry any real weight is showing them some old people – people who are clearly past 50."

"The problem with that," said Amanda, "is that until twelve months ago there was no one over fifty anywhere in the galaxy.

So the oldest people are only now beginning to turn 51. In fact, the oldest person in the whole colony is probably ..." she paused and looked at Zac.

"Me," he finished for her. "Yes, I am. I had just turned 52 when we left Altaria, a short time before the EI invaded that world and began its 'compulsory retirement' policy. We then journeyed across the galaxy, first to Polaris, then to Perdita and finally, here to this solar system. Accounting for the reduced rate of ageing during my time spent in cryogenic stasis on those various legs, by the time we destroyed the EI on Mars, I was 55. A month ago, I celebrated my 56th birthday. So that officially makes me ..."

"... the oldest person in the entire galaxy!" Amanda finished for him.

"Yes," he agreed. "Apart from the citizens of New Eden of course. They must have old people down there. But in terms of the rest of the galaxy, you are currently speaking to the oldest living person."

"Wow!" she said. "Can I get you a blanket or a mug of hot milk?"

"Very funny."

"Sorry. But I take your point," she said. "If we are going to convince them that the EI infection has been lifted and we can now live beyond fifty, you are the most convincing person to show them."

"Yes."

"So, what is the best way of doing that?" a councillor asked.

"Well I was thinking ..." he began. But Zac never got to finish the sentence.

A comm ping sounded and the face of Major Lea Chandra appeared on Amanda's screen. Lea was second in command of the colony's security forces.

"I apologise for interrupting your meeting, Mayor Robinson, but we've got a serious situation developing."

"What is it?"

"I've got a live video feed from the security cameras that we installed around the entrance to the access shaft on Wrights Hill. I'm seeing a squad of four of our soldiers in full battle gear approaching the metal door. One of them has begun laser cutting. They also appear to be carrying a couple of very high-powered EDs."

"EDs?" Amanda asked.

"Sorry. Explosive devices. Bombs."

"What the hell!" responded Amanda. "Who authorised this?"

"I was hoping you could tell me, ma'am. There's been no authorisation from our end. As far as I can tell, the squad I'm looking at is AWOL."

"Where is Colonel Carlisle?"

"I'm looking at him right now, ma'am. He's one of the four soldiers in the video feed."

"Damn it! Major, you call that operation off immediately! If they don't respond, get out there on a flitter and stop them!"

"Yes, ma'am."

Zac was already on his feet, running for the door.

"We've got to stop them! They'll ruin everything! Get me a flitter!"

Amanda was running now, too.

"Wait! I'm coming with you!"

**32**

—————

As was their custom, the four Primes entered the chamber first. They moved to their places at the four points around the polished metal table while Ludd and the other Seconds remained waiting in the doorway. Joram took his seat and the three other Primes followed his lead. After a respectful pause, Ludd led the seconds into the chamber. He took his position at his father's right side and waited until the other Seconds had reached theirs. The other First Born's looked toward him. He sat and they did the same.

Joram then stood and pronounced the words of formal greeting, declaring the quadracil commenced. He seated himself and was about to begin the discussion when there was a loud knock to the chamber doors. All heads turned toward the doors and Joram frowned. The quadracil was sacrosanct. No one could interrupt the meeting unless there was an urgent need.

"Enter!" he called.

The Captain of Security entered and came to stand at Joram's left. He bowed respectfully.

"I humbly apologise for my intrusion, but I felt that you

would want to know immediately. We have begun receiving a transmission from the surface people. The message is being transmitted in several languages, including Terran and English, and is being continually repeated. I have sent you a recording."

"Thank you. You may leave."

The Captain bowed and left the room.

Joram tapped the console in front of him and played the transmission.

"People of New Eden, we send you greetings and wish to assure you that we have come in peace. We have no desire for conflict and deeply regret the hostilities that have already taken place. We want to advise you that the malevolent Enhanced Intelligence that has oppressed mankind for so long has been destroyed. For the last twelve months, humans throughout the galaxy have lived free from its virulent influence. You have nothing to fear from us. Please, let us cease hostilities and begin again as friends."

The message began again, and Joram let it play a second time then stopped the recording.

Sterv spoke first.

"If this is true, then we have killed innocent people! People who were only trying to befriend us!"

"Yes, but is it true?" asked Avril, at the far end of the table. "This could simply be a ploy to get us to let our guard down."

"Of course it's a ploy!" spat Gord. "We would be fools to trust them! You can't honestly believe that the Enhanced Intelligence entity has been destroyed! It wiped out almost the entire population of humanity throughout our solar system. For millennia, all mankind's efforts against it have been completely futile. And now they expect us to believe that it has somehow magically been destroyed? Ha!"

"But what if it is true?" asked Sterv.

"It isn't!" declared Gord, vehemently.

"It is!" yelled Ludd, standing to his feet.

There were gasps of disapproval and shock, around the table, and even his friend, Garran, was looking at him wide-eyed in disbelief.

"Sit down! How dare you speak without being invited!" said Joram.

"I am sorry father, but the quadracil must be told the truth."

"I will ask you one more time to sit down and be silent, or you will be removed from the chamber!"

Ludd ploughed on, ignoring his father's request.

"I have seen the vid of the two attempted incursions. There are old people among them! People with grey hair! They do not have the virus!"

Joram looked at his son, a look of puzzlement now on his face, Ludd's breach of protocol momentarily ignored.

"What are you talking about? There is no vid of the attacks. The cameras were destroyed in the battle."

"No they weren't. You were lied to. I have a copy of the vid and I have just uploaded it to your data bank, father."

Ludd sat down, his legs shaking and heart pounding.

His father activated the vid. A square section of the metal desk in front of each Prime transformed into a transparent screen. Each of them leaned forward and watched the video intently as it played – all except Gord who was scowling and casting hostile looks toward Ludd.

The video ended and Joram spoke.

"It was difficult to see any detail ..." he began.

"May I speak again, father?"

Joram sighed.

"Speak."

"If you pause the vid near the beginning and zoom in, you will see."

Joram did as suggested, zooming in on a frozen scene of the battle.

"There!" cried Ludd. "You see? Old people! People clearly

over fifty! Look at that man with the pictures of palm trees on his shirt. He is definitely over fifty. And the fat man who is bald: he must be in his fifties too! These people are telling the truth!"

Joram was shaking his head, a frown deeply etched across his face.

Ludd manipulated his own touch pad and projected a new image onto their screens.

"This is a small corner of the last frame of the vid, showing a note that was part of their peace offering to us."

The image of the note filled the screen, its peaceful message clear to all.

"How did you ... where did you get this vid?"

Ludd glanced furtively at Garran who was looking at him pleadingly, shaking his head slightly.

"I ... I ... was browsing security files and stumbled across it. I am sorry if I acted inappropriately."

"We will deal with that later," responded his father. "In the meantime, I want to know why I was told there was no recording of the incursions."

He looked directly at Gord as he said this. Gord was clearly nonplussed, having been caught out in his blatant lie.

"I was told there was no recording by the security captain. I assure you I will look into this."

"Father!" cried Garran, unable to contain himself. "Please! Speak the truth!"

"What is going on today?!" cried Avril. "You Seconds have forgotten your place! Your interjections are unacceptable!"

Joram, however, chose to overlook Garran's breach of protocol.

"What is this truth you speak of, Garran?"

"Father?" Garran said, looking pleadingly at Gord. "Tell them."

"You will be silent in this quadracil!" exclaimed Gord to his son, his face mottled with anger and spittle flying from his lips.

"No," said Joram, firmly. "I will hear him. Speak, Garran. It appears your father is unable to."

Garran lowered his head and spoke tentatively into his lap.

"I ... I ... overheard my father telling the security captain to destroy the vid."

"Is this true, Gord? You deliberately withheld evidence from the quadracil?"

Gord was now glowering with anger.

"Yes! I ordered the file destroyed! But I did it to protect our city!"

"How would deceiving the quadracil protect our city?" interjected Sterv.

"Because I knew you would all be fooled by the intruders' deception!"

"Deception?" asked Joram.

"Of course! They have deliberately made themselves look old! They have coloured their hair and shaved their heads. It's the only possible explanation."

"Surely you don't honestly believe that?" asked Sterv. "Even their faces look old! How could they possibly fake that?"

"I am sure it can be done," replied Gord. "And the fact that you seem to believe what you are seeing is precisely why I ordered the vid destroyed. I knew their trickery would fool those who were gullible."

"Are you calling me gullible?" asked Joram, anger now bringing a spark to his eyes.

"I ... I ... did not mean to infer ..."

"How dare you!" continued Joram. "How dare you withhold valuable information from the quadracil! How dare you consider yourself a better judge of the truth than your peers! You have betrayed the fellowship of the Primes and placed yourself above the authority of this quadracil!"

Joram stood and was about to speak further when there was a loud knock on the door behind him and the Captain of

Security entered again, this time without waiting for an invitation.

"What is happening today?" cried Avril in indignation. "Has the city world gone mad? Has everyone forgotten their place in the world?"

"Forgive me," said the Captain. "But we are under attack."

## 33

The four soldiers arrived in a flitter, its pilot remaining in the aircraft as he and his three squaddies now approached the access shaft.

For the last few days Carlisle had grown increasingly frustrated at the inaction of the council. Civilian councils had no right having oversight of military decisions during a time of war. They were not trained in risk analysis and military strategy. The council's current passivity was a case in point. The enemy clearly posed a serious, ongoing threat to the colony's safety. The City Council was extremely naïve to believe that the problem would simply go away if they did nothing.

Over the last few days, he had studied the standing orders of his commission very carefully. They clearly stated that as Head of Security for the colony, he had the authority to act without consultation during a crisis. This was clearly a crisis, one that threatened the very existence of them all. He had no doubt that he was acting within the bounds of his commission.

There had been no difficulty in finding soldiers willing to accompany him on this mission. The whole company was itching to avenge the deaths of their comrades. He could have mobilised the whole base if he had wanted to, but three soldiers were all he needed for this operation.

They approached the access shaft quickly and silently. Each soldier knew exactly what to do, having been briefed in detail before they lifted off. Two of them clambered onto the concrete roof of the shaft and one began to cut a small hole with a laser cutter. At the same time another soldier began cutting a larger, person-sized opening in the metal door below which, by now, had been welded shut again. Carlisle stood slightly to the side,

The hole in the roof was completed quickly, the small chunk of concrete dropping to the floor inside with a dull thunk. The soldier with the cutter stepped aside and his companion knelt beside the small opening and held a baseball-sized sphere over the hole. The soldier who had cut the hole was now holding a remote control with a small digital screen in his hand. He gave a 'thumbs up' signal to his mate who released the sphere. It hovered over the hole momentarily and then slipped down through it as the soldier with the controls guided it. Nothing happened for a few moments and then there was an explosion from somewhere inside the shaft.

"The first booby trap was at the bottom of the second flight of stairs, sir," he whispered into his lapel com.

"Roger. Send down another floater. Keep sending them until all their movement sensor EDs have been defused – all the way to the bottom of the stairs."

"Roger that."

A second floater was activated and made it as far as the tenth flight of stairs before it tripped a movement sensor and another explosion took place. A third floater made it four flights further before tripping the next bomb. The fourth floater made it all the way to the bottom and was hovering in front of the door, relaying the video image of the welded patch.

"It's at the bottom, sir. No more bombs detected."

"Bring it all the way back up, just to be sure you haven't missed anything."

"Yes, sir."

Meanwhile the door at the top had been successfully breached, the cut-out section falling inward with a resounding clang. As soon as the floater emerged at the top of the stairs, Carlisle gave the command to commence the next phase.

"Go! Go! Go!"

All four soldiers raced down the stairs, the need for stealth long gone. They reached the bottom without incident and one soldier placed a metal circular disk with a hand grip against the door at head height. He activated the magnet and it stuck to the door. A second soldier stepped forward with a cutter and began cutting a hole around the magnetic grip, about the size of a basketball.

"Riley, get ready with the daisy cutter. The rest of you stay down. By now there will be a whole bunch of the bastards on the other side ready to drill us full of holes."

The final part of the cut was completed and a soldier who was holding the magnetic grip quickly pulled the circular cut-out clear of the hole and ducked down with the others who were crouching behind the door. An incandescent stream of laser fire immediately came blazing through the hole over their heads, drilling into the concrete walls and steps behind them and sparking off the metal railings like fireworks at a party. The laser fire kept up for several moments and then there was a lull.

"Daisy cutter!" whispered Carlisle.

A soldier lobbed a small device through the hole and they all hunkered down even lower. A massive explosion shook them accompanied by the rattle of dozens of pieces of deadly shrapnel banging against the door. Even through the ringing in their ears, they could hear the moaning and screaming of badly injured soldiers on the other side.

"Gopher!" said Carlisle.

"Another soldier stepped forward with a spherical metal bomb, the size of a small basketball and only slightly smaller than the hole. It had a small flat section on its underside and a series of tiny holes around the girth of its circumference. The soldier punched a code into the recessed keypad on its top and the device powered up, emitting a low hum.

"Set it for one kilometre," said Carlisle.

"Yes, sir" said the soldier, making the adjustment.

At the colonel's nod, he lobbed it through the hole and they heard it land with a thud and then roll for a few seconds before coming to a stop. A high-pitched whine could now be heard, accompanied by a sizzling sound. Carlisle used a small optic fibre periscope to look through the hole. The gopher had come to rest in the middle of the floor, in the midst of the carnage. Carlisle nodded appreciatively. There were no enemy soldiers left viable. The gopher's internal servo motors had righted it so that it was sitting on its flat bottom. Dozens of tiny laser beams were now firing down from the holes around its circumference. As he watched, the floor below the bomb seemed to dissolve and the device fell through a now perfectly circular hole.

"Bombs away! Let's get out of here."

They turned and retraced their steps up the stairwell, in no rush now but still moving swiftly. It would take many minutes for the bomb to reach the prescribed depth and, by then, they would be well away from here. They reached the top and were just emerging from the access shaft when all hell broke loose.

## 34

———————

The four Primes and their Seconds were in the Security Command Centre watching the attack unfold on the vid screens, their quadracil having been immediately abandoned when they learned of the attack. The explosions in the shaft had been monitored by their cameras and by the time the members of the quadracil arrived, the four enemy soldiers could be seen beginning their descent down the stairwell.

As the Primes and their Seconds entered the Command Centre, the security captain explained that a squad of ten defence personnel in full battle suits were already in position on Level 6 of the museum, with weapons trained on the stairwell access door. The captain's explanation was superfluous. One of the screens on the monitoring desk clearly showed a squad of bronze-clad soldiers kneeling in formation, their laser rifles pointing at the welded lower door.

"You see?" said Gord, triumphantly pointing at the screen showing the enemy soldiers descending the stairs. "Their message of peace was a ruse to lull us while they attacked. So much for their expressions of goodwill!"

"It doesn't make sense," said Sterv, shaking his head. "Why would they only attack with four soldiers?"

"And why bother with a false message of peace in the first place?" added Joram. "As soon as the first motion sensor bomb went off in the stairwell, they knew we would react anyway. Their message has bought them no time at all."

"What are they doing now?" asked Avril.

They watched the view from the hidden camera at the bottom of the stairwell. The soldier with the cutter was creating a small hole in the top of the door. Gord glimpsed a small spherical device in the hands of one of the other soldiers, and suddenly exclaimed.

"It's a hole for a bomb! Get our troops out of there!"

The captain opened a comm and had barely begun to issue his warning when the bomb was lobbed through. It exploded with devastating consequences. The carnage was catastrophic. No one was left standing and there were body parts strewn all over the vestibule.

Ludd watched in horror and shook his head, unable to make sense of what he was seeing.

Gord, however was scathing. He turned on Joram and his son, not bothering to hide his scorn.

"Where is your theory about their peaceful intentions now? The only peace they intend is the peace when they have utterly destroyed us! And you," he said, thrusting Ludd in the chest and pushing him backwards, "in future keep your mouth shut and leave these things to the adults!"

"You touch my son again, and you will regret it!" said Joram.

The two men glared at each other, but their stand-off was interrupted by the captain.

"They've thrown another bomb through!"

They saw the strange device land and begin its operation.

"Clear the museum! All floors!" ordered Joram.

"What about the enemy soldiers? Are you just going to let them get away?" asked Gord.

Joram was silent for a moment.

"Come on, Joram!" prompted Gord. "The time for peaceful negotiations is over! Now is the time to act!"

"Sadly, I think you're right," Joram replied.

He turned to the captain.

"Order a platoon of twenty soldiers out of the main hatchway! Deploy them on the small rise to the north of the shaft entrance. Shoot on sight."

"You're sending them onto the surface?" asked Sterv.

"Yes. It's time we took the fight to the enemy."

"And what about their town?" asked Gord. "As long as they continue to live there, they will remain a threat."

"Father, don't do it!" pleaded Ludd. "Something is not right here. It's not making sense. I'm still convinced these people are willing to make peace!"

Joram was silent for a moment, weighing up the options. He came to a decision.

"Prepare forty wasps for launch."

**35**

---

Two flitters landed at almost the same time. Major Lea Chandra had mobilised a platoon of twenty soldiers, with ten in each aircraft. As the platoon disembarked and formed up, a third flitter landed. Zac and Amanda emerged and quickly met up with the Major.

"Ma'am and sir, I suggest you stay back and let us handle the situation," said Major Chandra. "If there's any hostile action, I don't want either of you in the line of fire."

"Certainly," agreed Amanda. "Just get those soldiers out of there before they ruin our negotiations. As of this moment you are the new Head of Security. I want you to place Colonel Carlisle under immediate arrest."

"Yes, ma'am. We'll be on comm channel four if you need to communicate."

The platoon began moving down the hill toward the exposed access shaft entrance. They were only half-way down, however, when laser fire began sizzling down from a slight rise opposite them, directed at the entrance to the shaft below them and to their left. The four soldiers from the stairwell had just exited the doorway when they were caught in the deadly fire.

Major Chandra saw one of the four soldiers fall to the ground and remain motionless while the other three retreated back into the concrete shaft and begin returning fire through the open doorway.

"Take cover and return fire!" she commanded, crouching behind a small boulder.

The platoon took shelter behind the boulders and small bushes that dotted the slope, firing at the enemy position opposite them and starting to receive fire in return. As laser bolts cracked all around them, the major yelled instructions.

"Lieutenant! Take your squad around to our left. I want you on top of that rise above and to the left of the shaft. Lay down a crossfire!"

"Yes, ma'am!"

A few moments later there was a furious tangle of laser fire as the two squads of Major Chandra's troops fired upon the bronze-clad soldiers who were hunkered down on the opposite slope. The three soldiers in the bunker provided a third stream of fire from the middle of the triangle toward the Subterrans at the apex.

Amanda and Zac watched the battle from the top of the hill above Major Chandra's position with growing horror.

"No, no, no!" cried Zac. "This has got to stop! We aren't enemies! This is a terrible mistake!"

Without much thought he started running down the hill toward the Major's troops, calling into his comm at the same time.

"Major! Cease fire! Cease fire!"

At the same time, Amanda was yelling at him.

"Zac, get back here! Come back! You'll get yourself killed!"

Zac's comm crackled to life with the major's voice as he continued running down the hill.

"Say again? Say again? I didn't read that!"

"Stop firing!" yelled Zac as he continued down.

The firing continued, with the major unable to hear anything over the crack and bang of laser blasts sizzling all around her.

Zac made it to the major's position without being hit and dived to the ground beside her.

"What the hell are you doing down here!" she yelled, firing over the boulder as she spoke.

"Stop firing, Major! Cease fire immediately!"

Chandra looked at him for a moment then gave the command, yelling loudly into her lapel com, bending to almost touch her lips to it as she did.

*That's why she didn't hear me,* Zac thought. *I wasn't yelling into it closely enough.*

The firing died away from their own troops. They continued to receive fire from the enemy position for another minute, but then the enemy troops realised there was no further resistance coming from them, they switched the focus of their fire solely to the three men trapped in the access shaft.

"Now what?" asked the major. "We've got to get them out somehow."

"I'm not sure," confessed Zac.

"Zac! What are you doing?" asked Amanda through the comms.

"I don't know," he confessed. "I'm making this up as I go. I just know that we have to stop this killing before we reach the point of no return."

...

In the underground Security Command Centre, they were watching multiple feeds from helmet cams from their troops and had noticed the cease fire from the opposite slope.

"Why have they stopped firing?" asked the captain, sitting at the bank of monitors. Gord and Joram were standing directly behind him looking over his shoulder.

"My best guess is that they are calling for reinforcements," said Gord, speaking from his previous military experience. He turned to Joram, at his right shoulder.

"We need to send the wasps into the town now. If we level the town immediately, we can neutralise all their other troops before they can mobilise."

Joram hesitated. This was a step that they would never be able to undo.

"Joram!" said Gord. "It's now or never. Your troops need protecting. Make the decision!"

"Dad, don't do it!" pleaded Ludd. "This is all a terrible mistake."

"Quiet, son. This is not your decision to make."

"Sir!" said the security captain. "The bomb in the museum, hasn't gone off yet. It's eating its way down through the levels, using some kind of laser cutting mechanism."

"You see, Joram!" said Gord. "There is no going back now. We have to hit back with all our strength now!"

"Yes. I'm afraid you're right."

He addressed the Captain.

"Make it so. Launch the wasps. And get a security detail onto that bomb. Figure out some way of neutralising it!

...

"We're at a stalemate," said Major Chandra to Zac as laser fire continued to streak between the concrete structure and the opposite slope. "Those three are pinned down and aren't getting out of there without our help."

"If by 'help', you mean shooting and killing more of the other side, that's not acceptable, Major. There are bigger things at stake here than three soldiers stuck in a bunker."

"Then what do you suggest?"

"Right now, I can only think of one thing."

"What?"

"This."

Zac stood up with his arms raised high above his head and started walking slowly down the slope, yelling with all the strength he could muster, "Cease fire! Cease fire!"

Amanda was screaming into his comm for him to turn around and the major was yelling the same, but he ignored them and continued down the slope, yelling at the top of his lungs with his arms raised high.

Strangely it worked. The enemy soldiers, faced with an unarmed civilian dressed in a flowery shirt walking towards them in an obvious posture of passivity completely discombobulated them. The firing from the bronze-suited soldiers completely ceased, and the three soldiers in the access shaft ceased their fire as well.

Zac came to a standstill mid-way between the trapped soldiers and the enemy position. His arms were starting to get heavy, but he dared not lower them. Instead he continued his yelling, trying to reason with the troops opposite him.

"This is a terrible mistake! We have come here in peace! We do not intend to harm you! These four soldiers behind me have attacked you without authorisation. They acted illegally and will be punished. Please cease fire and let us talk together. We come in peace!"

He ran out of words to say. He didn't know what else to say, so he just stood there, in his Hawaiian shirt and jeans, with arms raised above his head, waiting for a response.

An eerie silence descended on the battlefield and no one knew quite what to do.

## 36

I n the underground Security Command Centre, the Captain peered at the screen, trying to make sense of what he was seeing. A civilian in some kind of floral shirt had brought the battle to a complete standstill.

"What is he saying?" asked Joram.

"I can't pick it up, sir. The audio level isn't strong enough," replied the captain.

Ludd leant forward, staring wide eyed at the scene.

"That's him! That's the old man in the vid! The one with the palm trees on his shirt!"

He turned to the others.

"You see! He's old! And they clearly want peace."

Gord could see the initiative rapidly slipping away. He needed to act quickly before peace broke out and these deceivers gained access to the city.

"Captain what is the name of the commanding officer on the battlefield?" asked Gord.

"Lieutenant Marlan."

Gord nodded. He lurched forward, brushing Joram aside and activated the comm.

"Lieutenant Marlan! Open fire! Resume the attack! Shoot that man now!"

"Belay that order!" yelled Joram, pushing Gord aside.

But Gord had already muted the channel, and he physically blocked Joram's path to the console, saying, "You'll thank me for this, later, Joram."

"Captain, cancel that order, now!" yelled Joram, as Gord continued to block his path to the console.

But before the captain had a chance to even unmute the comm, the deed was done. Ludd watched in horror as a single laser bolt hit the civilian in the middle of the chest and the man collapsed motionless to the ground.

"Nooo!" Ludd screamed. He turned on Gord and grabbed his shirt, pushing the much older man back against the back wall.

"What have you done?" he yelled into his face. He shook his head in disgust then turned and ran out of the room, muttering, "I've got to stop this."

"Ludd!" called his father. "Where are you going? Come back!"

But it was too late. He was gone.

...

Meanwhile, on the battlefield, all hell had broken loose again. Zac's tragic demise had broken the spell, and hostilities were now renewed with increased ferocity. Laser blasts ripped across the field of battle, exploding the rocks, gouging deep scars in the earth and occasionally finding their mark. The three men in the bunker returned fire haphazardly but were hopelessly pinned down.

"Sergeant!" yelled Chandra. "Hit them with mortar shells! Keep up a barrage! I'm taking three squaddies to try to flank them."

"Yes, sir!"

A few moments later, mortars began falling among the enemy, sending showers of rocks and soil into the air and filling the hillside with smoke. At the same time, dozens of wasps flew past them overhead, racing toward the colony East of their position. Meanwhile, Zac lay unmoving in the centre of the battlefield, laser fire streaking over his lifeless body as both sides desperately tried to gain the ascendency.

Then an unexpected sight brought the battle to a grinding halt yet again. Out of the smoke and chaos of the enemy position ran a young man. He was wearing white, loose fitting trousers and a red and gold flowing top that looked more like a dressing gown than a shirt. But it was his skin that was the strangest sight. He was an albino, with skin as white as porcelain, yet his hair was jet black. As he ran out in front of his own troops, they stopped firing out of fear of hitting him. He continued running down the hill into the maelstrom of incoming laser fire, with arms raised in the air, just as Zac had done. Major Chandra screamed a cease fire into her comm and the laser fire ceased. Miraculously, the young man had reached the bottom of the hill unscathed.

Silence descended over the battlefield once again as the young man came to stand next to Zac's fallen body. With arms raised in the air he called out in a strangely accented voice,

"We accept your offer of peace! Lay down your arms everyone! Let there be peace among us! Cease fire!"

Turning toward his own troops, he yelled,

"Tell my father to deactivate the wasps! There must be no more killing!"

Apart from one of the bronze-suited soldiers talking urgently into his comm, nothing happened and no one moved for nearly a minute. Then Major Chandra stood to her feet and shouted to her troops,

"Stand down everyone! The battle is over!"

Similar orders were issued on the opposing hillside, and soldiers from both sides began standing to their feet, uncertainly. In the eerie silence, the moans of injured men became obvious, and people began to treat the wounded.

A sudden movement at the entrance to the concrete bunker drew Major Chandra's attention. Colonel Carlisle had drawn his pistol from his holster and was raising his arm to aim it at the young man.

"Colonel Carlisle! Stand down! Drop your weapon immediately!"

Carlisle ignored the major and took aim at the boy, the frustration and rage that had built up within him over the last few days suddenly boiling to the surface. He aimed his pistol at the middle of the boy's chest, determined to take revenge on his fallen comrades.

The laser bolt streaked across the grass and hit him squarely in the chest, killing Carlisle instantly. Major Chandra lowered her rifle and nodded to herself. It was a good shot. Not just technically good; it was righteous.

Ludd was having difficulty seeing anything. The brilliance of the sun was blinding him. His eyes had never experienced the full light of day. He squinted in the piercing glare and tears coursed down his cheeks. He knelt down beside the fallen man in the colourful shirt and touched his shoulder. The man opened his eyes and looked back at him.

"Nice to meet you," the man mumbled.

Ludd stood up and turned toward the man's friends.

"The old man is still alive! Your friend is alive!" he yelled.

As a medic came running toward them, Ludd bent down and gently touched the wrinkles on the man's face.

"You're very old," he whispered.

Zac stared at the strange looking creature kneeling beside him.

"I feel a hell of a lot older now than I did about half an hour ago."

**37**

Zac almost died.

The laser blast had drilled through the right side of his chest and out of his back. The only reason he survived is that it had miraculously missed his heart and all of the major veins and arteries. But it smashed two ribs and tore through his right lung which filled with blood and began compressing his heart. By the time he arrived at the hospital, they had needed to shock him twice to restart his heart. He was rushed into surgery and they operated on him for nearly five hours.

Kit was an emotional wreck. It was the closest she had ever come to losing Zac and for the first 24 hours she thought she just might. It was 48 hours before they took him off life support and declared that he would make it. It was another 24 hours before they finally brought him fully awake and Kit was able to speak with him. She smothered him with kisses and stroked his head.

"Zac, my darling, you've got to stop saving the world."

He smiled.

"In that case, the world needs to jolly well get its act

together and stop needing to be saved," he replied, laughing slightly and then groaning in pain.

"Bloody hell, I'm getting too old for this crap."

The following day he was taken out of Intensive Care and given a private room, and by then he was starting to give cheek. Keo wasn't helping. Whenever he visited Zac, the two of them were insufferable. On the second day in his private room, a nurse came in and gave Zac a specimen jar to fill, stating that she wanted him to supply a urine sample. Keo had smuggled some mead in for Zac to drink and after the nurse left, they decided to play a joke on her, filling the specimen jar with mead. When she returned, she looked at the jar with concern, commenting on how cloudy his urine was. Zac reached out and took the jar back from her, saying,

"In that case, let me run it through the system one more time."

He opened the lid and gulped the contents down, to the nurse's utter astonishment.

On the sixth day, the doctors declared that the nanobots they had injected him with had done their job. His lung was healing nicely and his external wounds were mending. Zac was released from hospital and a celebration lunch was held at his apartment in his honour. The whole circle of friends and family were there and there was much laughter and banter that carried through into the late afternoon.

Finally, just Tash and Keo remained, and as the sun began to lower over the western hills, the two men sat together on the balcony while Tash and Kit cleaned up inside.

"I'm pretty sure mine's bigger than yours, Keo."

"No way, bro! Take a look!"

"That's nowhere near as big as mine dude!"

"Maybe not," conceded Keo, "But I lost a whole kidney, whereas you only got a puny hole drilled through your lungs. Loss of tissue mass has got to count for something, surely!"

"But I lost more blood than you," persisted Zac.

"I dispute that vigorously, bro. My whole stomach cavity was full of blood when they opened me up."

Zac considered the arguments on both sides and pronounced his final verdict.

"I declare a tie," he said holding his cup of mead out to Keo.

"A tie it is," agreed Keo, as they clinked glasses.

"Listen to them, would you!" said Tash. "Why does everything have to be a competition?"

"It's faulty chromosomes in the male genome," replied Kit. "There must have been some sort of genetic mutation that occurred somewhere back in the dawn of time, when two men were clubbing each other over the head and claiming that theirs was the biggest club."

The girls both chuckled as they listened to Zac and Keo's banter. They were currently engaged in a variation on their philosophical duel. This time it was a one-liner duel.

"If I'm a good dancer, does that make me a prime mover?" said Zac.

"If I'm a pacifist, are my jokes allowed to have punchlines?" replied Keo.

"I used to be a solipsist but I talked myself out of it."

"My narcissism is one of the things I love most about myself."

The girls shook their heads and settled down in the lounge room with a cup of tea.

Eventually the boys ran out of one-liners and sat in companionable silence, sipping mead and watching Wellington Harbour gradually turn to gold in the setting sun.

Later that night, Kit lay snuggled up to Zac, her fingers idly caressing the scar tissue on his chest.

"You know, back in our day, you wouldn't have proper scar tissue for another month. It would still be a weeping wound after six days."

"Yep," agreed Zac. "I'm very thankful for nanobot technology."

"And I'm very thankful you're still alive," she said, kissing him tenderly. "But I'm putting my foot down! No more saving the world for you! That's an order. You've done your bit; it's someone else's turn now."

"I hope there's no need for anyone else to take a turn."

But hope doesn't always translate into reality.

38

Mayor Amanda Robinson, met with Zac the following morning in her office, in order to bring him up to speed on developments that had occurred during his convalescence. Amanda had visited him twice in hospital but had deliberately not involved him in the wider concerns of the colony during his convalescence.

"A lot has happened over the last week, Zac," she began.

"I'm sure it has. I've heard some of it, but it will be good to get the full details."

"You missed the funerals, of course. Those couldn't wait. All told, we lost five good soldiers in the battle on Wrights Hill."

"Are you including Colonel Carlisle in the 'good soldier' category?"

Amanda sighed.

"I agree that he went off the rails and almost created a major war. If he had survived, I would certainly have initiated court martial proceedings. But I felt that a posthumous court martial would serve no useful purpose, so he was buried respectfully, but with no special military honours."

"What about the two surviving soldiers from his attack squad?"

"They've both been exonerated. They were only following the colonel's orders. In fact, one of them deserves some kind of commendation. Once the cease fire took place, he advised Major Chandra that they had unleashed a gopher in the underground city."

"A gopher?"

"A particularly nasty bomb that burrows to a specified depth before detonating. It would have been powerful enough to obliterate the entire district of the city underneath Wrights Hill. The soldier liaised with a lieutenant on the opposing army and provided the Subterrans with the deactivation code. It was a very close thing in the end."

"So, where are we up to with our new neighbours? I've heard bits and pieces, of course."

"I'm sure you have. Do you remember the young man who spoke with you as you lay injured on the battlefield?"

"Vaguely. I was drifting in and out of consciousness at that point. He had very white skin, as I recall."

"Yes. They all do, as it turns out. Thousands of years living underground will do that to a population. Anyway, his name is Ludd and he is the son of the President of New Eden. We owe him a debt of gratitude because he believed in our peaceful intentions when almost no one else did. He took a big risk coming out into the open without any breathing apparatus. In fact, as far as we can tell, he is the first Subterran to breathe fresh surface air for two thousand years. It was a bold move."

"I'm told he took a big risk, running down that hill into oncoming fire."

"Yes, he did. And he also defied the ruling council of their city, which they call a quadracil. If it weren't for the incredibly courageous actions of both of you, we would be in the midst of a full-scale war right now."

"So, what are we in the midst of?"

"A tentative but growing friendship. The leadership of New Eden are now convinced that the EI has been destroyed and that it is safe to venture onto the surface. Various gifts have been exchanged and we are in daily communication. A formal peace treaty is scheduled to be signed tomorrow. Which is where you come in."

"Me?"

"Yes. The reason the treaty has not yet been signed is that the Subterrans insist that you and Ludd be signatories to it, along with me and their President. They wish to honour the role that you and Ludd played in ending hostilities. The ceremony has been delayed until you are well enough to attend."

"I see. That's ... surprising."

"Not at all. You're a hero Zac – yet again! You seem to make a habit of it."

"It's a habit I'm hoping to break. Kit has expressly forbidden me to save the world again, upon threat of torture."

"She's a formidable woman," said Amanda.

"You can say that again!"

"She's a formidable woman."

"Um ... no ... I meant ... oh, never mind."

"Following the ceremony, they have invited a group of us to attend a formal dinner in their city. It will be the first visit of either group to the other's settlement. It should prove fascinating."

"Who will be going?"

"You and I will represent the City Council. I have also included Melody on the guest list, as she is Elizabeth Canning's daughter, although I have not yet indicated to the Subterrans her direct relationship to Elizabeth – I'll let that reveal itself tomorrow."

"That should be an interesting conversation."

"Indeed. The Subterrans have also requested that we

include a delegation of our oldest citizens – those who are over fifty. That means that Kit, Keo, Tash, Jaz and Karl will be going too."

"Why are they so keen for us oldies to attend? Surely, they have plenty of citizens even older than us, seeing they've never been under the EI's control?"

"Yes, they do. But apparently there is an undercurrent of doubt among some of their population regarding the truth of the EI's destruction. The President believes that parading our older citizens in public will allay those fears."

"I see. In that case I'll do my best to look as ancient and decrepit as possible."

"No need to go to any special effort," said Amanda with a twinkle in her eye. "You look extremely convincing just as you are."

## 39

The ceremony was held on Wrights Hill, on the very spot where Zac had been shot and where Ludd had made his courageous stand. A simple table covered with a red cloth was in place on the grass, with two copies of an official document awaiting signatures. They had decided on old-fashioned paper documents as a mark of historical respect for the ancient human ancestry that both groups shared. Ranks of soldiers in smart military uniforms were lined up on opposite sides of the table, facing each other. The flitter carrying the Wellington delegation landed on the hilltop, and Zac and the others disembarked and began walking down the gentle slope toward the table.

"Do I look old enough?" whispered Kit.

"Ancient, my love" assured Zac, who then received an elbow in his left side for his comment. He feigned injury and said, "That's not fair! That was a trick question!"

"What about me, bro? Do I look old enough?" asked Keo who had overheard their exchange.

"One look at you, dude, and they'll put you straight onto a respirator."

"Thanks, bro."

"Don't mention it."

They arrived at the table where a delegation of Subterrans, all dressed in white trousers and red and gold shirts, stood waiting for them. Once again, Zac marvelled at their intensely white skin.

A tall figure in their centre stepped forward and greeted them.

"Welcome, friends. I am Joram Taal, President of New Eden and Prime of District 1."

He introduced two other Primes – Sterv and Avril – and then the Seconds. Amanda then introduced the members of her own delegation.

"Please forgive us for wearing these sunglasses," said Joram. "We cannot tolerate the bright light on the surface. This is a strange and unsettling experience for us, as I'm sure you can imagine."

"No need for apologies, President Taal. We understand."

"Technically, it is President Joram, as we don't use our surnames in that way. But please, call me Joram."

"And you may call me Amanda."

They nodded to each other in mutual respect.

The president then addressed Zac.

"You were very brave, Zac."

"Some would say foolish," he responded.

"Your foolishness saved us from an even greater foolishness – one that we would have regretted forever."

"It was your son who saved us from that foolishness in the end," said Zac. "He is to be honoured."

"You are both to be honoured," agreed Joram. "We would not be standing here today as friends without your heroism. Which is why I would like you both to be the first signatories on this peace treaty."

Zac and Ludd were invited to step forward and sign the documents. As they sat at the table together, Ludd asked,

"You are feeling better now, Zac?"

"Much better, thank you."

"I see you are wearing a colourful shirt again. Is there a reason why no one else in your delegation wears such bright colours?"

"They don't have as good taste in fashion as I do."

"I see," nodded Ludd gravely.

"Don't listen to him," said Kit. "He is an anachronism."

"Anachronism? I do not know this word."

"It means I'm very special," said Zac, helpfully.

"Ah! Yes. I see that you are."

Kit and the others just shook their heads and smiled.

Zac and Ludd signed the treaty, followed by Amanda and Joram. At a nod from Joram, a trumpeter from the ranks of his soldiers stepped forward and blew a strangely eerie melody. At its conclusion, Joram made a brief speech.

"We have signed our names and ratified the peace treaty. We are now friends, not enemies. May there forever be peace and harmony between our peoples. Together, let us work toward the betterment of our world and the advancement of humanity! And now, let us adjourn to our city hall for dinner."

Zac and the others began to move toward the access shaft that had been the scene of so much violence in recent days, but Joram stopped them.

"No. Not that way, friends. Follow me. We will use the main hatchway."

"This is going to be interesting," whispered Amanda to Zac.

"You can say that again."

"This is going to be interesting."

"I'm going to have to give you a lesson in ancient idioms," said Zac.

## 40

J oram led the official delegation up the slight rise to the north of the access shaft. After about two hundred metres they came to a large rocky outcrop, with steep-sided granite.

"This is the main hatchway for District 1," said Joram.

"Where?" asked Amanda, looking around in puzzlement.

Joram stepped up to the granite cliff and placed his hand against a subtle indentation in the rock that they had not previously noticed but which they could now see was roughly hand-shaped. A huge section of the rock wall slid down into the ground, revealing a large chamber extending far back into the hillside. The visitors stood there, gobsmacked, gazing at the interior in wonder.

"There is a similar hatchway at the top of each of the four Districts, as well as separate launch hatches for our weapons."

At Joram's invitation, they entered the chamber, noting the presence of four large lifts, two on each side. As they approached one of the lifts it opened, revealing an interior spacious enough to accommodate both official delegations. After entering the lift, Joram spoke.

"Elevation 20, Level 10, please."

"Certainly, President Joram."

The doors closed and the lift began descending.

"You have artificial intelligence?" asked Amanda.

Instead of answering her directly, Joram addressed the entity that was obviously controlling the lift.

"Would you describe yourself as intelligent, D1?"

"Modesty prohibits me from being too boastful, sir, but I believe my intelligence surpasses that of any human's by a factor of many thousands."

"Aren't you concerned about your AIs evolving along similar lines as the EI?" asked Mel.

"No. The EI did not evolve or, more appropriately, devolve. It was deliberately created without fail-safe ethical coding. We have incorporated Asimov's Three Laws of Robotics into our Sentiums, as we call them."

"I assume that District 2 has a Sentium named D2?" asked Zac.

"Yes," replied Joram.

"So, if I was chatting with it about how intelligent D1 is, I could say to it, 'You are too, D2'."

Kit and the other ancient Terrans tried hard to stifle their laughs, while Joram simply replied,

"Certainly. All four Sentiums are equally intelligent."

The lift doors opened and Joram waved them forward.

"Welcome to New Eden."

They emerged into a wide, gently-curved corridor disappearing into the distance in both directions. The opposite wall of the corridor was the inside of the curve and consisted entirely of glass, whereas the outside wall, of which the lift was part, was solid and was dotted with doors.

Joram led them to the glass wall and they looked through with astonishment. They were looking down on a huge parkland, at least seventy metres below them. The huge park was perfectly circular, more than a kilometre in diameter, and was surrounded by a massive white wall. The glass-walled corridor they were standing in formed the top level of the wall, continuing around its entire circumference, like a glass-walled viewing promenade. Underneath them there were a further nine levels of windows built into the wall and extending all the way around its circumference. The park below them was absolutely stunning, with grass and trees and wide-open spaces, filled with people enjoying the 'outdoors' underneath the artificial lighting coming from the domed roof.

Joram explained proudly, "Each of District 1's twenty Elevations has a central park like this, surrounded by ten levels of domiciles and other facilities. Each domicile in each Elevation has a view of its Central Park. We are on Level 10 of the 20th Elevation. Level 10 is almost entirely dedicated to administration, medical and educational facilities for this Elevation."

"And there are nineteen more Elevations like this, below us?" said Tash, utterly amazed.

"Yes."

"This is ... absolutely mind blowing!" said Zac. "No wonder you've been content to live down here for thousands of years!"

"We are, indeed, very comfortable here. Of course, it wasn't always this grand," Joram reflected, as they continued to look through the window at the magnificent park below. "Our ancestors started very modestly. It took us over a thousand years to complete the top ten Elevations."

"It's stunning," agreed Amanda.

"Please, let us continue. Dinner awaits."

Joram directed them to the left and as they walked along the corridor, they encountered a constant stream of people passing in each direction, all of whom nodded politely but could not conceal their glances of curiosity.

"It appears that many of the citizens on the 20th Elevation have chosen this precise moment to go for a stroll along the

Viewing Corridor," chuckled Joram as he waved and nodded politely to various passing pedestrians. He smiled at Amanda.

"Please forgive them. You are the most exciting thing that has happened to our city in two millennia!"

They approached a large set of double doors on the left and two people in official looking garments opened the doors to let them in. They entered a large hall, with over two hundred guests seated at dining tables. As they walked through the doors, the guests all stood to their feet and applauded amid gasps and murmurs of surprise at various aspects of their different appearance.

"At last, I am being acknowledged for my greatness," muttered Keo. "I knew it would happen eventually."

"I think they're just amazed that a person of your girth can still be standing upright, my darling," said Tash.

**41**

———

Joram led then through the middle of the tables of guests, to a raised platform at the front of the hall, where a long, curved table faced the rest of the guests in a semicircle.

"I feel like I'm the bride at a 21$^{st}$ century wedding!" said Kit.

"And you look truly ravishing, my love," responded Zac. "Wait until you see what I've got planned for you tonight."

"Take it easy, tiger. You're still recovering, remember?"

"It will take more than a laser blast and a punctured lung to keep me from rising to the occasion!" he boasted.

Joram indicated the name cards on the table and they quickly found their places. Ludd was on Joram's right hand and Zac on his left – the two positions of greatest honour. Once they had all taken their seats, Joram stood and briefly opened proceedings. He welcomed everyone and pronounced a simple blessing over their meal. No sooner had he finished, than trays of steaming food arrived and were placed among them, the delicious aromas eliciting hunger pains in Zac and the others.

As they began eating, Zac asked Joram about the make-up of the quadracil. Joram explained the basic working of the quadracil as a council of the leaders of the four districts, with their First-Borns as Seconds – a kind of apprentice. As well as a Prime and a Second, each district also had a District Council which met to oversee matters of a more parochial nature.

"I notice that we have only met two of the other Primes," said Zac.

There was a moment's awkward silence as Joram phrased his reply carefully.

"The Prime of District 4 was dismissed immediately following the cessation of hostilities. He ... he deceived the quadracil and was instrumental in escalating the conflict unnecessarily."

"I'm sorry to hear that. It must be ... awkward for you at the moment."

"Yes. There has never before been a Prime who has been dismissed. I had to use my constitutional powers as President. We are still trying to work out how his replacement will be determined, as Primes are appointed by means of ancestral descent."

Zac nodded, appreciating the difficulty that Joram faced.

"I assume that 'quadracil' means 'council of four'."

"Yes. Hence the need to find a replacement for Gord."

"I hope you find someone soon."

Shortly afterward, Joram addressed Melody, who was three places to his left, on the other side of Zac and Kit.

"Pardon me for being inquisitive, but I notice that you share the surname of our first President, Elizabeth Canning. Do you know whether you are distantly related to her by any chance?"

"Yes. She was my mother."

"Indeed," agreed Joram. "She is the mother of us all."

"No. I mean literally. She was my actual mother. She gave birth to me. I am her daughter."

"What...?" asked Joram, confused. "I don't understand."

"I was here in the bunker – what you now call the museum

– when the GAE occurred. I was twelve years old at the time. I escaped just before The Scorching."

"No ... that's ... surely that's not possible? That was over 3,000 years ago!"

"Ours has been a strange journey," explained Zac. "There are seven of us sharing this meal with you today who were alive at the time of the Scorching – Tash, Keo, Jaz, Karl, Kit, Mel and me. We only barely escaped in a starship named Genesis, which subsequently became ensnared in the event horizon of a black hole while we were in cryogenic stasis. We encountered significant time dilation and when our vessel eventually broke free of the black hole's influence and we awoke, we found that the outside universe had aged thousands of years while we had barely aged at all."

Joram was staring at Zac with an incredulous expression.

"This is some kind of joke? Yes?"

"No. I'm completely serious."

Joram stared at him some more, then suddenly turned to a wait person behind him and whispered something. He sat silently, wrapped in his own thoughts for a few moments, until the wait person returned with what looked like a data pad. Joram took the pad and began furiously typing on its surface and manipulating the screen. Finally he stared at the screen for some time, then sat back. He glanced between the screen and Melody several times, then stood up and walked to her side.

"Forgive me for bothering you further, but I must confirm this."

Melody swivelled in her chair.

"By all means."

"The ancient records do, indeed, state that Elizabeth's twelve-year-old daughter, Melody, was initially with her in the bunker. This is the only photograph of her, kept by Elizabeth."

He showed Mel the photo.

"Yes that's me. And that's my teddy, Scruffy."

Tears welled up in her eyes as she looked into her past.

"Yes ... Scruffy ... that's what President Canning called the teddy in her diary," said Joram, a deep frown now on his face.

Joram continued reading, furiously.

"It says here that Melody broke her left arm badly when she was seven and had surgery to reconnect the bones. She never had the scar removed by cosmetic surgery."

Without saying a word, Melody rolled up her sleeve and revealed a long scar running down the back of her left arm, from the elbow to a point half-way toward her wrist. Joram's mouth opened in astonishment and he took an involuntary step backward. Then he looked at Zac and the others.

"So, all of you ... you are all from ancient Earth?"

"Yes," agreed Zac, with a mouthful of some kind of succulent meat. "If you want to get technical about it, we are all more than 3,000 years old. By the way, what is this meat? It's delicious."

"Darling, you've got gravy dribbling down your chin," commented Kit, helpfully.

Joram didn't register Zac's question; he was completely shell-shocked.

"So the ancient legends about the starship Genesis are true?" he asked, still struggling to process what he was hearing.

"Yep," agreed Zac, stuffing another wheelbarrow-sized portion of meat into his mouth. "But the food was pretty awful. Nothing like this. What did you say this meat is called?"

Joram suddenly clapped his hands loudly together several times, and the hall instantly became quiet.

"Ladies and gentlemen! I have just learned a truly remarkable thing! Some of these honoured guests were on board the legendary starship Genesis, when it left Earth over 3,000 years ago!"

Gasps of shock and astonishment were quickly followed by an eruption of conversation punctuated with bewildered expressions. Joram had to clap several times again to restore order before he could continue.

"As impossible as this sounds, I assure you that it is scientifically possible, and I have seen the proof of this claim with my own eyes. He went to stand directly behind Mel before he continued.

"But there is an even more astonishing piece of news! Our honoured guest, Melody Canning, is not merely named after the missing daughter of our first President, she is Elizabeth Canning's biological daughter, transported through time via the distortion of a black hole. We have the First President's daughter with us in our city tonight!"

Amid the gasps of astonishment, a man at a table toward the front of the hall stood to his feet and began clapping. He was joined by a growing number of others until, very soon, the whole crowd was on its feet, clapping and cheering.

Joram asked his son, Ludd, if he would consent to swapping places with Mel, and she was moved to the position of highest honour, at Joram's right side. The banquet was being broadcast throughout the four districts of the city, so within moments of the announcement, the whole of New Eden was abuzz. Melody was a sensation. And so were the other ancient travellers.

"You see!" said Keo. "My greatness is finally revealed!"

"You've dribbled gravy all down your shirt, dear," said Tash.

**42**

―――――――

The weeks that followed were idyllic. Winter gave way to the mild weather of spring and as the landscape around them burst into life, the new friendship between the two colonies also blossomed.

A steadily growing stream of New Edeners (as they were now called) began to venture forth from their cosy burrows, rising to the surface for the first time. In fact, the term, 'Eden rising' began to be applied to the growing proliferation of subterranean humans exploring the surface for the first time.

Unfortunately, for many of them, the experience was too much. The unending sky and vast horizon overwhelmed their senses, sending them scurrying back into the comfortably confined world that they had known all their lives. It was not unusual to see individuals and groups of people running out of the main hatchways to stand momentarily on the wide-open hilltop, only to run screaming and laughing back into the perceived safety of the hatchways. This practice became known as "surface diving", and groups of teenagers could often be seen timing each other to see how long they could last in the oppressive openness.

Not everyone succumbed to agoraphobia, however. Some adventurous souls never experienced fear at all, instantly revelling in the vastness of the surface. Others experienced initial unease but soon overcame it. The brightness of the unfiltered sun, however, remained a difficulty for all New Edeners. No amount of positive thinking could overcome the extreme light sensitivity that was a developmental vestige of millennia spent underground. A roaring trade in sunglasses resulted, with some New Edeners adopting a style of glasses known as sidewinders. These were more like slim-fitting goggles with sides all around that restricted their view to straight ahead, helping those who were agoraphobically sensitive.

Wellington Harbour became a popular day trip for New Edeners. They had never seen a body of water so expansive. A booming boat business soon sprang up, with the Wellington locals hiring out row boats and sailing boats and offering sailing lessons.

A thriving trade sprang up between the two colonies. Each community specialised in different varieties of fruit, vegetables and meat, with Wellington supplying seafood which had been completely lacking from the New Edeners' diets. Economically, a mutual currency was quickly established, the main unit of which they decided to call the Kiwi.

There was also an almost instantaneous desire to work together to share technology. Both communities had evolved different technologies over the millennia. While many elements were surprisingly similar, some were completely divergent. Teams of scientists from both communities quickly established a deep collaborative interchange and, in several instances, found that technological blockages to progress that one community had been unable to overcome had already been solved by the other. In this way, great progress was quickly made in many areas of science and technology.

Socially, the two communities initially remained quite separate, with visitors from one community walking through the streets of the other in homogenous groups like tourists. But gradually, the groups began to mix and friendships formed. An important common bond in the early days was soccer, for which both communities shared a passion. At first all games between the two communities were played in New Eden, in deference to the New Edeners' discomfort with the surface world. Over time, however, a growing number of games were played on Wellington oval, followed by community barbecues.

Politically, there was almost daily communication between the Mayor of Wellington and the President of New Eden, and every second week a combined meeting of the New Eden Quadracil and Wellington City Council took place.

It was at the second of these meetings that the most contentious issue arose; artificial intelligence. The four Sentiums in New Eden were highly advanced artificial intelligence entities who monitored and supervised the smooth functioning of the four districts. Their influence not only permeated the entire city, but also went beyond it. Each citizen of New Eden was almost continually linked to their Sentium via their communication devices wherever they went, even when they were in Wellington. This was because of the highly sophisticated transmission system that the New Edeners had designed, utilising a modified packet-waveform that was effective over vast distances.

The Wellington colony, however, had rejected the need for artificial intelligence up until this point. Having been established by colonists from Nova and Perdita, both of which had suffered under the cruel influence of the EI, the colony had decided that the use of artificial intelligence was best avoided. While they were not as vehement in their rejection of AI technology as the Altarian colony in Hobart, they were, nonetheless, reluctant to embrace it again.

The growing presence of the New Edeners in their midst,

however, meant that AI technology was now effectively entering their community whether they liked it or not. A whole hour of the second meeting of the combined councils was spent trying to find a reasonable way forward regarding the dilemma. Was it fair to ask New Edeners to leave all their electronic devices at home whenever they visited Wellington? Would it be practical to supervise and enforce such a policy if they decided upon it? How safe was artificial intelligence? Did Asimov's Three Laws of Robotics provide fail-safe protection against the possible corruption of artificial intelligence? How securely were the Three Laws encoded into the fabric of the Sentiums' consciousness? These were difficult issues that could not be resolved in a single council meeting.

In the end, Joram promised to bring a leading New Eden scientist to the next Combined Council meeting who could address the issue of the safety of their Sentiums. The Council agreed on the proposal and decided that in the meantime, no restrictions would be placed upon the New Edeners' use of Sentium-linked devices.

It was lunchtime when the second meeting of the Combined Council concluded. As the meeting broke up and people began dispersing, Ludd approached Zac as they walked out into the bright sunshine.

"Hello Zac."

Zac looked at the white-skinned young man with aviator sunglasses.

"Hi Ludd. Retro sunglasses I see. Very cool."

"Yes. I bought them yesterday for twenty Kiwis."

"Nice."

"Yes. I like them. I was wondering what you are doing now."

"I'm just heading home for lunch."

"Can I come? I would like to foster a close relationship with you."

**43**

---

The starship popped out of the wormhole like a cork out of a bottle. Due to the strange folding of space-time that wormhole quantum physics allows, the vessel had just traversed half the galaxy in a mere fourteen seconds. Now that it had re-entered normal space-time, however, it was travelling at the more sedate velocity of thirty kilometres per second. At that velocity they would reach Earth in approximately fifteen hours.

Starla was in no rush. She was standing behind and slightly to the side of the Captain's chair on the bridge, admiring the small blue-green sphere in the centre of the main viewing screen. *So that's my new home,* she thought, *at least for the next few years.*

Captain Jensen swivelled his chair to face her.

"Are you sure you don't want to take command on our final approach, Colonel Bree?"

"Not at all, Captain. This is your ship. I am just a temporary guest on board. Besides, I'm enjoying the view."

"Beautiful, isn't it? First time to Earth?"

"First time anywhere outside of Altaria," she admitted.

"Being Commander of Gateway Station kept me glued to our own solar system."

"How are your prisoners doing, Colonel?"

"Frankly Captain, they're proper pains in the arse. Mainly because they know that their status as prisoners is only temporary. Once they set foot on Earth, they are technically free, although they will all be on twelve-month good behaviour contracts, of course."

"Anyone in particular giving you curry?"

"Mainly their leader – Jurd Transid. He's done nothing but whinge and demand his rights ever since we locked him in his quarters. He's driving my sergeant batty. I try not to go near him because I'm likely to end up slapping his weaselly face."

"I heard you did a bit more than just slapping when you arrested one of them, Colonel."

"Yes. Carmen Orlando. Fractured her wrist and broke her jaw. I know they say that violence is not the answer, but I've gotta tell you, Captain, there was a certain amount of satisfaction involved in that arrest. I was quite happy that she resisted. She'd just killed one of my squad."

"So I heard. Terrible thing, that. How is she behaving herself now? Any trouble?"

"Nothing overt. But that's my worry with her. There's absolutely no emotion there at all. She has the coldest, deadest eyes I think I've ever seen. I get the impression that she would just as easily slit someone's throat as shake their hand."

"From what I hear, Colonel, she's done just that on more than one occasion."

"Yes. We know that she was directly responsible for a number of assassinations in recent years, but we just can't prove it in court. Jurd Transid might be the brains behind the reversionist movement, but she is definitely their deadliest enforcer."

"Well, I hope Hobart knows exactly what's coming their way."

"They certainly do. I'm the colony's new Head of Security. In fact, my appointment was the only reason the Mayor of Hobart was willing to accept their transportation at all."

"The Mayor must be happy about the free settlers we are also bringing," he said hopefully. "Over one hundred new colonists will surely be a big boost to the settlement."

"Yes. He's reasonably happy, bearing in mind that almost all of them are from reversionist islands. But as long as the colony sticks to its low-tech policy, there shouldn't be any problems."

A chime sounded, and they received an incoming message from the orbiting space station above Tasmania.

"Excuse me, Colonel, while I deal with this."

"Certainly."

While the captain discussed final course corrections and logistics for their approach to Earth, Starla reflected on the events that had led her here. Their bluff had worked. Despite a lack of evidence that would stand up in court, they had managed to convince the reversionist leaders that they were facing two years of solitary confinement while they awaited trial and decades more in prison when they were inevitably convicted. The prisoners – a group of thirty at the conclusion of all the arrests – had caved in very quickly when given the alternative of transportation to Earth. In the end, it was the Mayor of Hobart, Merv Portland, who was the source of greatest resistance. He was adamant that their ageing Head of Security was not up to the task of maintaining control of the reversionist leaders. He insisted that a replacement be made – someone strong enough and capable enough to handle the new challenge.

General Kellar gave her no choice. He advised Starla of her transfer, assuring her that she would only be there for six years, and hinting that this would be a very useful step toward gaining a star on her lapel. Starla had consented but insisted that she bring a crack unit of soldiers with her, headed by her two most trusted assistants, Lieutenant Ryeland and Sergeant Grimes. Kellar had agreed readily.

*What have you got in store for me?* she wondered as she now stood gazing at the image of Earth on the front screen.

She would soon find out.

## 44

They docked with the space station early the next day, Hobart time. The prisoners were kept locked in their quarters while the shuttles transferred the free settlers to the surface first. Finally, Starla told Sergeant Grimes to move them onto the remaining shuttle.

"How have they been, Sergeant?" asked Starla.

"Transid's been the main problem, ma'am. Whining like a little kid. Going on and on about his rights."

"The only right he's got at the moment is the right to keep breathing, and I've even got my doubts about that."

"Yes, ma'am," said the sergeant, smiling.

Starla stood at the airlock to the shuttle as the prisoners boarded. Most filed past her silently, thankful to be released from their quarters and finally heading toward freedom. Jurd Transid, however, was not so compliant. He stopped in front of Starla and spoke in his usual supercilious tone.

"Colonel, I must object in the strongest possible terms to our unnecessary incarceration."

"And I object to your murder of innocent men, women and children on Altaria. I win. Now move your arse."

Starla turned to Sergeant Grimes.

"Sergeant, if he makes another complaint, shoot him."

"Happily, ma'am," he replied with a wide grin.

Transid stood staring at her for a moment longer, then turned and moved into the shuttle, shaking his head and muttering. Carmen Orlando was next to board and as she walked past Starla, she glared at her captor with icy cold eyes.

*I'm going to have to watch that one very carefully,* thought Starla.

Thirty minutes later, their shuttle touched down in Hobart and the prisoners were transferred by ground car directly to the Mayor's chambers where they were made to stand in two lines facing his desk.

Mayor Merv Portland, lived up to his name, sporting a slightly portly belly, despite his average Altarian height of two metres. He gave the prisoners his sternest look and explained their conditions of release.

"Let me make a few things clear to you," he began. "I don't really want you here. If it were up to me, I would have locked you all up for the rest of your miserable lives. But here you are. And each of you has a chance to make a fresh start. As soon as you walk out of this office, you will be free citizens. But remember this: you are all on a strict twelve-month good behaviour contract. That means that any breach of the law, any unlawful activity of any kind, will result in the rescinding of your freedom and immediate incarceration. Make no mistake; we will be watching you very carefully! Each of you has been given a small studio apartment and you have been assigned jobs in various industries. Play your part, become responsible citizens, and you will have no trouble from me. Bend the rules even slightly, and you will wish you had stayed in Altaria. My staff will direct you to your lodgings. That is all!"

The group filed out of the chambers with Lieutenant

Ryeland, Sergeant Grimes and several soldiers in attendance, while Starla remained behind.

"Nice to have you with us, Colonel," said Portland. "You have quite a reputation. I'm looking forward to working with you."

"Thank you, Mayor. It's a beautiful colony you've got here."

The two of them walked to the large window that looked down over the growing settlement. The town hugged the shores of the beautiful river harbour to the East and was bounded by thickly-forested hills to the West.

"Yes. It certainly is easy on the eye," he agreed.

He turned to face Starla.

"You might find discipline a bit slack here, Colonel. I'm hoping you might fix that. It's why I was pushing so hard for a new Head of Security. Major Rathborne was definitely passed his best years of service."

"I'll get things tightened up pretty quickly, Mayor. The addition of new troops will help as well."

"I'm sure they will. I have every confidence in you. I'll let you get settled into your quarters for the moment. This afternoon I'd like to show you and Lieutenant Ryeland around the town; help you get oriented."

"Thank you, that would be good."

"And just a heads up: tomorrow you and I will be flying to Wellington. It's our monthly get-together with our cousins across the Tasman Sea. We will meet with our counterparts over there – the Mayor and the Head of Security, as well as a special liaison officer they've recently appointed. It'll be a good intro for you. I don't envisage there'll be anything too controversial on the agenda."

But they were in for a surprise.

**45**

———

Mel was now a celebrity among the New Edeners. In fact, she was more than a mere celebrity; she was royalty – the daughter of their revered First President. She could no longer go out in public without people wanting to meet her and take her photo. As much as it inconvenienced her, Zac and Kit were glad for the distraction it gave her, as she was still grieving deeply for Phil. Mel was constantly being invited to functions in New Eden and asked to speak of her memories of her mother and the events leading up to The Scorching.

Meanwhile, Ludd had latched onto Zac, wanting to know more about the ancient history of Earth. At first, Zac found it mildly annoying, as Ludd would often come visiting and would spend hours questioning him. But Zac quickly overcame his annoyance as he discerned in Ludd an intelligent, enquiring mind, and found him to be someone who was not bound by conventions or tradition.

"He's like a younger version of you," said Kit one day, after Ludd had visited.

"But a lot whiter," added Zac.

"I don't know about that. You've got a fair bit of white happening on top of your head these days."

That afternoon, Amanda called to say that the delegation from Hobart would be present at tomorrow's council meeting. It would be Zac's first meeting with the Altarians and Amanda warned him that Mayor Portland could be a little abrupt.

"Don't worry, Amanda, I'll be at my diplomatic best," he promised.

The meeting next morning got off to a pleasant start, with Zac and Starla renewing their acquaintance.

"Starla! It's great to see you!" Zac exclaimed, shaking her hand in the old-fashioned way. "I had no idea you were on Earth."

"Nice to see you again too, Zac. It was a last-minute arrangement. I'm the new Head of Security at Hobart."

Introductions were made all around, and Starla noted the competent demeanour of her counterpart, the newly promoted Colonel Lea Chandra. She sensed they would get on well.

The tone of the meeting degenerated, however, when Mayor Portland learned of the existence of artificial intelligence in New Eden. He had previously been advised of the discovery of the underground city and had been kept apprised of events during the conflict, but this was entirely new information.

"It can't be allowed to continue!" he said angrily. "We must insist that all artificial intelligence be deactivated immediately!"

"It's not as simple as that, Merv," Amanda responded.

"Why the hell not? We've all committed to an AI-free world. They should be no different."

"But they were here first," Amanda argued. "We are the newcomers in their world, not the other way around."

"But surely they can see the danger inherent in artificial intelligence? We've already had one instance go horribly wrong!"

Amanda shook her head.

"That was because some crazy scientist on Mars deliberately omitted the safety coding from the programming. The Sentiums in New Eden have Asimov's Three Laws of Robotics built into their coding. Yesterday, we met with the leading scientists from New Eden who assured us that the Three Laws are embedded deeply into the consciousness of each of the four Sentiums. The same thing is not going to happen here."

"I don't give a damn how deeply the Three Laws are embedded! If they've been removed once, they can be removed again! It's not worth the risk to the safety of this planet, and of the whole galaxy!"

For another thirty minutes, Zac and Amanda tried to talk Mayor Portland down from his belligerent position, but he wouldn't budge. Then, toward the end, he took offence on another front.

"Why isn't the Mayor of New Eden here to meet me?"

"President," corrected Amanda.

"President? It's just a city, not a whole damn country! Who the hell does he think he is?"

Ignoring the incendiary comment, Zac tried to explain.

"We thought it might be better to delay their meeting with Altarians. The people of New Eden are still adjusting to *our* presence among them. We look different enough, with our olive skin. Given the ... ah ... more considerable differences in your appearance, we thought it best to delay introducing them to the Altarian community."

Merv Portland stood up, his two-metre height towering over them. He leaned forward, resting his strangely elongated fingertips on the table and stared at them with his oversized eyes.

"I'm not interested in pandering to their sensibilities! I want a meeting with this so-called president ASAP! Call me when you've set it up!"

He turned and walked out of their meeting room. Starla stood and said, somewhat apologetically,

"I guess that's my cue to leave too. I'm sorry I didn't have more time get to know you. I hope there will be more opportunity in the future. It was nice to meet you. Zac, please give my regards to Kit and the others."

"I will. Thanks Starla. Good luck with him," he said, indicating the departed Mayor.

Starla raised her eyebrows and nodded, then left.

"Well this is going to be interesting," said Zac after she had left.

But it was going to get a lot more than just interesting.

**46**

---

The meeting between the Altarians and the New Edeners, just three days later, was equally ineffective. The four Primes of New Eden were present, along with the five leaders from the previous meeting. Amanda had briefed President Joram on the different appearance of the Altarians, so he and the other Primes knew what to expect. To their credit, the Primes did not display the merest hint of discomfort or surprise when they were introduced to the taller, genetically modified humans. Joram introduced the other Primes, including the newly-appointed Prime of District 4, a mild-looking man named Larne.

Portland didn't beat around the bush.

"Mister President ..."

"Joram, please."

"Very well, Joram, I'm not going to blow smoke up your arse ..."

"I'm very grateful," replied Joram. "That sounds a very peculiar and uncomfortable custom."

"What I mean is, I'm not going to spend time buttering you up and tiptoeing around the issue ..."

"That also seems a peculiar custom. What do you call it? A butter dance? Is it a welcome ceremony of some kind?"

Portland decided to give up on figures of speech.

"What I'm saying is, I want to get straight to the point."

"That's peculiar," said Joram, "because it seems to me you've already taken up a lot of time not doing that."

Zac was trying hard not to laugh. He was really starting to like Joram. Joram had, of course, previously been briefed by Amanda and Zac regarding Mayor Portland's concerns.

Portland ploughed on ahead.

"I've come here today to ask, in the strongest possible terms, that you deactivate your Sentiums."

"And what are your terms?"

"I beg your pardon?"

"What are these 'strongest possible terms' that you speak of? Are you threatening us?"

"No. Of course not."

"Then are you demanding or asking?"

"Asking, of course."

Joram nodded, thoughtfully.

"In that case, your request is politely denied."

Zac watched the colour begin to rise in Portland's jowly face.

"Mister President ..."

"Joram, please."

"Joram, surely given our history, you can see how dangerous artificial intelligence is?"

"No, I cannot see that. All I can see is how foolish the ancient scientists were to remove the fail-safe moral coding. Even my six-year-old nephew could predict the tragic consequences of that."

"But if it happened once, Joram, surely it can happen again!"

"No. It cannot. The Three Laws of Robotics are embedded

within the foundational coding of our Sentiums. Firstly, a robot may not injure a human being or, through inaction, allow a human being to come to harm. Secondly, a robot must obey orders given it by human beings, except where such orders would conflict with the First Law. And thirdly, a robot must protect its own existence as long as such protection does not conflict with the First or Second Law."

"Yes, I'm completely familiar with the Three Laws, thank you!" said Portland, gruffly.

"Good. Then you know that they are unable to be circumvented, provided they are embedded deeply into the coding. In the case of our Sentiums, these laws cannot be removed without killing them. The mistakes of the past will never be repeated."

"Are you willing to bet your life on that, and the lives of everyone else on this planet?"

"Merv, you are welcome to share this planet with us," said Joram, changing tack. "After all, it is the birthplace of humanity, and all humans should be free to live here if they choose. But we have been living here for over 3,000 years and you have only just arrived. If you do not like what you find here, you are free to leave and find somewhere else that suits you. But do not come knocking on our door and ask that we change in order to accommodate your baseless fears."

Portland was not used to being denied. He leaned forward as if to press his point home.

"I have a whole colony of people who have moved to this planet on the promise that it will be free from artificial intelligence!"

"That is your problem, not mine. I've always believed that it is foolish to make promises to people before you are certain you can deliver them."

"I need to warn you, Mister President, that among our colonists, are violent activists who have previously demonstrated a willingness to use extreme measures to destroy AI technology."

"So you *are* threatening me now, are you?"

"I am warning you, sir, of the extreme feelings that some of our colonists have in regard to this issue."

"Thank you, Merv, for sharing your feelings and the feelings of your people. If you think it would help, I would be very happy to welcome a delegation from your colony to our city. I will make sure they have full access to our scientists who can explain, much better than I, the absolute safety of our Sentiums."

"Let me get this straight," said Portland, his face bright red with indignation by now. "You aren't willing to even consider changing your technology?"

"That is correct."

"Then we're done here!"

Portland stood up and stormed out of the room, leaving Starla to once again make her apologies.

After they had left, Joram turned to Zac.

"That's a shame. I didn't get a chance to see the butter dance."

**47**

---

TEN MONTHS LATER, the Hobart riots had escalated to a dangerous level. News of the existence of artificial intelligence on Earth had leaked out among the Hobart population within days of the failed negotiations with the New Eden President. The source of the leak was never identified, but Starla strongly suspected that it was the Mayor himself, hoping that the combined ire of his entire colony would bring pressure to bear upon New Eden. If that was his purpose, however, it failed. New Eden remained resolute, continuing to declare the absolute safety of their technology and refusing to bow to the unreasonable, phobic demands of the Altarians.

Although the leaking of the news failed to achieve its ultimate purpose – the removal of AI technology – it was spectacularly successful in achieving its preliminary goal – making the citizens of Hobart very angry. As the days and weeks went by, shock turned to anger, and anger to outrage. The outrage birthed mass demonstrations which had now, ten months later, metastasised into riots. Each night over the last week, citizens had taken their anger to the streets, destroying public property and creating havoc.

In their minds, their cause was just. They had been cheated, swindled, lied to. They had been promised a world free from the dangers of artificial intelligence. On the basis of that promise, they had uprooted themselves and their families, and travelled half-way across the galaxy, to find that the promise was not true.

Over ninety-five per cent of Hobart's population had come from reversionist islands on Altaria. They had spent decades arguing and advocating for the removal of AI technology on their home world, but their pleas had fallen on deaf ears. When the promise of an AI-free life on an almost pristine Earth had been presented to them, it had seemed like a dream come true. But now their dream had become a nightmare. They were in exactly the same situation they thought they had left behind, and they were furious.

Just who they were furious with, wasn't entirely clear. The world, probably. Life, the universe and everything. But their anger was so great that it was now exploding in violent expression throughout the entire colony. Starla and her security team of trained soldiers were completely overwhelmed. The base had comprised twenty soldiers when she had arrived ten months ago, and she had brought with her an additional twenty. But even a platoon of forty soldiers was hopelessly inadequate to contain an entire colony of several thousand people who were in uproar. Each morning over the last week, as Starla had gone to bed exhausted, the council workers had awoken to more broken windows, burnt facilities and overturned vehicles.

The City Council had been meeting every morning during the last week. On the morning after the sixth night of rioting, Mayor Merv Portland opened the meeting with a surprising announcement.

"I think I've found a way of ending the riots."

They all looked at him expectantly.

"Jurd Transid has offered to speak to the colony via a public broadcast. He will make a plea for peace and calm."

There was a moment's stunned silence.

"But he's their leader!" exclaimed one councillor.

"He's probably orchestrating these riots himself!" added another.

Starla silently agreed. She strongly suspected that Transid and his team were behind the riots, but she hadn't been able to find any hard evidence. Transid had maintained a squeaky-clean profile over the last ten months, never being late for work and refraining from anything illegal. He had also been conspicuously absent from all of the riots. But she was convinced that he was behind them. Someone had to be working behind the scenes, orchestrating all of this: it was too well-organised to be spontaneous.

She had expressed this opinion to Portland on several occasions, but he had strangely brushed her concerns aside. What was even more concerning was that yesterday, she was sure she had briefly spotted Transid and Portland sitting together in the back of a council ground car, driving into the underground carpark under the science complex. Now, the Mayor's surprise announcement was deepening her suspicions further.

"I don't believe Jurd is behind the riots at all," said Portland. "There is absolutely no evidence that points to his involvement, and all of you have to admit that he has been a model citizen since arriving here."

"What is his reason for offering to calm the colony?" asked Starla. "There may be no evidence implicating him in the riots, but he would surely be strongly sympathetic to their cause."

"Yes," admitted Portland. "He is sympathetic. He remains strongly opposed to artificial intelligence. But then, so do almost all of us! If you're going to condemn him for his views, you may as well lock me up as well, and yourselves while you're at it!"

A couple of the councillors chuckled, and Starla could see that Portland was winning them over.

"So what's his angle?" asked one of them.

"He believes that violence and rioting is counter-productive. The people must be shown that they are only hurting themselves. These riots are having no impact on New Eden. Jurd is going to ask for calm and plead that the colony gets behind us, its leaders, as we continue to push for a wind-back of technology in New Eden."

"It might just work," said someone.

"It certainly can't hurt," said another.

Two minutes later, the motion was passed almost unanimously.

Starla abstained.

**48**

---

J urd Transid's video broadcast was impressive. The man was made for the camera. He exuded an aura of authority and calm, and his soothing voice could have been that of a movie star.

"Fellow citizens of Hobart, I am Jurd Transid, former leader of the reversionist movement on Altaria. I share your deep disappointment at our recent discovery of AI technology on this planet. We came here believing that we had escaped from all this. We believed we had a chance to build a new simpler world, a world that was safe for our children to grow up in, a world that was free from the possibility of ever again experiencing the cruel oppression of a demented artificial intelligence. Instead, we have arrived to find that we are faced with the same terrible risk that we thought we had left behind.

"I share your pain and frustration. You have every right to be angry! You have every right to be outraged! And I join you in your outrage. But we must focus our anger in the right direction. These riots that are destroying our city are only hurting ourselves. The City Council is not to blame. Your leaders are just as angry as you! They have been let down, just as you have been. No, it is not them we must be targeting. We must direct our rage and our anger toward those who have created this problem. We must direct our energies toward those who refuse to listen to common sense – who have not learnt from the mistakes of the past and are leading us once again toward a path of destruction.

"At the moment, we are a divided community. We are fighting with ourselves, while our true enemy is laughing. Today I am asking that we stop punishing our own leaders, who are as much the victims in this situation as we are. Today I am asking that we unify behind our City Council and give them our full support as they continue to fight on our behalf for the redemption of this world from AI technology.

"I want to finish with a request. Tonight, I want every man, woman and child in Hobart to come together in solidarity. Let us meet together in the square outside our City Hall, at 5:00 pm. And instead of throwing rocks and burning vehicles, let us demonstrate our unity and determination in a show of support for our City Council. Together, we can present a stronger, more powerful voice to the rest of the world!"

The broadcast went out on all comm channels at midday and was replayed several times throughout the afternoon. The City Council had not been aware of the exact wording of Transid's message until it actually went to air and were somewhat surprised at the concept of appearing in public before the crowd. But by 5:00 pm, over four thousand people were packed into the square outside City Hall, cheering instead of jeering, waving coloured banners instead of throwing rocks.

"It's incredible! Almost the whole of Hobart must be out there!" said one of the councillors, as they stood inside the foyer, preparing to go out.

"I told you he could do it," said Portland, proudly. He looked around at the rest of the council. "Are we ready?"

They all nodded.

"Let's do this."

The City Council walked through the double doors onto the front steps. Immediately the crowd went crazy, cheering and clapping. The applause and adulation went on for a full five minutes before the mayor raised his hands to speak. He gave a brief speech, not nearly as eloquent as Transid's, but along the same lines. The crowd lapped it up and cheered some more. Then Portland spotted Transid to the side of the crowd, joining in the cheering. On an impulse, Portland called out,

"Ladies and gentlemen, I can see Jurd Transid with us in the crowd this afternoon. Jurd, come on up here and let the people of Hobart show their appreciation for your wise words."

As Transid walked up the steps and stood beside the mayor, the crowd went wild again, except this time they cheered even longer and louder. The mayor grabbed Transid's hand and they held up their arms together as the crowd continued to cheer and applaud.

Starla watched from the sidelines and noticed Carmen Orlando in the middle of the crowd. She wasn't cheering or clapping. She was just staring at Transid and Portland, a cold glint in her eyes and a satisfied sneer on her face.

Starla thought to herself, *I've got a very bad feeling about this.*

**49**

———

Mayor Portland called an extraordinary meeting of the City Council the next morning. To say that he was pleased with the previous afternoon's rally was an understatement. He was delighted. The crowd had stayed and cheered for over an hour, with an impromptu speech from Transid eliciting further cheers. At the end of his speech, Transid asked that as a show of goodwill and solidarity, the crowd do a clean-up walk through the town, helping to right the wrongs of the previous riots. As a result, the town was now spotless and peace had returned to their picturesque colony.

Without wasting any time, Portland got straight to the point.

"I would like to move a motion that we invite Jurd Transid onto the City Council."

The council took a few moments to reflect on Portland's suggestion.

"Isn't he still under a good behaviour contract?" asked someone.

"And doesn't that mean that he is still on parole?" added another.

"What does our constitution say?" asked a third. "Can someone with a criminal history be elected to Council?"

"As to that last question," answered the mayor, "Jurd has never actually been convicted of a crime. He was arrested on Altaria, but he was brought here before the charges could be heard. And in terms of him still being on a good behaviour contract, there is absolutely nothing in that contract that prohibits him from taking public office. As far as I can see, his appointment to Council would be perfectly legal and within the bounds of our constitution."

"I have to admit, he did a remarkable job yesterday," admitted someone.

"Yes, he did," agreed Portland. "In fact, I'll go so far as to say he is the only person in the colony who could have achieved that outcome so quickly. The people love him and trust him. He was their hero on Altaria and he is still their hero here. Which is exactly why I want him on the council."

"I guess it makes sense," agreed someone.

"Of course it does!" agreed Portland. "It makes perfect sense! Appointing Jurd to the council will ensure the complete trust and support of our entire population. And that, in turn, will enable us to present a stronger, unified front in our bid to remove AI technology from this planet."

"I'd like to speak against the motion," said Starla.

There was an awkward silence, then Portland nodded.

"Go ahead."

"What if Transid orchestrated this whole thing to achieve this very end? What if the riots, followed by his speech and then the remarkable turnaround in crowd behaviour were all deliberately planned and manipulated by Transid and his organisation to get him elected to Council?

"Do you have any proof of those claims?"

"Nothing solid, just a very strong gut-hunch."

"Well, the Council doesn't operate on 'gut-hunches',

Colonel. We operate on solid evidence. And all the evidence points to the simple fact that this man has united our community and single-handedly ended a situation that was spiralling out of control."

"That may be, Mayor, but consider another fact. Just ten months ago he was deported from Altaria, charged with multiple counts of murder, conspiracy to murder and inciting civil unrest. Those are also facts, and this is the man you are considering appointing to the leadership team of this colony. I seriously recommend that you take at least another year to continue to evaluate his behaviour. A leopard doesn't change its spots, but it can disguise itself."

"Very eloquent, Colonel. And if we weren't faced with an urgent crisis involving delicate political negotiations, perhaps we would take your advice and wait a few more months. But we need him on our team right now. His negotiation skills could make all the difference in our current crisis."

There was no further discussion. A few moments later, the motion was passed by eleven votes to one. Jurd Transid, the self-proclaimed leader of the radical and violent reversionist movement, was elected to Hobart City Council.

**50**

---

The riots in Hobart hadn't been completely ineffective in garnering support for their cause elsewhere. News of the riots had filtered through to Wellington and had reinforced the concerns of a small but growing number of citizens regarding New Eden's Sentiums. Could they turn malevolent, as the AI on Mars once had? Were they completely safe? Was it possible to absolutely guarantee that a malignant entity wouldn't arise again? Wouldn't it be safer to downgrade all technology and remove artificial sentient control of infrastructure completely?

These were questions that began to be discussed around dinner tables all across Wellington. New Edeners began to notice scowls sometimes directed their way when they were out in public. Not a lot, but enough to begin to make them feel uneasy. Most Wellington citizens were hospitable and welcoming to their New Eden neighbours. But occasionally, a business would refuse to serve a New Edener or a passer-by would mutter a derogatory comment about their Sentiums. It came to a head when three Wellington teenagers accosted two similar-aged girls from New Eden and smashed their data pads, telling them to "keep your filthy AIs out of our town."

Amanda called a meeting of the Wellington City Council to discuss the issue.

"The problem seems to be growing worse by the day. I hardly noticed it at first, but now I am catching dirty looks and snide comments being directed at New Edeners fairly regularly. Yesterday's attack on those two girls has raised it to a whole new level. We need to act before this gets out of control."

"But how is this phobia continuing to gain momentum?" asked Zac. "The riots in Hobart came to a stop two weeks ago. Something else is feeding this, fanning it into flame."

"I may have an answer to that," suggested Colonel Chandra. "Our security monitoring station has been noting regular coded, short-burst compressed-wave transmissions every night at precisely 2200 hours. We haven't been able to break the code yet, but we've triangulated their source."

"Let me guess," said Zac. "Hobart."

"Yes."

"So you think someone in Hobart is feeding inflammatory information into our community?" asked Amanda.

"Yes, I do," said Chandra. "And equally concerning, it also means that there are people here in league with them – to the point where they have a shared code system."

"It would be nice to know what they're saying," Amanda mused.

"We're working hard to break down their code, Mayor."

"I'm sure you are, Lea. Let us know as soon as you have anything. In the meantime, what are we going to do about this phobia that is spreading?"

"Fight fire with fire," suggested Zac.

"Meaning?"

"The best way to fight misinformation is with accurate information. We've been pretty passive about this up until now. I think we need to take the fight to them – whoever 'them' turns out to be. Let's get a couple of science gurus from Wellington and New Eden and broadcast a series of interviews with them, explaining the fail-safe moral coding that is built into the Sentiums. And let's not do just one broadcast. Keep them going. Make it into a science series covering all aspects of technology that relates to our dual colony. If someone's feeding biased propaganda into the community every night, we need to reinforce the truth regularly. Give our people the facts. Give them something positive to talk about over the dinner table."

"That's a brilliant idea, Zac," said Amanda. "Let's get onto that straight away."

"There's another possibility regarding the coding that's worth mentioning," said Colonel Chandra.

"What's that, Lea?"

"The coded messages might not just be propaganda. They could be something more sinister."

"You mean some kind of plot?" asked Amanda.

"Yes."

"To do what?"

"That's just our problem. Until we crack that code, we have no idea."

"We need to bring New Eden in on this," said Zac. "At the very least we need to warn them that there could be some kind of plot in the wind. But beyond that, maybe their Sentiums could be of assistance in cracking the code."

"Yes. Let's do that," said Amanda. "I'll contact Joram ASAP."

"I'll tell you who else we should contact," said Zac.

"Who?" asked Amanda.

"Starla."

"Colonel Bree, in Hobart?" asked Lea.

"Yes."

"Can she be trusted?"

"Definitely. She's not a reversionist sympathiser, and she's a damn fine soldier. She might be able to help us track what's happening from her end."

"How can we contact her securely, without our conversation being overheard by unwanted ears?" asked Amanda.

"There's only one sure way," said Zac.

"What?"

"A personal visit from the Wellington City Council Multi-Cultural Liaison Officer."

Colonel Chandra looked confused, glancing around the conference table, so Zac leaned across to her and helped her out.

"That's me," he whispered.

## 51

Zac's flying visit was arranged under the pretence of meeting with Mayor Portland to clarify the Hobart colony's demands for New Eden. The meeting unfolded as Zac expected, with Portland belligerently insisting on the immediate deactivation of the Sentiums and refusing to compromise on even the smallest point. Zac was in the process of winding up their brief discussion when the door opened and in walked Jurd Transid.

"Ah, Dr. Perryman. How nice to see you again," he said as he took up a third comfortable chair in the mayor's private chambers.

"I see you've got out of prison again, Transid. What was the issue this time? Didn't like the food?"

"Touché, Zac. Very funny. Always the wit, aren't you?"

"What are you doing here, Transid? This is a private meeting."

"Jurd is our new Deputy Mayor," explained Portland. "He was voted in this morning. I thought it would be good for him to sit in with us."

"I thought our meeting was basically concluded," said Zac. "We've said all that needed to be said."

"I wanted to contribute one small point to your pontifications," interjected Jurd.

"OK. What do you want to say?"

"I wanted to ask you to come over to our side."

"Side with you?"

"Yes."

"Why on Earth would I do that?"

"Because we will win this, Zac. Of that I am sure. We will rid this planet of AI technology, one way or another."

"That sounds ominous."

"I prefer the term, 'inevitable'."

"I'm leaving now," said Zac, standing. He nodded to Portland. "Thank you for the meeting. I'll convey your message to New Eden."

After he left, Portland turned to Transid.

"You didn't really expect him to change sides, did you?"

"No. Of course not. I just like pushing his buttons. But I do wish we had someone like him on our team."

...

Zac had arranged to meet Starla for a cup of juvo – an Altarian import that Zac sorely missed in Wellington. At Zac's suggestion they got take-away cups and walked down to the harbour. Sitting on the harbour wall and sipping his favourite drink, he explained the situation back in Wellington.

Starla was deeply concerned at the escalating tensions between Hobart and New England and seemed relieved to be able to talk candidly about it.

"I'm convinced Transid is planning something more than mere negotiations," she said.

"How did he get to be Deputy Mayor?"

"The previous deputy died yesterday of a mystery illness. She was found dead in her bed."

"Transid?" asked Zac.

"Carmen Orlando, I'd say. But, of course, there's no evidence. She's a pro."

"Whatever it is they're planning, we have to stop it before more lives are lost," said Zac.

"I agree. I'll try and track the source of the transmissions from this end. If I find out anything, how do I contact you?"

Zac took a small black disk from his pocket and handed it to Starla.

"This is an encrypted tight-beam comm that is relayed via the Perditan battle cruiser in orbit over Wellington. Press to speak. I've got an identical one. They're paired to each other."

"How romantic," she said, smiling.

Zac stood up.

"Take care, Starla."

"You too, Zac."

**52**

―――

Starla decided the time had come for some clandestine work. For the next week after her meeting with Zac, she tailed Transid as much as she dared. One thing became immediately obvious: Transid and Portland spent an enormous amount of time together. Whatever they were up to, it involved long meetings almost every day. Some other issues also came to light. She had seen them meet with Carmen Orlando, twice. On both occasions the meetings appeared to be clandestine, taking place in the park beside the harbour. The other interesting thing she discovered was that the two men visited the science complex together on three occasions during the week. The Academy of Science was only fifty metres from the Council Chambers, but on each occasion, instead of walking there, they drove out of the council basement carpark and into the basement carpark of the science building. It looked to her like they were trying to avoid being seen entering the building.

On their third visit to the science building, Starla decided to act. She waited for about five minutes after she had seen them drive in, then she crossed the road and paused outside the glass entry doors. The entry foyer was empty. She walked boldly through the revolving doors and approached the reception desk.

"Good afternoon. My name is …"

"Colonel Bree!" finished the receptionist. "Welcome to our facility."

Starla wasn't surprised. She was a well-known public figure in Hobart, especially after the riots.

"How can I help you, Colonel?"

"I was meant to meet up with the Mayor and Mr. Transid here somewhere, but I'm running late. Can you tell point me in the right direction?"

"Research and Development, first floor. Just use those lifts over there," she said. smiling.

"Thanks."

Starla looked toward the bank of lifts and noticed a doorway with a sign saying, "Stairs".

"I think I'll take the stairs," she said to the receptionist with a smile. "I prefer the exercise."

She walked across the foyer and entered the stairwell, climbing two sets of stairs until she came to a doorway with the number one affixed to it. She cracked the door slightly and peeked out. The stairwell opened onto a corridor with no one currently in sight. She opened the door a little wider and glanced furtively in both directions. There were glass-walled science labs all along the corridor, but she could only see into the one directly opposite. There was no sign of Portland or Transid.

Starla closed the door again and sat down on the stairs to wait. She couldn't risk being seen by either of the two men, as she didn't want them to know that she was monitoring them. She settled down to wait.

She stayed in the stairwell for an agonisingly slow hour, occasionally walking up and down some stairs to ease the boredom. No one entered the stairwell in that time, and Starla was thankful that the science boffins appeared to be a lazy bunch, preferring to use the lifts rather than expend unnecessary energy on stairs.

Finally, she gauged that Portland and Transid must surely have left by now. She opened the door and walked slowly along the corridor, looking into the labs as she went. She quickly realised that she would have absolutely no idea what any of the scientists were working on. In almost every room, white-coated scientists were bent over benches, working on their projects, surrounded by all kinds of anonymous equipment. The entire floor was apparently taken up with R & D, and the labyrinth of labs and corridors soon overwhelmed Starla. She couldn't just walk into every lab and ask if this was the lab that was working on the mayor's secret project. She admitted defeat and was walking back toward the lifts, when a distinguished looking man stepped out of an office and asked,

"Can I help you, Colonel? Are you looking for anything in particular?"

Starla noticed his name tag. Dr Albert Reinhardt.

"Nothing in particular, Dr Reinhardt. I had some free time and have always wanted to see the Academy. I just popped in to have a wander around."

Reinhardt gave Starla a suspicious glare, then quickly covered it up with a false smile.

"No problem. Unfortunately, I'm very busy at the moment, otherwise I would give you a guided tour myself. Perhaps some other time?"

"Yes," agreed Starla. "That would be nice. I'll leave you to your work." She walked to the corner to the junction with the adjoining corridor. As she turned into the next corridor, she glanced into the reflection in the lab window in front of her and saw Reinhardt still standing in the corridor, looking at her suspiciously.

She turned the corner, out of sight, and opened a comm channel to her next in charge, Lieutenant Ryeland.

"Lieutenant, do you copy?"

"Yes ma'am," he answered instantly.

"I want an immediate comm trace placed on Dr. Albert Reinhardt, at the Academy of Science. Record all messages in and out."

"Right away, Colonel."

Starla left the building a few minutes later, thinking that she might not have wasted her time after all. Arriving back at her security headquarters shortly afterward, she summoned Ryeland.

"Any action on that comm trace yet, Lieutenant?"

"One call, Colonel, almost immediately after you called me."

"Let's hear it."

She sat back in her chair as the recording played.

"Jurd, it's Albert."

"What are you doing calling me directly?" asked Transid, annoyed.

"Sorry, but I think you'll want to hear what I've got to say."

"What?"

"Colonel Bree was just here, snooping around."

Transid swore.

"There's no cause for alarm, though," assured Reinhardt. "There's nothing here for her to see anymore. As you know, final assembly was being done elsewhere."

"I'm still concerned. She shouldn't be this close. I'm moving the shipment forward."

"When do you want to move them?"

"Immediately. Are they ready?"

"Yes. As I told you this afternoon, all four are now fully assembled and ready to go."

"Good. I'll get them picked up immediately."

"Is our naïve little earth-burrower still in play?" asked Reinhardt.

"Yes. Everything's set at the receiving end. He has no idea," replied Transid, smugly.

"And what about Portland?"

"Our puppet on a string is dancing to our tune very nicely. It's all too easy, really. Like taking candy from a baby."

There was a pause in the conversation, and then Transid continued.

"We need to tie up all the loose ends. And the loosest end is Dr. Sandborn. That man is a quivering bowl of jelly. He'll sing like a canary as soon as someone even looks at him."

"What do you want me to do?" asked Reinhardt.

"Nothing at all. Leave this to the professionals. I'll pay him a little visit myself. Where is he?"

"At home sick. He's got a bad case of hay fever – all this springtime pollen in the air."

"Excellent! Where does he live?"

Reinhardt gave him the address and then asked,

"When are you going to visit him?"

"No time like the present."

The call ended abruptly and Starla sprang into action.

"Lieutenant, I want you to take twenty soldiers and lock down the airport. Search every shuttle and flitter that comes in or out. Especially any that are heading to Wellington."

"Yes, ma'am."

"Secondly, get Sergeant Grimes to take charge of the remaining soldiers and ground every other flitter in the colony. Most of them are in the Council transport pool, but there are always at least a few that are in use. Track them all down and search them. I don't want anything leaving Hobart until we find whatever it is they're trying to move."

"Yes, ma'am. Where will you be?"

"I'm going to intercept Transid."

"What about support, Colonel?"

"I can handle Transid on my own. We need every available soldier locking down the town."

Fifteen minutes later she wished she had made a different decision.

**53**

---

Starla parked her ground vehicle two hundred metres from the apartment block, in a cul-de-sac where it wouldn't be noticed. She exited the vehicle and looked back along the road to the apartment block. She was fairly certain she had arrived before Transid. She ran back along the road and into the building. Dr. Sandborn's apartment was on the second floor. Ignoring the lift, she ran up the stairs and quickly found the right door number. She put her ear to the door and listened. She could hear classical music – probably a live stream from the colony's classical music station.

She touched the door sensor and heard a pleasant chime somewhere inside. After a moment she activated the chime again. The music continued in the background, but no one came to the door. Something was wrong. She unholstered her laser pistol, then took a security decoder out of her pocket and held it against the door's sensor. The door hummed briefly and then opened.

Starla was in full battle mode now. She was standing to the side of the doorway with her back to the wall and her pistol in a two-handed grip. She quickly poked her head around the corner and glanced into the apartment. There was a small lounge room with a hallway leading off to the right and a kitchen to the left. There was no one in sight. She moved quickly into the lounge room, putting her back to the right-hand wall and traversing her weapon across the lounge room and kitchen. Nothing. Kitchen and lounge room were empty.

She moved along the wall until she reached the corner of the hallway, leading off to her right. She could see the body now. Sandborn was lying on the lounge room floor in front of the large sofa, face down in a pool of blood and gore. A neat hole had been drilled through the back of his head. It looked like he had been shot from behind as he sat on the sofa and had then slumped forward onto the floor.

With her back to the wall, she risked a peak around the corner. The hallway was empty. There was an open door halfway down on the right and a closed door to the left. She turned the corner and began walking slowly down the hall with her weapon raised in front in a two-handed grip.

The sizzling laser bolt hit her from behind, directly between her shoulder blades. She collapsed to the ground in agony, finding it difficult to breathe. She rolled over and attempted to bring her weapon to bear on her assailant, but her movements were too sluggish and Transid was upon her before she could fire. He kicked the pistol out of her hand and stood over her with a satisfied grin, aiming the pistol at her head. Looking back down the hallway, she glimpsed the kitchen pantry door now standing ajar.

"Colonel Bree, how lovely that you dropped by," he said facetiously. "And thank you for being so polite. Sounding the door chime like you did gave me ample time to tuck myself away out of sight."

Starla was still trying to breathe, and only managed a groan in response.

"I see you are wearing a battle vest under your shirt. Very

sensible. You'd be dead now, without it. Of course, you've probably got a couple of broken ribs. I imagine they hurt like hell," he said, smiling.

"You won't get away with this," she managed to gasp.

"By 'this' I assume you are referring to more than the dispatching of a simple-minded egg-head. You must have tapped into Reinhardt's comm call to me. A foolish mistake on his part. But then he's not a professional like us, is he?"

"Where are the bombs?" she gasped.

"Very good, Colonel. Although it wasn't too hard to guess was it? Words were never going to resolve this situation. I've always been a big believer in the old adage, 'actions speak louder than words.' And I can assure you, this particular action is going to be very, very loud indeed."

"How are you getting the bombs into New Eden?"

"No need to worry your pretty little head about that, Colonel. Let's just say that I have some inside help. But I think it's time I said farewell. This conversation is boring me, and I have things to do."

He straightened his arm, sighting his pistol on the middle of her forehead.

"Goodnight, Colonel. Sweet dreams."

The flash of the laser bolt lit up the dim hallway, and a sickening mixture of blood and brain matter splattered the floor and walls. Transid's arm dropped to his side and he stood there for a moment, teetering on the edge of balance before toppling to the floor like a felled tree. He lay beside Starla with his head turned toward her, his sightless eyes staring at her and his open mouth only inches from her ear, as if whispering a final secret.

Starla sat up painfully and saw Lieutenant Ryeland still standing with his weapon pointing down the hall.

"Are you OK, Colonel? Any injuries?"

"Mainly my pride. What are you doing here? I told you to supervise the troops at the airport."

"Sorry, ma'am. I thought you might need some backup," he said as he swivelled around and switched off the music.

"Remind me to reprimand you for disobedience after this is all over."

"Yes, ma'am."

He reached out his hand and she grasped it, standing to her feet and groaning.

"Transid might be right. A couple of my ribs are giving me curry. I've gotta get this vest off, it's killing me. I'll be right back."

She stepped through the open doorway into the bedroom. She unbuttoned her shirt and removed it, laying it on the bed. The vest was a little more difficult to remove. It was lined with a maranium and carbon nanite-tube composite which, although light, made it difficult to get on and off. She unlaced it at the front and gingerly eased it back over her shoulders, sighing with relief as she dropped it onto the bed. She could see the large indentation in the back where the laser bolt had impacted.

She was just reaching for her shirt again when she heard the deadly sizzle of a laser bolt in the lounge room followed by the sound of a body hitting the floor. She moved silently to the doorway, dressed only in her bra, her shirt and vest now forgotten on the bed. She listened but heard nothing. She reached for her pistol but then cursed herself in her head as she spotted it still lying on the floor further down the hallway.

She was having a very bad day.

**54**

—————

Carmen Orlando stood silently in the lounge room, the smell of ozone still lingering after her single shot. The lieutenant lay dead near the entrance to the hallway. But where was Jurd? He had sent an emergency text message, giving her the address and asking for backup. What was he doing here? The address wasn't familiar to her.

She stood absolutely still for three whole minutes. Not moving. Barely breathing. Just listening. She could hear her own heartbeat. She slowly moved her head around, altering the angle of her ears and noting the subtle frequency shifts in the apartment's ambient soundscape. She heard nothing else. Either she was alone here or the other person was very good.

She peeked around the corner of the hallway and saw Transid's body. She had expected it. If Jurd was alive she would have heard him. He wasn't disciplined enough to remain completely silent for this long. She shook her head in disgust. The fool had the gift of the gab, but he was incompetent as an operative. Whatever he was doing here, he should have brought her with him.

She saw his pistol lying on the floor further down the hall

and began walking toward it when she froze. That wasn't his pistol. She could now see Transid's pistol poking out from underneath his body, where he had fallen on it. The pistol down the hall belonged to someone else! Someone who was very, very good. Because whoever it was, was obviously still in the apartment and was absolutely silent. Either that or the person was dead. *Assume the worst,* she thought. *Someone is still here, but unarmed. I have the advantage.*

She stood completely still for another minute. Nothing. The apartment was completely silent. It was time to move; she couldn't stand here forever. Check the bedroom first. She put her back against the wall to the side of the open doorway and took a tiny mirror from her top pocket. She eased it past the doorframe and moved it around. The bedroom appeared empty, but there was a discarded soldier's shirt and vest on the bed. Someone was in there, somewhere. The only place she couldn't see with her mirror was directly on the other side of the wall, behind the open door which pivoted that way. It would be a cliché if there was someone hiding behind the door, but clichés can still kill you. She stepped back and drilled a vicious laser blast through the wall, not worrying about the noise she made. If someone was here, they would have already heard her when she killed the soldier. She stopped and listened. Nothing. There hadn't been anyone behind the door.

There was an open door on the other side of the well-made bed that must lead to an ensuite – a small private bathroom. She moved into the bedroom with her pistol extended in front of her.

Starla dropped from above the doorway, planting her feet squarely between Carmen's shoulder blades with the full force of her weight behind her. She had been balanced on the tiny ledge of the open doorway's lintel, squatting with her arms pressed against the ceiling to stop herself falling. As a consequence her arms were on fire; in excruciating pain after nearly five minutes of continuous strain.

Carmen was knocked to the ground and her pistol went flying under the bed. Starla's momentum carried her over Carmen's head. She hit the ground slightly off balance and rolled to her right groaning as she did so. She sprang to her feet and turned to face Carmen, and nearly lost her life in that second. Carmen had regained her feet more quickly and the knife that she now viciously swiped across Starla's exposed throat barely missed, as Starla bent backward just in time. Starla backed away, raising her hands in the defensive position, and the two women squared off. Carmen had a savage glint in her eyes and a wicked smile on her face. She lunged in with a series of lightning quick attacks, which Starla only just managed to fend off.

"You're injured, aren't you?" Carmen said as they circled each other, both looking for an opening to attack. "You're slow. Sluggish. Reaction time way down. In pain. What is it? Ribs? Yes, ribs! I can see it in the way you're holding yourself. Around the back, mid-way down."

She feinted with her knife hand and watched Starla's reaction.

"Yes! Very slow! And it hurts to breathe too, doesn't it?"

She feinted again, this time lunging with an immediate second attack that Starla only just managed to fend off, the knife opening a cut on her elbow that immediately began dripping blood onto the carpet.

"You know you're about to die, right? That was very impressive, by the way – wedging yourself above the door like that," Carmen said, glancing back at the chest of drawers beside the open doorway that Starla had obviously used to climbed up to the top of the doorframe. "But it must have taken a lot out of you. You're tired now, aren't you? You weren't expecting me to take so long."

She feinted and lunged, then feinted and lunged a second time, this time managing to cut Starla across the bottom of her ribs, on the left side. Blood immediately started oozing from the wound, and Starla was struggling to breathe now, with her ribs aching and her lungs on fire.

"Soon. Very soon, now. It's coming. You can feel it, can't you? Last drinks, everyone. It's closing time. Lights out."

Carmen came at her then, with another series of lightning strikes that were so fast they blurred into each other. All Starla could do was duck and weave and block, backing around the room as she did so, finally only driving Carmen back with a desperate front kick. Both her forearms were bleeding now, with deep gashes. Starla had tried to manoeuvre herself toward the doorway so she could try to retrieve her laser from the hallway, but Carmen was too smart and too fast to allow that, constantly shepherding her away from the open door. Carmen's pistol was under the bed but was no use to Starla either; Carmen would pounce on her before she could ever reach it.

Starla was standing now with her back to the curtained window, panting heavily and blood flowing from the wounds on her arms and chest. Carmen sensed that Starla was almost completely spent, and she made her first mistake. She switched her knife grip from the reverse to the forward grip, deciding that she wanted to experience the thrill of plunging the blade directly into her opponent, rather than simply slashing her open. Carmen attacked with lightning speed again, with a series of feints designed to weaken Starla and open her to the final thrust. But Starla knew what was coming. She responded to the feints predictably and opened her left side to exposure, feigning a slow recovery from her last defensive bloc. Carmen attacked the opening, going in for the kill, but Starla was ready.

She twisted to the left, her right hand coming across and grabbing Carmen's right forearm as the knife plunged passed her side, narrowly missing her. Starla kept the movement going, continuing to twist to the left, pulling Carmen's right arm through even further, so that it smashed through the glass window. Her back was now momentarily toward Carmen, but she continued to rotate to the left, swinging her left elbow up and around behind her as she did so and smashing it into Carmen's left temple. The massive blow to her head caused Carmen's knife hand to open involuntarily as it hung out the smashed window, and the knife dropped from her grasp, clattering to the driveway two storeys below.

But Starla wasn't finished. She released Carmen's right arm and turned her pivot into a full-blown spin. She was poetry in motion now, her training taking over, muscles acting instinctively and a kind of pure, joyous energy coursing through her as she became immersed in the perfection of her lethal ballet. She was pivoting on the ball of her left foot now, and as she completed her 360-degree rotation, she transferred all her remaining momentum to her right arm which swung in a wide arc. Her fist connected with Carmen's left temple in a solid roundhouse punch.

The whole single, fluid movement, involving an arm grab, twist, elbow strike, pivot and punch, had taken less than a second. Starla had finished the movement in a perfectly set martial arts strike position, and Carmen had finished lying on her back, dazed and confused.

"Holy crap, you're good!" she mumbled.

"Yes. We've already had this conversation, if you remember."

But Carmen wasn't ready to give in. She got to her feet, unsteadily, and assumed the attack position.

"Really?" asked Starla. "Look at your wrist. You're dying."

Carmen looked at her wrist in confusion. It had been slashed to the bone on the jagged windowpane and blood was spurting out of her artery. She shook her head, as if to deny what she was seeing, and when she looked at Starla again, it was with a cruel, deadly glint in her eyes. She attacked again with ferocity, using her bare fists, but without a weapon she was no match. Starla executed two swift blocks and a simple front kick to Carmen's solar plexus; there was no need for anything fancy, now. Carmen was driven back a few steps and was growing visibly weaker from blood loss.

"Carmen Orlando, you are under arrest for the murder of Lieutenant Ryeland and ... well ... for a whole lot of other crap, too. You have the right to remain silent. You have the right to an attorney ..."

Carmen gave a primal scream and charged at Starla who stepped to the side at the last second and watched as Carmen crashed through the broken window and fell to the concrete two storeys below.

"... or you have the right to attempt your first solo flight if you choose to do so," she finished.

She looked through the window at Carmen's lifeless body, splattered on the ground below.

"Good effort. Terrible landing."

**55**

———

Starla found some bandages in a first aid kit in Dr. Sandborn's kitchen and wrapped both her forearms and her ribs to reduce the bleeding. Her first aid wasn't completely effective but it would do for now. She retrieved her shirt and battle vest from the bed, and gingerly put the now-damaged shirt on. Now that the adrenalin of battle was wearing off, she was in a lot of pain again. That would have to wait, too.

She retrieved her weapon and called Sergeant Grimes.

"Sergeant, where are you?"

"At the transport pool, behind the Council building, Colonel."

"What's your progress?"

"We've checked all the flitters in the colony, ma'am. Nothing suspicious in any of them."

"Alright, leave some squaddies to keep all the flitters impounded. I need two of your team to get to the address I'm sending you now. Get there ASAP. There's a crime scene that needs to be secured. Send another two to meet me outside the Science Academy. I've got to arrest someone. While I'm doing that, I want you to take two more and arrest the Mayor. The charge is planning an act of terrorism."

The sergeant was silent for a moment.

"Begging your pardon, ma'am, but wouldn't you or Lieutenant Ryeland be better suited to make that arrest?"

"Yes, we would, but I can't be in two places at once and the Lieutenant can't make it either. Just carry out my orders, Sergeant."

"Yes, Colonel. I'll get the job done. Where will I take him, ma'am?"

"Throw him in a holding cell back at headquarters. And Sergeant?"

"Yes, ma'am?"

"No need to be too gentle with him. I don't mind if he has a few bruises."

"Message understood."

## 56

———

Mayor Portland and Dr. Reinhardt were stewing in separate holding cells. Both were blustering but Starla knew they would break down pretty quickly. She certainly needed them to break down quickly, because the bombs were on their way somewhere and she needed to neutralise the threat ASAP. Upon returning to base, she uploaded the file from her ARD – automated recording device – which had started recording as soon as she pulled her pistol from its holster. That recording would prove helpful in the enquiry that was sure to take place eventually. She then called Zac and her own opposite number in Wellington, Colonel Lea Chandra, to apprise them of the situation. The airport at Wellington was placed in lock down and all flitters were grounded. As far as Starla could see, the bombs now had no means of access to Wellington. She concluded that they must still be somewhere in Hobart, and she was determined to find them.

After some quickly administered stitches to both arms from the medic on base, she strode into Reinhardt's cell with a fresh shirt on and a determined glint in her eyes.

"Colonel, there must be some kind of mistake ..." began Reinhardt.

"Shove it, Reinhardt," interrupted Starla. "I haven't got time for games. Here's what we've got on you; a recording of your call to Transid, discussing the plot to kill Dr. Sandborn. On that same recording, we have you discussing your role in manufacturing and assembling bombs intended for use in terrorism. We also have a recorded confession from Jurd Transid at the scene of Dr. Sandborn's murder, admitting to the manufacturing of your bombs. You have been charged with conspiracy to murder, accessory to murder, conspiracy to commit an act of terrorism, illegal manufacturing of a weapon of mass destruction and misuse of public facilities for the purposes of crime. There's fifteen to twenty years prison for each one of those, and our evidence against you is rock solid. I don't need any more to secure a conviction and send you away for the rest of your life.

"But here's what I'm going to do. I'm going to offer you a reduced sentence, so that you might walk out of jail in a mere twenty years, if you cooperate. If you don't, you'll die in jail. I promise you that, you miserable bastard."

Reinhardt's bluster completely disintegrated. His bottom lip started trembling and he spoke in a meek voice.

"I ... I ... thought I was doing the right thing ... protecting our world ..."

"I don't care what you thought. I just what answers."

"What do want to know?"

"Tell me about the bombs. We know there are four of them."

"Yes, but they're only EMP bombs – Electro Magnetic Pulse. All they're designed to do is wipe out computer circuitry. No one was going to get hurt."

"That's the story you're sticking to, is it?"

"Of course!"

"Really? Then explain to me what role Dr. Sandborn played in the construction of the bombs."

"He ... um ... he just assisted with some of the technical details."

"What details?"

"Just some of the complex issues regarding electromagnetic pulses."

"Don't lie to me, Reinhardt! During the last two hours we've discovered quite a lot about Dr. Sandborn. He was a nuclear physicist who, for the last fifteen years, has been refining nuclear fission processes to obtain maximum explosive force with minimal radioactive residue. He has never worked in the field of electromagnetic pulses in his life."

Reinhardt looked deflated.

"Plus," continued Starla, "I have Transid's own recorded admission that the effect of the blasts was going to be catastrophic."

Starla walked around the table to where Reinhardt was sitting with his hands chained between his legs. She leant down and whispered menacingly.

"I'm going to make you a rock-solid promise, right now. You lie to me one more time – just the tiniest little lie – and I will walk out that door and our deal is off, and you will spend the rest of your life in prison."

She walked back around the table and stood looking down at him.

"Now. Let's try that one more time. Tell me about the bombs!"

Reinhardt seemed to collapse in upon himself. He slumped in defeat and began talking.

"They are high-yield nuclear fission bombs with low fallout ratios. Each one was to be planted somewhere in each of the four districts."

"Where are they now?"

"I don't know."

Starla began moving toward the door.

"It's the truth!" Reinhardt yelled, desperation clearly in his voice now. "They were in a science storage facility, in the industrial area on the southern edge of town, but less than fifteen minutes after I called Transid, some of his men arrived and took them away."

"Where were they taking them? How were they going to transport them to Wellington?"

"I don't know."

Starla turned and opened the door.

"It's true! It's true! Please! You've got to believe me!" he was sobbing now. "Transid wouldn't tell me how he was planning to get them there. He said it would be better if I didn't know. My job was simply to oversee their construction. He was going to take it from there."

Starla sensed he was telling the truth.

"How big are the bombs? What do they look like?"

"They are shaped like an old-fashioned gridiron football, except twice as big and with a slightly flattened bottom. They're completely black and have a recessed keypad in the top."

"How much do they weigh?"

"forty kilograms"

"What sort of damage would they do?"

Reinhardt hung his head for a moment then looked up and spoke in a pleading tone.

"You have to understand! If we don't eliminate the threat that the Sentiums pose, our entire galaxy could one day be plunged into chaos again! The sacrifice of a few people is for the greater good of all!"

"How much damage!" yelled Starla.

Reinhardt hung his head in shame.

"Each bomb will completely atomise everything within a one-kilometre radius and its kill-reach is twice that."

The corporal in the room with Starla swore, then looked at Starla apologetically.

"Sorry, ma'am."

"And the Mayor is OK with this?" asked Starla, ignoring the soldier.

"No. We told him it was an EMP bomb and that no-one would get hurt."

"And he believed you?"

Reinhardt laughed.

"Of course he did. He's a fool!"

"Yes. That's the first reasonable thing I've heard you say."

She turned to the corporal.

"Take him back to his cell."

She walked out of the interrogation room, muttering,

"Now all I've got to do is find those damn bombs."

## 57

The two fishing trawlers met up in the middle of the Tasman Sea, almost exactly half-way between Hobart and Wellington. Each was over 1,000 kilometres from their respective hometowns. The trawlers were nothing like fishing boats of the past, that puttered along at twenty knots. These were super-fast hydro-flyers, that skimmed a metre above the surface of the sea. They were capable of speeds of up to 180 knots in a very calm sea. It meant they had extraordinary reach; able to access distant fishing grounds and return home in a single day. But on this occasion, it wasn't fish that they were focused on.

Today was a particularly calm day, and the Hobart vessel had reached the designated coordinates in less than six hours but had sat waiting for the Wellington vessel for almost forty minutes. The Captain wasn't happy with the delay, but he'd been paid handsomely for his trouble, so he could hardly complain. He didn't want to know what he was carrying and he didn't ask any questions. Four small, wooden crates marked "Tasmanian Apples", sat on the floor of his cramped bridge, just behind his captain's chair. He wasn't a particularly intelligent man, but he was smart enough to know that there was something more than just apples in those crates. You don't get paid this kind of money to transport a few cases of fruit. And certainly not involving a clandestine, mid-ocean transfer. Whatever was in those crates, he'd be very glad to get rid of them.

The Wellington trawler eventually appeared on the radar and soon afterward they were lashed together, with huge padded fenders squeezed between their gunwales.

The transfer was made swiftly. The four crates were manhandled over the side and passed into the waiting hands of the Wellington crew. As he watched the Wellington crew carry the crates out of sight, the captain wondered if they knew any more than he did. He shook his head and turned away, keen to have the whole episode over and forgotten.

The two vessels soon parted and the Wellington vessel, 'Arthur's Dream', accelerated up to its top speed, its hover jets gouging deep furrows in the sea beneath it. Arthur lit a pipe and sat back contentedly in his chair. They'd be back in the harbour in a little under six hours. It would be nearly dawn by then. He hoped that the pale-skinned New Edener would be at the dock as promised. The earth-burrower sure was a surly bugger and hadn't been pleasant to deal with, but his money was good.

Arthur took another puff of his pipe. He glanced at the radar and then checked his course, adjusting the wheel slightly. He yawned and rubbed the back of his neck. As far as he was concerned, the sooner this night was over, the better.

**58**

---

"You're going to prison, Portland."

"How dare you address me in that manner, Colonel! I am the Mayor of this colony!"

"You ceased to be the Mayor when you decided to commit a crime."

"Everything I've done has been to protect this colony. I should be praised as a humanitarian, not locked up like a criminal!"

"And how does murdering hundreds of thousands of people fit into your role as a humanitarian?"

"What are you talking about? The bombs are completely harmless to people! They're EPMs for god's sake!"

"You mean EMPs. And, no, they're not. They're advanced nuclear fission bombs that have enough yield to wipe out the entire population of New Eden."

"Rubbish! You can't fool me, Colonel. I know how these interrogation techniques work; you exaggerate and bluff and wear the suspect down until he admits to things he didn't do. Well it's not going to work on me!"

Starla just shook her head and sighed.

"Listen very carefully to me, Portland. I'll try to spell it out in words of two syllables or less. You were lied to. Transid fooled you into believing that they were just EMP bombs. But they aren't. I have recordings of both Transid and Reinhardt confessing that the bombs are actually high yield nuclear weapons. We've also just found Dr. Sandborn's schematics for the bombs. These bombs make the nuclear weapons of the past seem like firecrackers. These pals of yours weren't just planning on destroying the Sentiums: they were going to eliminate the entire population of New Eden."

"You're ... you're lying," said Portland, with doubt now creeping into his eyes.

"Congratulations, Portland. You get my DSOB award."

"DSOB?"

"You're officially the Dumbest Son of a Bitch I've ever worked with."

"How dare you!"

"No! How dare you!" retorted Starla. "How dare you allow a known criminal to be elected to Council! How dare you elevate him to Deputy Mayor! How dare you conspire to launch a terrorist attack on another city! Make no mistake about it, Portland, you're going to jail for a very long time!"

"I want to see a lawyer."

"I bet you do. But under the Anti-Terrorism Act, I don't have to provide you with one for quite some time. In fact, if I play the system right, I can leave you stewing in a cell for months before you have access to legal advice. But you've got a more immediate problem to face. If these bombs go off and hundreds of thousands of people die, you won't just be charged with conspiracy to commit an act of terrorism, you'll be charged with genocide. You'll spend the rest of your life in prison."

Portland had gone pale; white as a sheet.

"However," said Starla, allowing a pregnant pause to hang in the air, "if you can help us track down these bombs before they are detonated, the court will be very positively disposed toward you. If you help us save the lives of these people, you could get a significant reduction in your sentence and may even have your terrorism charge downgraded."

"What about Jurd?" he asked. "Has he said anything?"

"He's dead. One of my officers shot him."

Portland blinked, trying to process the news.

"Which means, by the way, that if you help us, you don't have to worry about your buddy showing up unexpectedly one day and drilling a hole through your head."

Portland blinked again, processing.

"You're welcome," added Starla.

She looked at the quivering, pot-bellied fool, trying to hide her disdain.

"So tell me. Where are the bombs? How were they supposed to be smuggled into Wellington?"

"I'll tell you."

"Good."

"But only after I've seen a lawyer. I want a signed, watertight legal document offering me leniency before I say another word!"

"You bastard!" she said. "That's going to take hours! You're gambling with people's lives!"

"It's my life I'm concerned about here," said Portland. A smug expression filled his face as he realised that he currently had the most powerful bargaining chip at the table.

Starla opened the interrogation room door and yelled.

"Sergeant! Get a lawyer in here! On the double!"

**59**

———————

It was Mel's fortieth birthday, and President Joram had insisted on hosting a banquet in her honour. The people of New Eden had come to love Mel and had adopted her as their own. She was a living, breathing piece of their history, and wherever she went in the city, she was approached by people wanting to speak with her. The banquet would be in the form of a luncheon in the main reception hall on the 20th Elevation of District 1, and the tickets for the event had been sold out within minutes of them becoming available two weeks ago. The event was due to start at 11.30 am with various speeches, followed by the meal commencing at 12:00 noon. By 7:00 am preparations were well underway. Decorations were being arranged, chefs were frantically cooking and food supplies were arriving from all over the city and beyond.

At 8:00 am, an emergency Combined Council meeting was held to discuss the overnight developments in Hobart. Starla was present via satellite link, as she could not leave Hobart with her investigations ongoing.

Without preamble, Amanda invited Starla to bring them up to date.

"OK, let me give you a brief summary of overnight events here," Starla began. "We've uncovered a plot to detonate four high-yield nuclear fission bombs in New Eden, powerful enough to destroy the whole city. The main ringleaders of the plot were Jurd Transid, Mayor Portland and a scientist, Dr. Reinhardt. Transid and a key member of his team were killed in a fire-fight, in which my Lieutenant also lost his life. Portland and Reinhardt are under arrest. Further arrests are anticipated as we identify other members of the conspiracy. We were able to shut down the airport and ground all aircraft in Hobart within a few minutes of learning of the plot, as well as advising Colonel Chandra at your end. I believe you were just as quick in locking down your city."

"We certainly were," agreed Chandra. "All shuttles and flitters were grounded within minutes."

"In that case," said Starla, "I believe that the bombs must still be here in Hobart somewhere. Subsequent intel has revealed that they were still in a storage facility on the southern edge of town, even as we were locking down the airport. They were removed from the storage facility by some of Transid's followers shortly afterward and taken somewhere. We're still looking for them but I can't see how they could have left here since then."

"Do you have any leads?"

"We think Portland might have some idea where the bombs were taken, but he's withholding that information until he has a signed legal agreement granting him leniency. It's 6:00 am here – we're two hours behind you. Drafts of the agreement have been flying back and forth between his lawyer and ours for a few hours and I'm hoping they're nearly ready."

"The conniving bastard!" muttered a councillor.

"I heard that and I agree," said Starla. "But unless I beat the information out of him, my hands are tied."

"How were they actually going to smuggle the bombs into New Eden?" asked Joram. "Surely they couldn't do that unless they have inside help?"

"That's right," agreed Starla. "I've just come from a further interrogation of Dr. Reinhardt and he says that there is someone in your city who was in regular contact with Transid and was going to arrange for the bombs to be smuggled in. Transid never told Reinhardt the name of the person. He kept referring to him as a 'naïve little earth-burrower'. No offense intended, Mr. President."

"That doesn't make sense!" said Joram. "Why would one of our citizens want to destroy his own city?"

"He was apparently told that the bombs are only EMPs – electromagnetic pulse bombs – and was assured that no one would be injured. Hence the reference to his naïvety."

"Even so," continued Joram, "why would a citizen of New Eden want to destroy the Sentiums? They are at the heart of our whole technology. The entire city would grind to a halt without them."

"I'm only guessing, Mr. President, but it would have to be someone who has been swayed by the reversionists' fear-mongering to believe that the Sentiums are unsafe."

"So, what should we do? Should we evacuate the city?" asked Joram.

"That's your call, Mr President. All I can say is that I am fairly confident the bombs haven't left Hobart."

The Combined Committee met for a further hour, discussing every possible security measure. The decision was made to not evacuate. Normal life would continue, but with enhanced security measures. Everyone entering the city would be searched. Soldiers had already been placed at each of the four hatchways from dawn that morning and the number of troops would now be doubled. The committee was confident that no bombs would be able to enter the city undetected from this point forward.

They were absolutely correct.

The bombs were already there.

The lawyers finally came to an agreement at 6:25am, Hobart time. If the information Portland provided led to the seizing of the bombs, the charge of conspiracy to commit an act of terrorism would be downgraded to conspiracy to commit public affray, which would only require a brief custodial sentence, if any.

Starla was now facing Portland in the interview room again.

"OK, spill the beans. Tell us what you know."

"Jurd was going to ship them by sea."

"By sea?" Starla said, her mind racing. "But there aren't any vessels of any kind operating between here and Wellington."

"He said he'd found a fisherman here who could be bought."

"Who?"

"I don't know. He never mentioned a name."

"When?"

"It was supposed to get shipped today some time. I don't know exactly when."

"And the explosion? When was that supposed to happen?"

"I don't know. I think it depended on how quickly the gopher could get the bombs in place."

"The traitor in New Eden?"

"Yes."

"Give us a name."

"Jurd never mentioned a name. He just said he had someone on the inside."

"What else can you give us?"

"That's it. Truly. I don't know anything more."

Starla stood up.

"If I find out you've held any information back, the deal is off and you'll rot in jail."

She stormed out of the interview room into the briefing room where Sergeant Grimes and Warrant Officer Tanya Becker, Starla's personal assistant, were waiting.

"The bombs are planned to be shipped by fishing trawler. Becker, find out how many fishing boats we've got in Hobart capable of travelling to Wellington. Grimes, take a squad and get down to the marina. Search every fishing trawler, from top to bottom."

"Three," said Becker.

"Three what?"

"Three trawlers, ma'am. That's all we have."

"That was quick."

Becker looked up from her data pad.

"What can I say? I'm good."

"Get me the contact details of the captains, or whatever the hell they call themselves. Then you and I are going to pay each of them a visit."

---

## 61

The search of the trawlers struck out. Two were currently at sea, having left before dawn. Starla ordered them back to harbour immediately, and her comm officer tracked them via satellite as they began their journey back. The remaining trawler had not gone out today and was sitting empty at the dock. The harbour master informed Grimes that he had heard it coming back sometime before dawn, its distinctive engine sound giving it away."

On learning this, Starla and Becker decided to visit that Captain first. And they were glad they did. They had to rouse him from his bed at 7:30 in the morning, and when he saw their uniforms, he became extremely agitated and nervous. Starla and Becker glanced at each other. *He knows something.*

It took exactly three minutes to break him down and get him talking. A man had approached him, offering money to ship four crates half-way to Wellington.

"Half-way?" asked Starla.

"Yes. To give to the other boat."

"What other boat?"

"The one coming from Wellington."

"When is this supposed to take place."

He looked awkward.

"Last night."

Starla jumped to her feet.

"The crates have already gone?"

"I'm sorry. Am I in trouble? I don't want no trouble."

"What kind of crates were they?"

"Wooden. About this big," he said, indicating with his hands. "The writing on the top said, 'Tasmanian Apples.'"

"You gave the crates to another boat?"

"Yes."

"What can you tell me about it? What did it look like? Did it have a name?"

"A bit smaller than mine. Blue gunwales. Arthur's something. Couldn't see the other word. It was dark."

Starla and Becker sprinted to their ground car.

"Straight to the airport!" said Starla.

As Becker raced to the airport, Starla called up her counterpart in Wellington, Colonel Chandra. When she answered, Starla got straight to the point.

"Lea, I've made a major stuff up. The bombs are already there!"

## 62

They took off from Hobart at 7:50 am and the flight took ninety minutes, with the shuttle pilot pushing the engines to their absolute limit. Adjusting for Wellington time, they landed at 11:20 am. Colonel Lea Chandra met them as they disembarked, and Starla introduced Becker.

As they transferred to a flitter, Chandra filled them in.

"'Arthur's Dream' got into port at 4:50 am this morning. We haven't been able to locate the captain. We've searched the vessel, as well as the docks and storage areas. No sign of apple crates anywhere."

They were in the air now, heading toward New Eden, and Chandra continued.

"President Joram has been informed, and both our entire security forces are now searching the city. Our advice to the President is that everyone who can, should leave the city, but Joram doesn't want a panic at this stage. He's resisting a full-scale evacuation."

Chandra's comm pinged and she answered.

"Go ahead."

"Colonel, two developments. We've found the captain of

Arthur's Dream. He's dead. Shot with a laser and dumped in a refuse bin at the docks. Secondly, we also just located his wife. She'd been out shopping all morning. She tells us that a New Edener came to visit her husband about a week ago and made some kind of business deal. Her husband wouldn't talk about it with her. The same man came back yesterday at about 4:00 pm. He spoke urgently with her husband and her husband left immediately. She hasn't seen him since. We haven't broken the bad news to her yet."

"Did she give a description of the New Edener?"

"Yes, ma'am. Short, bald and aggressive, and he has a scar above his left eye."

"Good work sergeant. Leave two female soldiers to break the news to the wife, then get on a flitter with the rest of your squad and join us at New Eden. We've got some bombs to find."

"Right away, Colonel."

She had barely finished speaking when Starla's comm chimed and she took a call from Grimes, back at Hobart.

"What is it, Sergeant?"

"Colonel, we've had a bit of a breakthrough."

"Give it to me."

"I visited the trawler captain again. I took an identikit artist with me and got him to describe the man who paid him. It turns out we both know him."

"Who is it?"

"One of the prisoners we transported to Earth, ten months ago. Ex-Deputy Police Commissioner Warland. I arrested him and brought him here for questioning. Gave him the whole spiel about being locked away for the rest of his life. I might have laid it on a bit thick, but it worked. He started singing like a bird. No backbone that man."

"Get to the point, Sergeant."

"Yes ma'am. Turns out, he was the one sending coded

messages to the contact in New Eden. The contact's name is Gord. Used to be top dog of one of the Districts there."

"Colonel Chandra is nodding at me, Grimes. Looks like she knows who you're talking about. Anything else?"

"Yes, ma'am. Warland's last transmission was in the early hours of this morning. Apparently Gord responded and advised him that the bombs would be going off at 12:00 noon, today."

Chandra swore in the background and looked at her time display.

"Excellent work, Lieutenant," said Starla.

"It's Sergeant, ma'am."

"Don't contradict me, Lieutenant."

"Yes, ma'am! Thank you, ma'am!"

She disconnected before Grimes could get mushy.

As the flitter raced westward, toward New Eden, Chandra tried to raise Joram, but he wasn't responding to his comm.

"Damn!" said Chandra, looking at her time display. "The luncheon's already underway, and we've got thirty minutes until the whole place blows!"

**63**

———

The hall was packed, mainly with citizens from New Eden but also with a scattering of people from Wellington. Joram gave a very brief but warm welcome speech and reminded everyone of how fortunate they were to have someone in their midst who had not only been alive prior to The Scorching but was, in fact, the daughter of their revered First President.

Joram finished his speech and sat down as a musical recital began. No more than a few bars had been played, however, when Colonel Chandra entered and rushed to the President's side. As the music continued playing, she bent down and spoke clearly.

"President Joram, we've just learned that Gord is the collaborator. He's already planted the bombs in the city and they are going to be detonated at 12:00 noon."

The president's fork froze half-way to his mouth. Zac was sitting next to Joram and heard Chandra's grim news, too. Joram looked at his time display. It was 11:40.

Joram stood up to leave the room and Zac started to rise as well. Kit gripped his arm, leaned over and asked,

"Zac, where are you going?"

"Just some committee business my love," he said loudly enough for people around him to hear. Then he leant down and whispered to her,

"There's a bomb. If we're not back in ten minutes, get out of here and get to the surface. Grab a shuttle and get as far away as possible. Take Mel and the others with you."

He turned and left with Joram, leaving Kit worried.

The two men exited as discreetly as possible. Once they were in the corridor outside, they found that Ludd and Zac's daughter, Dayna, had followed them out.

"Dad, what's going on?"

"We've got a bit of a problem," he replied, in his usual understated way.

Colonel Chandra briefly explained the situation, and as she finished, Zac checked his time display.

"We've got seventeen minutes."

"Shouldn't we at least evacuate the banquet hall and get those people to the surface?" asked Dayna.

"It wouldn't make a difference," said Starla. "From what I can gather, the combined force of the four bombs will leave a crater kilometres wide. Even on the surface, the people wouldn't stand a chance. Either we find these bombs, or we're all dead."

"Where should we start?" asked Joram.

"I've got both our security forces searching throughout the four districts," said Chandra, "but it's like looking for a needle in a haystack."

"How quickly can you evacuate the entire city?" asked Starla, who had been waiting in the corridor, not wanting to startle the guests with her sudden appearance.

"Not quickly enough," answered Joram. "It would take many hours to process the citizens in twenty Elevations through the hatchways of each District, and even longer to get them far enough away."

"The key is finding Gord," said Zac. "He knows where the bombs are. Can the Sentiums locate him?"

"We've already tried that," said Chandra. "The Sentiums say that Gord has switched his personal comm off. They can't find him if he's offline."

"Damn!"

"I know someone who might be able to find him," said Ludd.

"Who?" asked Chandra.

"Garran. His son. I'll contact him."

As Ludd chimed Garran and began talking, Joram spoke to the group.

"This is my fault. I allowed Gord to go free after I dismissed him from his position as Prime. He should have been arrested for the part he played in escalating our conflict, but I was too soft. I wanted to avoid the additional furore that arresting a Prime would create."

"It's not your fault, Joram," said Zac.

"Yes, it is. I should have been stronger. My people needed to be protected, and I failed them. I have allowed someone with a dangerous phobia to threaten our entire city."

"Garran thinks he knows where Gord is!" interrupted Ludd. "He says that his father often goes to the museum to be alone and remember our past."

Joram began running down the main corridor toward the museum entrance.

"Wait!" called Chandra, running after him. "He could be dangerous!"

"I must speak to him!" cried Joram. "He will listen to me. I must make this right."

The entrance to the Museum was four hundred metres

from the banquet hall. It was closed today due to the celebrations, but Joram used his code to open the main doors.

"Could Gord have gained access, if it's closed?" asked Starla.

"Probably. Yes, I think so. We may have neglected to change his security code. Again, my mistake."

The group ran through the foyer and pushed open the double doors into the statue room. Gord was there, staring up at the statue of Elizabeth Canning on the far side of the room. He spun around as they entered and a moment later he had a gun in his hand.

"Stay where you are!" he cried, pointing the laser directly at the President.

The group froze, and both Chandra and Starla drew their weapons.

"Where are the bombs?" demanded Chandra, pointing her laser at Gord.

Gord merely smiled and shook his head.

"If you shoot me, I will shoot Joram."

"Gord, please! Help us!" pleaded the President. "You are going to kill us all!"

"No. I am saving us all. Saving us from your weakness, Joram. Once you opened our city to the surface, you left me with no choice. You have allowed evil to enter our city. The Sentiums must be destroyed now, before they become corrupted by the virus that must surely still be out there, somewhere."

"Gord! The bombs will destroy the entire city!" said Chandra.

"No. They will only destroy the circuitry of the Sentiums."

"No they won't!" said Starla. "The people you have collaborated with lied to you. My team have arrested them now. The bombs are not EMPs like they told you. They are high-yield nuclear fission bombs that will completely obliterate New Eden and all of its citizens!"

The look of confidence faded from Gord's face.

"You are lying!"

"No, she isn't," said Joram. "It is you who have allowed a great evil to enter our city, not me. You aren't saving the city; you are about to destroy it."

"No ... it can't be ..." said Gord.

"It's true," said Starla. "We've obtained the specs for the bombs from the scientists who created them. They're going to atomise the entire population of your beloved city."

A look of horror crept across Gord's face and his arm fell to his side. He dropped his weapon to the floor and looked at Joram, pleadingly.

"I'm ... I'm sorry. I thought ..."

"It doesn't matter what you thought," interrupted Chandra. "Tell us where the bombs are!"

"They are where I could be assured they would be most effective. They are in the Sentium server rooms on Elevation 10 in each District."

"How do we disable them?" asked Zac. "Is there some kind of code?"

"You can't disable them. Once the timer is activated, it can't be switched off."

"What time are they set for?" asked Chandra, hoping their information was incorrect.

"Twelve noon."

"Damn!" said Chandra, checking her time display. "Twelve minutes."

She activated her comm.

"Attention all security personnel. The bombs are located in each of the Sentium server rooms. They cannot be disarmed so they must be removed. Retrieve them and get them to the surface. I want a flitter at the exit of each of the four hatchways. Get those bombs away from here and drop them in the ocean if possible. We have twelve minutes!"

"There's another complication," said Gord apologetically.

"Spit it out!" said Chandra, angrily.

"I have others working with me. There are two people guarding each server room. They are armed, with orders to shoot anyone who tries to enter."

"Contact them now!" said Chandra. "Tell them to stand down."

"I can't. I told them to switch their comms off, so they couldn't be traced."

"You bloody fool!" said Zac.

Chandra was back on her comms, warning her security teams and advising them to use extreme force.

"Eleven minutes," said Starla, checking her time display. "It's going to be very close."

"Now what do we do?" asked Ludd.

"President Joram, let's get you to the surface," advised Chandra. "A flitter will take you and your son to safety."

"No. I am going back to the banquet hall. If my people are about to die, I choose to be with them at the end."

**64**

---

Zac was standing outside the main hatchway to District 1. The flitter beside him had its engine running and the pilot was ready to lift off as soon as the bomb arrived. *If* it arrived. Zac looked at his time display.

Six minutes.

To his left, Chandra was on her comm, talking with various security teams. The sound of laser fire could be heard in the background over the comm, as her teams engaged in a deadly battle with the defenders at the server rooms.

Kit, Keo, Tash and Dayna emerged from the hatchway and came to stand beside him. The rest of their group followed a few seconds later.

"Dayna has explained the situation to us," Kit said. "We managed to leave the banquet while another musical recital was taking place. Mel chose to stay."

"What's the current situation?" asked Karl.

"The security teams are trying to fight their way into the server rooms," said Zac. "If they can get the bombs back to the surface in time, there is a flitter at each hatchway ready to get the bombs to a safe distance."

"What about other flitters, for evacuation?" asked Tash. "Can't we at least fly some people to safety."

"Unfortunately, no. We made a major stuff up. Every single member of our security force was flown out here to deal with this emergency, and we only brought four flitters. There are plenty of other flitters back in the town, but there's no one left there who can fly them."

"Can't we help people to run to a safe distance?" asked Jaz, fear showing in her eyes.

"We can't possibly outrun these four bombs. They are going to make the Grand Canyon look like a mere scratch on the surface."

He looked at his time display.

Five minutes.

In the distance they heard a flitter lift off, and Chandra called to them.

"That's District Four. The bomb is on board!"

A moment later, the flitter flew directly over their heads, accelerating rapidly toward the ocean.

"That's one down," said Zac.

Kit reached out and held his hand.

"I love you, Zac."

"I love you, too."

"At least it's not you who is trying to single-handedly save the world this time."

"No. I wouldn't dare. You'd kill me."

The others in the group began to reach out toward each other, some holding hands, others standing with arms around one another.

Zac checked the time.

Four minutes.

Chandra's comm crackled to life again, as one of the teams reported in, with the crack and whoosh of laser fire in the background.

A flitter could be heard lifting off and the pilot reported in. Chandra turned to them.

"District 2 is clear!"

As the flitter raced overhead toward the coast, another flitter could be heard increasing its revs and taking to the air. A moment later it streaked past them, close behind the other aircraft."

"District 3 clear!" said Chandra.

Zac checked the time.

Three minutes.

They stood together in silence, each caught up in their own reflections.

Time slowed to a crawl.

"Will it hurt?" asked Kia, Tash and Keo's daughter, as she clung to her parents.

"Not at all my little one," said Keo kissing her. "In the blink of an eye we will be with the angels in heaven."

Zac checked again.

Two minutes.

Chandra was monitoring the time as well.

"Alpha team, do you copy?"

There was no answer.

Chandra checked her time display again.

"Even if the bomb gets here now, we can't get it safely to the ocean in time."

Zac turned to Keo.

"Dude, have you got anything profound to say?"

Keo nodded and looked at Zac.

"I feel a deep sadness, bro. There was roast chicken on the menu – my favourite."

The sound of boots came from the hatchway and a group of soldiers burst from the entrance, carrying the football-shaped bomb.

"One minute!" yelled Chandra to the pilot as the bomb was

placed in the passenger compartment. "You'll never make it to the coast!"

"I know what to do," yelled the pilot. The flitter lifted off and instead of heading toward the ocean, it raced to the west, toward the forested hills of the wilderness beyond New Eden.

"Into the hatchway, everyone!" yelled Chandra.

They ran into the large cavern and activated the door mechanism. The huge slab of rock lifted slowly from its recessed cavity in the floor and soundlessly kissed the top lintel, sealing them in. There was silence, then. No one spoke. They just stood there, waiting and wondering if the bomb would be far enough away when it exploded. Time seemed suspended. Then it came. The ground shook and fragments of dust and rock showered them from above. The dust settled and they began to laugh and hug each other, with several shedding tears of relief and joy. They were alive! The city was saved!

As they brushed the dust from their clothing, Keo slapped Zac on the back and said,

"Let's get back to the banquet, bro. It would be a shame to waste all that chicken!"

**65**

———

It had been a week since the foiled terrorist attack. Memorial services had been held for those who had lost their lives. All eight misguided defenders who had tried to protect the bombs had been killed. Five security personnel had also lost their lives in the battles – three from New Eden and two from Wellington. Gord had also been killed. He had gone to the server room in District 1, thinking that he could call off his defenders but had been caught in the deadly crossfire of the battle.

The flitter pilot carrying the bomb from District 1 survived. She had dropped the bomb into a deep ravine to the west and managed to clear two high ridge lines further west before the bomb went off. Her flitter was knocked into a spin, and she crashed into a thickly wooded slope. She was quickly located and airlifted to Wellington hospital in a critical condition and underwent life-saving surgery. She was now making a strong recovery and Colonel Chandra had awarded her the Star of Honour.

Starla returned to Hobart where, over the next few days following the bomb attack, the rest of Transid's gang was rounded up and arrested. As promised, Mayor Portland's charges were downgraded to conspiracy to commit public affray, attracting a light sentence of only six months in prison. Starla, however, had another ace up her sleeve. Her investigating officers scanned the recordings of Portland's comm calls with Transid and found an instance of him suggesting that Dr. Sandborn be eliminated once the bombs were complete. They also found glaring evidence of misuse of public funds in a whole range of areas. The added charges of conspiracy to commit murder and illegal use of public funds meant that he would be spending the next twenty years in a cell.

Starla, herself, was now the acting Mayor of Hobart, awaiting the arrival of a new appointment from Altaria. As the temporary leader of the Hobart colony, she had broadcast a number of interviews with leading scientists from New Eden who had explained in great detail the fail-safe moral protocols that were built into the Sentiums – protocols that made it impossible for the mistakes of the past to ever be repeated. The broadcasts and discussions were ongoing and were definitely having an impact. The fears of the Hobart settlers were gradually being allayed and Starla was confident that, in time, they would grow to accept the co-existence of artificial intelligence on Earth.

It was a warm spring day and lunch was just finished. The bones of two large trout lay in a tangled mess on a serving platter in the middle of the gazebo table, and Zac and Keo were contentedly sipping Keo's latest batch of mead. The two couples were having a well-deserved weekend away at their "beach shack", as they liked to call it.

Zac looked at Keo and said,

"A Catholic priest, a Baptist minister and a rabbit walk into a bar, and the rabbit says, 'I'm pretty sure I'm a typographical error.'"

Keo raised his cup and toasted Zac.

Zac leant forward and stared at Keo carefully for a moment, then pointed his finger accusingly at him.

"You smiled!"

"I did not!" Keo replied indignantly.

"Yes you did, dude! I saw the corners of your mouth go up!"

"That was just a twitch, bro!"

"It wasn't! It was a smile! I win!"

"No it wasn't. I was merely dislodging a piece of fish from my cheek."

Kit and Tash came out from the drop-pod carrying some fresh fruit and a refill of mead for their cups.

"Kit! Help me out here! You saw him smile, didn't you?"

"Didn't see. Don't care. Here, have some fruit."

They refilled their cups and Tash took a sip and grimaced.

"You know, I think you're actually getting worse at this, not better. This batch tastes like dirty underwear."

Zac took a large gulp and smacked his lips together, expertly savouring the flavour while he considered Tash's critique.

"No," he finally declared. "I wouldn't say dirty underwear. I would describe it as a bold mead with an initial burst of rotten fruit followed by a lingering, crisp finish of salty armpit. Very refreshing."

"Thanks, bro. I knew you'd have my back," said Keo.

"Don't mention it," said Zac as the two of them clinked mugs together and had another gulp.

The two girls merely shook their heads and smiled.

The afternoon's lazy aura was broken by the sound of a flitter coming in from the south. It landed on the beach just in front of them, and Amanda strode up the sand toward them.

"Amanda. What brings you here?" asked Zac.

"You need to come with me, right now. All four of you. We've found something."

**66**

---

The flitter landed at the bottom of the deep canyon created by the bomb that had exploded to the west of New Eden. True to the bomb's design, there was almost no residual radiation now, barely distinguishable above the natural background radiation of the natural environment.

"It's over here," said Amanda, walking toward the freshly exposed canyon wall.

As they approached, they could see the layers of rock that had been laid down long ago, exposed now for the first time since their creation. Sticking out from between two layers of rock and shale was a shiny metal cylinder. It was still half buried in the rock layers but the exposed part was miraculously undamaged from the blast that had uncovered it. Zac reached out and touched it, gently.

"It's made of untarnished maranium. It looks like ... it can't be ...it looks like a time capsule or canister from the 24th century!"

"Exactly what we thought," said Amanda. "That's why we waited for you. You're the most qualified historian in the colony."

Zac examined the rock layers around the canister.

"It doesn't make sense! These rocks are from the Cambrian layer in the geological column, but this canister is definitely 24th century."

"What does it mean?" asked Keo.

"It means that our dating of the geological column is shot to pieces," answered Zac.

"What do you want to do?" asked Amanda.

"This," said Zac.

He grasped the cylinder and pulled. Surprisingly, it slipped out easily and he held it in his hands. They gathered around and looked at it closely. It was about eighty centimetres long and twenty-five centimetres in diameter, and one end of the cylinder looked to be a lid that could be screwed off. As Zac turned it over in his hands, they saw a date and writing, etched along the side.

24 July 2351
Wellington Public School
Year Six History Class
Time Capsule

"Holy crap!" said Tash. "That's a month before the GAE! A month before we left Earth! This is from our time!"

"But how did it get here, down at this level in the rock layers?" asked Kit.

"The blast from the Scorching, travelling at 30,000 kilometres per hour, probably caused major geomorphological upheaval and redeposition of the sedimentary layers," offered Zac.

"You wanna run that one by me again, Doc?" said Tash.

"The shockwave would have reshaped the surface of the Earth."

"Why didn't you say that in the first place?"

"I wonder what's in it," said Keo, switching the direction of the conversation.

"Only one way to find out," said Zac. He gripped the lid and twisted. After some initial resistance, it grudgingly gave way. He unscrewed the lid and laid it aside. Amanda had brought a small tray from the flitter and Zac carefully tipped the contents onto it.

A variety of things tumbled out. Various pieces of kid's jewellery – a ring, some earrings and a necklace. A small sling shot. A 24th century turbo-top. A small rubber ball. There were various other mementoes and small toys, all of which apparently meant something to the children in the history class. In the midst of the mementoes, however, was a metal plaque with writing engraved on both sides. Zac reverently picked it up and read it aloud to the group.

*"To whoever finds this. Enclosed in this capsule are the small treasures of 6G history class, from the year 2351. However distant in the future you live, we hope that you never forget that our children are our true future. Mrs Edith Garrett."*

Zac turned the thin plaque over and looked at the writing on the back.

"It's a piece of literature," he offered. "Here, Keo, you read it."

Keo took it and adjusted the angle so that the afternoon sun lit up the words, as if they were made of fire.

*"In vain we search for meaning amidst the shifting sands of this world. Riches will perish and civilisations will crumble. Only by looking beyond the stars will we find the True Path that is set for us. And only by trusting in an Infinite Goodness will we finally lay to rest the strivings of our troubled hearts. Kevin J Simington. 2020."*

"Wow! 2020! That's ancient!" said Amanda.

"Have you ever heard of the author, Keo?" asked Zac.

"No."

They studied the words in silence for a few more moments.

"What do you think it means, Keo?" asked Kit.

"I think the writer is expressing the viewpoint that although the universe can often seem chaotic and meaningless, he still believes in an ultimate power who is keeping everything from completely unravelling."

"Do you believe that?" asked Zac.

"You know I do, bro."

"Even after everything that's happened?"

"*Especially* after everything that's happened. Just think about it. The odds of us surviving everything we've been through are so astronomically small as to be virtually impossible. The most logical explanation is that Someone has been watching over us, and we have been allowed to play a small part in a grand plan that is much bigger than we can possibly imagine. We are just tiny ripples in the ocean of history, but together, our ripples make a difference."

"Well, I don't know about all that profound philosophical stuff," said Tash. "But I've got a very simple, practical question."

They all looked at her expectantly.

"If there really *is* some Great Ultimate Goodness or whatever you want to call it watching over us ..."

She paused.

"Yes, my love?" prompted Keo.

"... the least he could have done is not make your mead taste like dirty socks! I mean, is that too much to ask?"

Kit and Zac chuckled, but Keo turned and started walking back toward the flitter.

"Keo! Bro! Where are you going?" called Zac.

He stopped and turned, looking back at them with a cheeky grin on his wide olive face.

"I'm going back home for some more of that beautiful mead. Is anyone else coming?"

They all laughed.

"Wait for us! We're coming too!"

Arm in arm, the four friends walked back to the flitter and back to the life that they had created on a world that had been made anew.


THE END

## 67

# ORIGINAL FINAL CHAPTER

*Thank you for reading this fourth and final book in my quadrilogy (that's what I'm calling it and I don't care if it's not a real word!). The series has been an absolute delight for me to write, and I hope that you have enjoyed reading these four books as much as I have enjoyed writing them. What follows is the original final chapter of this book. I still prefer it to the one you have just read, but my two wonderful editors had some reservations about it. Based on their reaction, I wrote the alternate ending that was finally published, but I couldn't help including the original one here as an appendix. Feel free to let me know which one you prefer!*

Kevin J Simington
kevin@kevinsimington.com

.......................

THE FLITTER LANDED at the bottom of the deep canyon created by the bomb that had exploded to the west of New Eden. True to the bomb's design, there was almost no residual radiation now, barely distinguishable above the natural background radiation of the world around them.

"It's over here," said Amanda, walking toward the freshly exposed canyon wall.

As they approached, they could see the layers of rock that had been laid down long ago, exposed now for the first time since their creation. Sticking out from between two layers of rock and shale was a small, brown leather satchel. It was still half buried in the rock layers but the exposed part was miraculously undamaged from the blast that had uncovered it. Zac reached out and touched it, gently.

"It's real leather. It looks like ... it can't be ...it looks like something from about the 21$^{st}$ century!"

"Exactly what we thought," said Amanda. "That's why we waited for you. You're the most qualified historian in the colony."

Zac examined the rock layers around the satchel.

"It doesn't make sense! These rocks are from the Cambrian layer in the geological column, but this satchel is definitely 21$^{st}$ century."

"What does it mean?" asked Keo.

"It means that our dating of the geological column is shot to pieces," answered Zac.

"What do you want to do?" asked Amanda.

"This," said Zac.

He grasped the satchel and pulled. Surprisingly, the satchel slipped out easily and he placed it on the ground at their feet. On the front flap of the satchel was a single word in embossed gold metal lettering: STARPATH.

"What does that mean?" asked Tash.

"No idea. Only one way to find out."

He bent down and opened the satchel. Inside, was a single sheet of white paper in perfect condition, as if it had been placed there yesterday. Zac carefully removed the paper and held it out in front of him so they could all see. There was writing on the sheet and as they looked, they all gasped in astonishment.

Zac read the words aloud.

*"Dear Zac, Kit, Keo and Tash, you are all imaginary characters in my quadrilogy of novels, called the STARPATH SERIES. It has been my great joy to have created you and grown to know and love you over the course of these four books. I apologise for having put you through such pain and heartache, but your journey is now over. The story is at an end, and I leave you in this beautiful, restored world to live out your lives in peace and happiness. You deserve it. All the best. Kevin J Simington. P.S. I'm sorry for making you bald and fat at the end, Keo."*

The four friends looked at the paper in amazement.

"You mean, we're not real?" asked Kit.

"Apparently not," said Zac. "I always suspected there was something weird about my passion for Hawaiian shirts."

"So, none of this actually happened?" Kit persisted. "We're just imaginary characters in some guy's book?"

"Yep. It appears so. But look on the bright side, my love: we had some great imaginary sex."

"So, is he writing this dialogue even now?"

"Probably," answered Zac.

"He must be pretty clever," said Kit.

"That's not really your own opinion," said Zac. "He's just making you say it."

"I'm confused," said Tash.

"Check the other side of the paper, bro," said Keo. "There's a photo on it."

Zac turned the paper over.

"It's a photo of the author," he said.

"Do you think he looks a bit like you, Zac?" asked Kit

"No. I'm much better looking."

Keo turned and started walking back to the flitter.

"Where are you going, dude?" asked Zac.

"Back to drink some more of that imaginary mead."

"Wait for us! We're coming too."

Half-way there, Kit stopped. She turned around and looked vaguely up into the sky.

"Hey! Mr Simington! If you can hear me, can you please make the mead taste better? That was just plain cruel, dude!"

*Sorry about that. I'll fix it right away.*


THE END
Really and truly.

# LEAVE A REVIEW

If you enjoyed this book, I would be extremely grateful if you would leave a review on Amazon, Goodreads and other review websites. Reviews are hugely important for me as a self-published author. In Amazon's case, reviews impact Amazon's algorithms, helping the book to climb higher in the charts, thereby making it more visible to potential readers. Every single review really does help!

Leaving a review is very easy. To leave a review, just go to the relevant Amazon page for your country (see below), search for my book and click on the reviews link next to the stars. A review of 4 or 5 stars is considered to be a positive review and a review of 3 or less stars is considered to be a negative review. (Unfortunately, Amazon only allows reviews from people who have spent at least $50 on Amazon over the preceding 12 months).

Click your country's Amazon link and scroll down to "Write a customer review":

AMAZON UNITED STATES

AMAZON UNITED KINGDOM
AMAZON AUSTRALIA
AMAZON CANADA

# SOMEONE ELSE'S LIFE

About to be released in 2020 ...

## SOMEONE ELSE'S LIFE

*"A page-turning thriller by a master story-teller!"*

What if you weren't who you thought you were? ... And people will kill to stop you finding out!

**DUE FOR RELEASE IN THE SECOND HALF OF 2020**

A FASCINATING GLIMPSE INTO THE
WONDERS OF THE UNIVERSE
WELCOME
TO THE
UNIVERSE
A POCKET GUIDE
FOR VISITORS
KEVIN J SIMINGTON

# ABOUT THE AUTHOR

Kevin J Simington is an acclaimed fiction and non-fiction author whose books are renowned for their intelligence, clarity and wit. He is a very popular conference speaker on the topics of philosophy, apologetics and science. He also writes for several international magazines.

Website:
https://kevinsimington.com

Amazon Author Page:
amazon.com/author/kevinjsimington